REAL CHANGE

ANDRE ERASMUS

D1528433

ACKNOWLEDGMENTS

I am grateful to have lived during a period of real change in South Africa and for the characters in its history that showed such bravery during those troubled and turbulent times.

Thanks are also due to the many friends and family who have contributed and encouraged me.

That said, I also record my undying gratitude to my wife Lynne for all her support in producing this book. For that and the many other things you have done in my life, I love you.

1

SOUTH WEST AFRICA/ANGOLA BORDER - 1977

Inside the hut it was blindingly dark compared to the white heat and glare outdoors.

But that was where the scream came from - ignored by the soldiers further into the village compound.

In a split second, his eyes frantically adjusting to the darkness which was punctuated by bullet holes through its mud walls, like laser lights piercing the gloom, Daniel Jacobs took in the scene.

A woman crouched against the wall. Fear was visible in her eyes as two or three beams caught her face. Her eyes were wide open and glistening tears mingled with the dust on her cheeks. Backed into a dark corner of the hut on her haunches, she looked like a fragile buck awaiting the hunter's final death-bringing bullet.

She was already wounded!

The whites of her eyes and her teeth almost glistened in the subdued light – a sudden contrast to the harsh Southern African sunshine and glare outside. Her chest heaved and her mouth was drawn back in a grimace, mixing her fear with anger.

Anger at being violated.

The South African soldier was towering over her, strobes of light catching his ginger hair. He was unaware of Daniel being there, his broad rugby player's back was to the door as he re-buttoned his combat trousers.

The man was tall, well over six foot and, as he reached for his R4 semi-automatic rifle propped against the wall of the mud hut, he muttered in Afrikaans and more to himself than the woman, "If I shoot you now, no-one will know what happened and they will think you were a bloody terrorist, too."

He pointed at the corpse of the older black man lying crumpled and discarded to the left of the woman, about 10 feet away, part of his face blown away by the shot that had left a small hole at the back of his head, just above the nape of his neck.

On the wall of the hut where the body lay, highlighted by one of the rays, was a reddish-yellow smear - as if someone had struck the wall with an over-ripe peach. There was a pervading rusty, musty, smell of blood, sweat, semen, death and fear. The young woman would not look at the corpse. Too scared perhaps to take her eyes from the huge white man looming over her.

As his eyes adjusted to the gloom, Daniel realised instinctively that he had to act even though the man was bigger and, presumably, stronger than he was. But surprise was on his side. Frantically he lunged at the soldier. He hit him between the shoulders with his elbows and forearms, his own rifle held high and parallel to the ground, pushing him away from the weapon he was reaching for against the wall.

The man gasped, winded and taken by surprise at the assault. He tumbled against the mud wall, cracking its brittle strength with his weight and allowing even more light in which counted in Daniel's favour.

As the soldier turned, stumbling to his knees, cursing and dazzled by the added light, Daniel swung his rifle, striking him across the broad cheek and bridge of his thin nose with the butt. The soldier's head jerked backwards, his eyes rolling upwards at the same time as Daniel heard the dull crunch of his cheekbone or nose crumbling and the taller man fell stunned in an untidy heap.

His chest heaving with the exertion and shock of it all and his heart thudding in his chest, Daniel realised everything had taken place in a few seconds and in comparative silence - the loudest sound being the curse by the man and then the crunch of the rifle hitting his face. Gasping, his breath raw in his throat, he turned to the woman.

Her fear was now mingled with confusion. "Was this man to be her next rapist? Or was he trying to protect her?" She turned her back to him and curled into a self-protective foetal ball, trying to hide her exposed flesh by pulling the torn remnants of her clothing around her.

Taking her now unconscious assailant by the collar of his sweat-stained shirt, Daniels dragged him to the doorway of the hut and into the bright sunlight and heat beyond, saying to her soothingly in English: "Don't move. I'll be back with help. Don't worry."

A few minutes later and after much haggling with Captain Derek du Toit, who was of the opinion that the 'terrorist bitch should be left to rot', he returned with the platoon's assigned medic.

Daniel was struck by the look in the young woman's eyes, begrudging gratitude mixed with fear as the medic tended to her. She looked at Daniel with huge dark-brown eyes, this ravaged Ovambo woman, as if memorising his features.

***

Her assailant, a corporal Frans Jonker, was now conscious and under guard for a later court martial. His cheek had already swollen and his hatred for Lieutenant Jacobs palpable as the officer walked past the prisoner at the military vehicle 500m away from where his young victim had lain.

"I'll get you, you bloody English rubbish," he promised, his pale, icy blue eyes glinting with anger as he looked down at the shorter officer.

Four days later, a hastily-convened court martial was held at the regiment's bush headquarters. The officer commanding the regiment presided over proceedings in the huge tent which also doubled as the officers' mess. He seemed keen to get the whole affair out of the way as quickly as possible. With no-one prepared to give evidence on Frans's behalf, the rapist was found guilty of gross misconduct. Daniel's evidence and that of the medic about the woman's injuries were enough to earn Frans a dishonourable discharge and three months in military prison.

As he left the court martial room, his nose swollen and the bruises under his eyes starting to go yellow, he looked at Daniel with his piercing blue eyes and muttered menacingly in his strong Afrikaans accent through thin, cruel lips: "I'll get you for this. I do not forget."

Frans was taken to Grootfontein for internment for the remainder of the regiment's three-month active service stint, three weeks before the rest returned home. This left the corporal imprisoned for a further two months - a long time to let his anger and resentment fester.

2

PORT ELIZABETH - MARCH 21, 1985

Driving to work on a sunny Thursday morning Daniel wondered if he'd have to do another stint of border duty for the army and be subject to more *Military Madness* as sung by Graham Nash.

The radio news was chattering on about Kissinger's withdrawal of support leading to South Africa's military withdrawal from Angola. Not, he mused, that life as a journalist was without military madness. The country's security forces were trying to keep the covert ANC and the masses under control so townships were being patrolled by police with army backing at times.

But things were getting out of hand. A State of Emergency had been declared by the government which restricted the press from getting coverage of what was really going on in the townships.

So, a lot of what happened in the townships to quell the unrest went unreported and, as a result, many white South Africans were blissfully unaware of the full extent of the troubles, learning only from rumours. Journalists were banned from reporting what they saw and every press report on the unrest that was allowed to be published had to be vetted by the police and carry a full police comment - even if the comment flew in the face of the facts, which it often did.

Daniel chuckled wryly to himself as he approached work and the radio news report ended.

"Interesting, too," he reflected, "that the government-supported broadcasting stations only carry sketchy and bland reports on the unrest almost subliminally supporting the government and police point of view - that this unrest is a temporary blip."

***

The first thing he saw on entering the newsroom was a man in a suit sitting in his chair looking at the newsdesk diary and another suited man standing further away, with his back to Daniel talking to a frightened looking June Purdon, the newsdesk secretary.

It was 8.05 and the reporters only started arriving at 9, so the room was empty. "Who are you, what are you doing at my desk and who let you in?" Daniel demanded as he approached.

Seemingly unfazed, the smug looking man slowly looked up, closed the diary and said, with an Afrikaans accent: "Morning Mr Jacobs. The security guard downstairs owed me a favour. I'm Du Preez, Captain Arrie du Preez, Security Branch. We need to speak about the weekend and last night."

The other man had taken June by the arm and moved her around the corner, without even turning round.

It was just Daniel and the policeman in the newsroom.

"Speak? You're going through my stuff! Do you have a warrant?" As Daniel spoke he realised his question was futile.

"A warrant? I don't need one. We make the rules. Anyway, I have the right to demand reporters' notes and films if you guys attended a banned event. We know there were meetings in Uitenhage at the weekend and last night. We know your reporter John Temba was there and taking pictures." The captain sat back, as if waiting for Daniel to spring into action and fulfil the request.

Playing for time, Daniel replied: "I can't do that without the editor's permission and, anyway, I was not on duty last night ... so I don't know about any notes or film". He moved to pick up the newsdesk diary, which would contain notes made by the duty news editor, Gavin Patterson, who would not be on duty today.

Putting his fleshy hand on the diary, Du Preez smiled thinly and said: "OK, I'll wait. Maybe I'll look through your drawers and send my man up to the darkroom to look for negatives while we wait."

Playing for more time, Daniel responded: "But with your

vast network of informants, why do you need our notes? Surely you guys know what went down at the meetings?"

He hoped, as he watched, that Gavin, John and the duty photographer had not left anything in the office - a rule the newspaper had introduced at the outset of the State of Emergency Press rules.

"And," he added quickly as Du Preez made to talk, "if we wait a bit I can get the photographer to take pictures of you searching our offices. That'll look good in tomorrow's paper, showing you care about the English Press so much that you paid us a visit to see how we work." Daniel wondered if Du Preez would pick up the sarcasm.

At that moment, the editor Jake Swarts, walked round the corner. "Indeed, that would be interesting news. I've heard most of this conversation. I suggest you leave now while we seek legal advice. Daniel, come with me." With that comment, he walked off calmly and entered his office.

Du Preez stood up as Daniel took his diary from the policeman. "Okay, fine. I'll be back, I'll get a Section 205 order which will force you to give us what we want."

He paused and then said, almost confidentially: "But if you tell us how to find them, it will look good because I won't say how we got the information.

"However, believe me, if we are forced to search for it or have to get a Section 205 forcing you to give it to us, we will tell everyone we got the information voluntarily from the Herald. It will look like the Press is on our side and our image will improve. Not too sure about yours though."

As the two stared at each other, the other policeman and June came back into the newsroom.

Daniel started as he recognised former Corporal Frans Jonker - last seen under arrest on the Border eight years ago.

"You bastard, Jacobs," he said moving forward aggressively.

Du Preez stepped forward, beckoned Frans and walked out followed closely by his subordinate.

June stood open mouthed as Jake called from his door, "Come on Dan, I'm waiting."

Daniel quickly told June to get photographer Clive Brent into the office, even though he was only due to start work at 2. "I'll explain everything when I'm done with Jake," he said as he walked into the editor's office.

***

Jake, a stocky, businesslike and brisk man with curly hair and heavy glasses, sat behind his desk with the morning edition in his hands.

He looked up as Daniel entered. "Well, an interesting start to the day. There's not much in the paper about Uitenhage. What was that cop going on about?"

Daniel sat opposite Jake.

"Gavin called me yesterday evening, saying John had come in wanting to write about some meeting the UDF had held, concerning a funeral planned for today, that they wanted to give the Press their list of speakers, hoping to draw more people."

Jake snorted derisively as he answered. "The United Democratic Front? They don't seem so united or too democratic at the moment do they?

"So why was that not in the paper? Although I see that lightning strike at the motor races in Jo'burg took up quite a bit of space. More than I would have imagined necessary."

"Well," said Daniel, "by the time John had finished his copy and Clive had processed his film, it was almost 11pm and the newsdesk had just been told that an order was to be issued banning the funeral. As the first edition deadline is 11.15, it would have taken too long to sub and place John's story and the banning order - due at 11.30 according to the police PR - could have affected that and its content. So then Peter decided to run the paper as it was, with the lightning story uncut to fill the gap."

Jake smiled. "I suppose that is the chief sub's right. Pity as that edition would have been well read in the Uitenhage townships this morning."

There was a sharp knock on the door and it was opened before Jake or Daniel could say a word. An ashen

June stood there looking worried.

"Sorry, but you'd better come quick Dan. It appears there's been a shooting."

Jake dismissed his news editor with a wave of the hand as he turned back to reading his paper.

3

THE HERALD NEWSROOM THAT SAME MORNING

Back at the newsdesk June told Daniel there seemed to be some trouble about to brew in nearby Uitenhage. There'd been a report of a shooting.

Reporters for the day shift were arriving and setting up for another day. The phone rang and, as she answered, police reporter Shaun Riley came rushing up to the desk.

"I guess you know that late last night the police issued a banning order for the funeral in KwaNobuhle."

Daniel looked around for the photographers. "Where's Mark Daly?" he asked June who'd put the phone down.

"Out photographing a golden wedding anniversary couple in North End for Liz," she said, adding that Clive was on his way in with John's film.

Just then both phones rang at the newsdesk. Daniel took the one closest to him. "Herald newsdesk."

"Dan, Des here. You're not going to believe this," said Des Hughes who was the deputy chief of the local emergency paramedic unit and one of the Herald's better contacts. "But I understand the police have been involved in a shooting in Langa. Something about a funeral which had been banned but nobody, as usual, bothered to tell the people."

Daniel asked about the extent of the shooting.

"This is the weird part. I believe it's over 20."

"Dead?"

"Yes, really scary. This means the shit will hit the fan in a big way. Look. I've got to run, must get some guys out there.

"Got that? It's in Langa, on the Maduna road. Look, got to go."

Daniel put the receiver down just as June, looking startled, said: "That caller, a black guy, said there've been shootings near Uitenhage. Wouldn't give his name, said he'd seen it."

Shaun rushed off to make calls, Daniel summoned senior reporter Jamie Nelson and told him the news. "Get ready to go. Clive's on his way, meet him downstairs. You're to head for Uitenhage. There's been a shooting near Kwanobuhle township. On the Maduna Road, Clive knows the area well," Daniel ordered as he got June to get a contact number for the wedding anniversary couple from social editor Liz Jones and instruct Mike to be ready to go at a moment's notice. Daniel reckoned he could deal with Liz's anger at having her precious wedding anniversary story put on the backburner. But he had more pressing needs now.

Jamie was given further instructions, including being told to phone in with any further updates, before Daniel got other reporters manning phones to get more information from hospitals, council contacts, people in the area or whatever they could find at this stage to help put the story together.

He looked across at the newspaper's day shift black reporter, John Temba, who had walked in a minute or two earlier, and summoned him over. "John, what's the word out there?"

The young and enthusiastic man looked worried. Daniel decided not to tell him about the security police visit.

"Well, boss, as you know there was to be that funeral today - of four comrades who were shot and killed. There've been vigils in Langa, and KwaNobuhle, organised by the UDF. I went to the Langa one last night. It was very political. Oliver Tambo is using this International Youth Year to aid his call for intensification of the struggle to make South Africa ungovernable and apartheid unworkable."

As he paused, Daniel recalled the reports, published abroad about Tambo, the president of the banned ANC, making such calls. Nothing was reported in South Africa of this.

"Anyway, there was a rumour going around yesterday," John continued, "that buses hired for the funeral would be blocked by the police and that the mourners would meet at Maduna Road bus stops anyway and if the buses were not there, they'd walk to the funeral."

Daniel knew from past events that funerals were an opportunity for political speeches and incitement to continue the struggle. Funerals were not only an event for mourning a death but for dreams of a new life without apartheid, of democracy and the ANC being unbanned. Banned leaders like Steve Biko, Robert Sobukwe and others had used sporting events and funerals to defy their banning orders and get their message across.

"Then late last night the banning order for the funeral came through - I was here.

"I think there'll be thousands who wanted to go to the funeral. It is the anniversary of Sharpeville and the word is that Mathew Goniwe, Sparrow Mkonto or Fort Calata might speak. I was going to head out there now. Then I heard you telling Jamie and others about the shootings. Can I still go?"

Daniel knew that if Goniwe, leader of the UDF in nearby Cradock, or his colleagues were to be in the area, John would track them down for their comment on the shooting. Too good an opportunity to miss. He instructed John to meet Mark in North End and to head out to find the Cradock men.

"If that doesn't work, track down Des Hughes or head for the hospital and then call in."

It was time to tell the editor it was going to be a busy day.

***

And it was.

Daniel then realised this 25th anniversary of the infamous Sharpeville Massacre was significant. On 21 March, 1960, in the Transvaal at least 180 black Africans were injured and 69 killed when police opened fire on demonstrators protesting against the pass laws at the township of Sharpeville, near Vereeniging.

Now, apparently, it's happened again.

Daniel briefed reporter Monica Davis to get information and files from the newspaper library and to write a piece on the date coincidence.

"That day," he told the young woman, "Robert Sobukwe's Pan Africanist Congress launched a series of pass law protests. There was a similar demonstration at the police station in Vanderbijlpark, where another person was shot. And later at another Langa, the township outside Cape Town, police baton charged and fired tear gas at the gathered protesters, shooting three and injuring several others.

"But the Sharpeville Massacre was the start of armed resistance in South Africa."

As she left other reporters came to the desk with phone call updates. He told them to compile everything so they could be checked later.

Shaun, in the meantime, was trying to get comment from the police.

He told Daniel: "They're not happy that we did not publish the banning order. I told them it came through too late. Carl Strydom disagrees." Carl was the PR officer for the police.

"So," Daniel asked, "any official comment on the shooting?"

"Well, Carl says he'll check it out. Claims he's heard nothing. But, he says if it did happen, it's on our heads because the banning order was meant to stop that happening."

Again the phone rang and Daniel answered. "Newsdesk."

"Hello, I'm at a phone box in Langa. I called earlier. We saw the shooting, the police just opened fire for no reason. Then we saw them moving the bodies - those that were running away when the shooting started."

"Where are you?" Daniel asked quickly as the caller drew breath.

"Hendricks Street is where my house is, will you send a reporter? I'm Arthur Shipalana, I want to tell you what happened."

Daniel knew the paper was on to something big. As he rushed off to tell Jake, he told June to call him if either team in Uitenhage called in.

4

PORT ELIZABETH, EARLIER THAT MORNING

Police sergeant Jimmy Jonker was not a happy camper as he clambered into the armoured troop carrier, known as a Hippo, used by the police for township patrols.

His head throbbed from the previous night's brandies and coke during the darts evening, probably his last social event as a serving policeman as he would be a civilian once more from the end of the month , some nine days away.

"Hey, you lucky bugger, don't look so sad," Jimmy's fellow policeman Hendrik Alberts punched him on the shoulder in greeting as he pushed past other men to get next to his friend.

"Hell, that hurt," muttered Jimmy as they took their seats down the centre row facing outwards.

"Well, that's because you drank so much last night. But you still played good darts, man. And we thrashed that Humewood team solidly. You deserved every drink."

Trying not to talk too loudly and trying not to let the vehicle's rocking make his head move, Jimmy smiled and said: "Just think, in six weeks I'll be in London, riding in a black cab, not a bloody troop carrier. I'll be checking out the Limey girls on the busy roads there, not you ugly lot or the township streets."

The young lieutenant in charge of the two armoured troop carriers, Cas Smit, had earlier told his patrol they were heading off to block an illegal march in Langa, not far from their base in Algoa Park, in the city's northern areas.

Cas leant forward and caught Jimmy's eye.

"And remember Jimmy, Guinness tastes better in Ireland not England where the beer is served warm, the Scottish are called Scottish not Scotch - that's the whisky."

Others joined in the light-hearted banter as Jimmy reflected on the fact that joining the police instead of doing army National Service like his brother Frans had stood him in good stead.

After nine years he was a sergeant, with a degree in criminology and psychology, and was due to move to the UK where he'd been accepted for further study in criminal behaviour and forensic psychology in London. Still single at the age of 33, Jimmy felt he had the world before him.

"Unlike my brother."

He realised he'd spoken aloud when Hendrik said: "What about your brother? He's the new Security branch guy here isn't he?"

Jimmy paused, and then replied: "Yes, just arrived here. He's had a few problems in his life. But I have to do this patrol, unlike my brother who has a cool company car and no need for a uniform."

"Problems?" enquired Hendrik.

"Yes, he was kicked out of the army some eight years ago and became a bit of a drinker. He then joined the police and did border duty with Koevoet."

Hendrik looked surprised. "Koevoet? The counter-insurgency guys? Hell, they're an effective fighting force but also notorious for some brutal stuff too."

Conversation stopped as the Hippo entered the dusty township roads.

Hendrik then said, "I heard that Koevoet members were paid through a bounty system, for kills, prisoners and equipment they captured. This gave them a lot more than their normal salary."

"Yes," Jimmy said. "Frans was one of those. He made a lot of money but got into trouble again. His platoon was accused by the International Red Cross of killing more people than taking prisoners and also of torturing prisoners for information.

"Anyway, to avoid trouble with the UN, he was transferred back to SA, did a course at Pretoria and is now here, checking on what he calls the English Press and their all-too liberal ideas."

***

16

About 10 kilometres west of Algoa Park, Frans Jonker was back in his office at the Security Branch offices in Strand Street, near the Port Elizabeth harbour. Capt Du Preez was sipping the coffee Frans had just made.

"Well, now what?" asked Frans as he sat in the Captain's small second floor office with the barred window overlooking the harbour - the view marred by the freeway which now bypassed the city's main street.

"This is an historic office," said Du Preez, wincing as he took a sip of the coffee which was way too hot. "Ja, this is where that Steve Biko guy was questioned in 1977 and it is from here he was taken to Pretoria where he died." Du Preez blew on the coffee and took another tentative sip. Less pain this time.

"Biko? Stephen Bantu Biko? The Black Consciousness guy who was a political activist of note? Yes, I knew about that, my uncle on my mother's side, Harold Snyman was one of the officers who interrogated him. Didn't know it was right here in this room. Uncle Harold said Biko was a tough man, often tried to attack them, so they had to hit him around a bit."

The room went quiet as the two men sipped on their coffee and contemplated the Biko Affair - the death of a man who was instrumental in starting the June 1976 uprising in Soweto which, to many observers, was the beginning of the end of apartheid and the start of resistance.

Du Preez spoke first. "Yes, I remember his funeral in King William's Town. I was one of the officers there, trying to control the crowds and, despite the bannings, there were thousands, man, from all over. And that Desmond Tutu did the funeral service. It was a marathon funeral and, it seemed to me, more of a protest rally against the whites than a proper funeral."

"And the English papers made a big fuss," Frans added. "I remember the Rand Daily Mail saying he was the 20th to die in security police custody in just 18 months. Hell man, didn't they realise these guys want to run the country? Run it into the ground they will."

Du Preez, finishing his coffee, coughed and said: "Yes, the bloody English Press. There was that Donald Woods guy, editor of the Dispatch in East London, who said we, the police, killed him. And this despite the then police minister Kruger telling Parliament Biko had been on a hunger strike and that the best doctors had treated him."

Frans quickly jumped in. "Yes, I remember him calling Biko his 'most valued friend' and saying he was a man of peace. Not according to my Uncle Harold."

Du Preez dug in his desk drawer and pulled out a newspaper clipping. "And it wasn't just the English papers hey? Even the Burger, a government-supporting paper from Cape Town, said this, 'The death of detainees in South Africa is an emotional matter which generates much heat. But never before has it been as bad as in the latest case of the black power activist Steve Biko. Concern over detainees' deaths becomes deep dismay when the hysterical propaganda against authorities is observed. A vehement campaign is in progress which surpasses all previous protests'. See? we're suddenly the bad guys here.

"But so far a court of law has never established that we have been responsible for torturing or killing a single detainee, although all cases are thoroughly investigated."

Frans flushed and said: "Yes, the bloody newspapers and guys like that Daniel Jacobs. A do-gooder, I know him from way back, from my army days. He's trouble too. We must seek these guys out."

Du Preez calmly said: "Don't worry, that's our job and we have people on the newspapers who tell us things. But I saw today at the Herald that you didn't seem to like Daniel Jacobs. Why's that?"

Frans looked away. "It's a long story. I'll tell you someday."

5

LANGA, EARLIER THAT MORNING

It was already warm in the dusty African township of Langa near Uitenhage as Arthur Shipalana emerged from his small family home to wash and make a fire for early morning coffee. It was just gone 6am. The sun was already an orange ball in the eastern sky.

In the distance, he heard the diesel sounds of a South African Police patrol vehicle – one of many that had spent the past few months patrolling the black townships of the Port Elizabeth/Uitenhage metropole in an effort to quell the rising political unrest against the apartheid regime. They were called Hippos because of their ungainly shape and the hippopotamus was the animal responsible for the most deaths of people in Africa. "Maybe that's why they chose that name," Arthur mused as he lit the fire.

"Hello Arthur," a woman's voice made him turn away from trying to see where the patrol vehicle was heading and back to the house where he saw Nancy Nujomba emerge from her sleeping quarters.

Nancy was an Ovambo, from northern South West Africa who had fled the unrest in the region - like many others from neighbouring states - and entered South Africa illegally about six months ago, working her way down to Uitenhage and the Eastern Cape, just about as far as she could get from Ovamboland.

Despite the apartheid government, there was more security for people in South Africa and entering the country was not that hard.

She was a 26-year-old mother of an eight-year-old boy called Sam, and was actively seeking work in the area to pay rent to the Shipalanas who had offered the destitute pair the shack in their backyard.

Arthur, about the same age as Nancy, quite fancied her but she seemed distant and reluctant to get involved, almost scared of men. He had noticed her flinch and seem scared when security force patrols passed nearby.

Although it was early, the township was alive and many people were moving about, making the long walk to public transport to get to their jobs or, for the many unemployed, going to the side of the main road in the hope of some businessmen seeking temporary labour.

Or, for many others, it was just another day. But today was different. There was an air of anticipation and expectancy. Most knew there was a big funeral due to take place and many were aware that it would be a major political event with the security force in close attendance.

"Hey," Arthur turned to Nancy, "Fancy a cup of coffee to mark Sharpeville Day?"

"Coffee, yes please. Sharpeville, wasn't that was long ago?" Nancy stretched in the warming sun and then moved to sit near Arthur.

"Yes, it's a part of this country's history. If you were from here you'd know the details." Arthur finished making the coffee and sat down to tell Nancy the story.

"In 1960, the year I was born, there was a confrontation between the police and demonstrators in Sharpeville, in the Transvaal. It was the build up of opposition to Verwoerd's Nationalist government's apartheid policies. The police opened fire when the people did not disperse. More than 60, all unarmed, were shot and killed."

"But," Nancy interrupted, "The ANC was all about peaceful change then. I know a bit of the history."

Arthur, surprised that this girl from rural South West Africa knew some of the details, continued his story. "Yes, that was in the 1950s. But when Verwoerd was elected in 1958 and the Nats replaced the United Party at the top, the laws changed. First the Mixed Marriages Act was brought in and the segregation laws just went on and on.

"And, yes, the idea was to protest within the law against all forms of racial discrimination but the arrest of many leaders, like Mandela, and the treason trial, changed that. Some ANC members had become disillusioned with the peaceful response. These Africanists were opposed to a multi-racial future for South Africa. So they had a philosophy that a racially assertive sense of nationalism was needed to mobilise the masses, and they advocated a strategy of mass action. Boycotts, strikes and so on.

"Then Robert Sobukwe - from Graaff Reinet just up the road," Arthur indicated in the direction of the hinterland, "became president of the Pan Africanist Congress, the PAC, in April 1959, and the Sharpeville demonstration was called to protest the need to carry passbooks."

"So, 60 were shot and killed. At a peaceful protest about the pass laws?" Nancy seemed shocked.

"Yes, we say 69, the authorities say fewer. Maybe some stones were thrown at the police. But there were about 300 cops there. They had armoured cars and rifles.

"Yes, the pass laws. The government had recently decided all blacks in white urban areas had to carry a passbook to show they were allowed to be in the area. If they didn't have one, they were jailed.

"Anyway, in similar demonstrations that day at the police station in Vanderbijlpark, another person was shot and killed and, later that day at another Langa, a township outside Cape Town, police baton charged and fired tear gas at the gathered protesters, shooting three dead and wounding others."

They sat for a while in silence, soaking up the sun's warmth and drinking their coffee - reflecting on this turbulent period.

"It's strange, I remember at school being told that the Boer War, when the Dutch farmers and the English occupying army fought over who owned South Africa, marked the beginning of the end of the worldwide British Empire. Now some of our leaders are saying Sharpeville signalled the start of armed resistance here. It has prompted worldwide condemnation of apartheid and it could be the start of our path to full democracy."

Just then Nancy's son emerged from their room, rubbing sleep from his eyes and went to his mother for a hug. Almost simultaneously, more police vehicles came past and Nancy flinched and hugged her son.

"Why are you scared?" Arthur asked, "They're not

interested in us. They have other things to worry about."

Nancy quickly finished her coffee, turned to Sam and said, "I'll make some breakfast," and then, looking at Arthur, said softly. "It's a long story, I'll tell you one day. But now I must get Sam ready and we must go to the shops."

Arthur, concerned about his friend and her fear of the police, said: "OK, I'll walk with you. It's quite a way and I am worried about this funeral and all the police about." He was warmed by Nancy's grateful look.

They gave themselves some time to get ready before the long walk to the township shopping complex. A walk of about two kilometres there and back - not too far for township dwellers.

But on that day, March 21, 1985, it was a walk that would change their lives.

***

Hangovers, hot sun and the smell of diesel fuel did not go well together, Jimmy Jonker realised as the Hippo bucked over the township's bad gravel roads and he struggled to hold the rising nausea down.

"Jeez," he thought, "All I need to do now is puke and I'm no longer the darts hero but just some sissy who can't hold his drink."

Focusing on the tip of his rifle and trying to ignore all around him, Jimmy zoned in on the crackle of the radio being held and used by Cas. He heard the Lieutenant say he'd head for Maduna Road - in response to some static-laden instruction from base.

Cas passed on an instruction to the driver and the vehicle lurched to the right, the sun now directly in Jimmy's eyes, making the growing alcohol-induced headache even worse.

"I must remember not to mix beer with brandy-and-coke," Jimmy thought, recalling the after-match switch to hard tack, maybe a few more than he should have had. But, hey, what a way to bow out, winning the last match and getting the police trophy for the second year running.

His thoughts were interrupted by Cas's shout to halt.

Jimmy then realised that, while he and the other policemen were sitting swaying and rocking in the vehicle, the officer had stood, holding onto the hot metal side of the troop carrier and staring ahead, something like a Roman centurion leading his forces, Jimmy thought. Although this was a rather one-sided war - heavily armed police and troops against township dwellers with stones and, at best, knives and pangas.

Cas was getting excited in his conversation with headquarters, something about a gathering crowd heading for the funeral in KwaNobuhle. He was being told, it appeared, to block off the side roads and funnel anyone who was walking in the area into the main road, making it easier for crowd control should there be a need.

"Oh no," Jimmy thought, "this is going to be a lousy day. It would have been far nicer to have a quick ride around the area, see nothing out of the ordinary, and head back to base. A cold shower, some strong coffee and a nap - that's the ticket."

But now he had to contend with a throbbing head, the radio crackle, nausea, a full bladder and some work. Then Cas called to Jimmy.

"Hey, you're at the back. There are some people walking up the road. Tell them to go away."

Jimmy looked up. In front of the Hippo were a young black man, a slim woman in jeans and a child. It was unusual to see a black woman in jeans – and so slender. Normally the women of the Xhosa tribes in this area wore skirts or dresses and were often round and a bit overweight. The trio was walking towards KwaNobuhle.

"Get out and turn them around. These buggers obviously don't understand. Tell them that's what I want. And that's what they will do."

His helmet falling into his eyes as he clambered ungainly out of the vehicle, Jimmy was not happy. He walked up to the trio, the kid looking at him with big wide eyes, apparently fascinated by the rifle he was carrying. The woman with her head turned as if not wanting to be aware of his presence and the man was defiant, standing, protectively, slightly ahead of the other two.

"I'm sorry," Jimmy said speaking English and pushing his helmet back so he could see them properly, "but you guys will have to go back to the main road. The officer says no people are allowed on the side roads. Not today at any rate."

The black man looked at him with surprise, obviously wondering why this soldier was being so courteous. The norm would have been for the soldier to swear, prod them with his rifle and push them away.

"OK. But I don't think that's a good idea, there's a huge crowd of people coming. I think there will be trouble," said Arthur, feeling compelled to be friendly, too. Nancy still faced the other way, sneaking looks at the white man while she held firmly on to Sam's hand.

"Ja, we know," said Jimmy, after all, the police were meant to know everything. "Best you just go home then."

As the trio turned away, Jimmy struggled back into the Hippo. The Lieutenant was talking on the radio and issuing orders for the soldiers to cock their weapons.

"There's hell to pay. Appears there's an illegal march in the main road. These buggers just won't listen."

On the road, as they started walking back to the main road, Arthur looked at Nancy. She was crying.

"What's wrong?" he asked, putting his arm comfortingly around her shoulders. She leant against him.

"I'm sorry, I can't talk about it now. Maybe later."

Just then they were covered in dust as the Hippos roared past, heading for the main road about 200 metres away, Arthur's puzzled expression lost to Nancy as the tears blurred her vision and left tracks in the dust on her cheeks.

6

LANGA, THE SHOOTING

It was a standoff.

About 3,000 people wanting to head southwest, from Langa to KwaNobuhle, were strung out across the road and its wide unkempt verges, stretching back about 100 metres. The crowd formed a formidable mass.

In front of them parked across the road with its engine still running and diesel exhaust fumes filling the back compartment where the troops stood were two Hippos. They held a total of 14 men, including the drivers and the Lieutenant who was still taking orders on his crackling, static-hissing radio.

Jimmy was really feeling bad. The radio noise, the diesel fumes and the hangover were not what he needed right now. The sun was beating down and his head was throbbing, sweat trickling down his face from under the helmet. Around him, the young policemen were wary of the mass of people near them on the road.

Most of his colleagues were young men like him. They were living with the prospect of being attacked and having to shoot to protect themselves. It was a tense time and their nervous tension almost crackled in the air.

Jimmy half heard Cas say into the radio, "Okay, I'll warn them".

Then Cas picked up a loudhailer and said, in Afrikaans and then in his broken English: "This is an illegal gathering. You have been warned. You have five minutes to disperse."

The crowd edged closer. What was that man saying? The loudhailer was ineffective against the hum of the crowd and the steady rumble of the idling Hippo engines. Only those in the front two rows and nearest the Hippos had heard what he said. Further back, people were asking what was happening. Why had the walking stopped? They pushed forward. Keen to find out what was going on. The front rows had to take a step forward to stay standing as the crowd behind edged forward.

"Stop where you are! Do not come closer!" Cas shouted into the loudhailer, his raised voice only serving to create a screeching feedback, making his words unintelligible. Panic was becoming obvious on his face. Sweat was running down his pink cheeks.

A Rastafarian at the front of the crowd took a step forward seemingly ignoring the officer's instruction, and asked: "Why? All we want to do is go to a funeral and bury our dead. What's wrong with that?" He was not aggressive. Bold, perhaps, in questioning the white man, but not aggressive.

Cas told him, through the loudhailer, that the funeral had been banned. This message got to the second row and was relayed backwards, the voices causing a rising rumble through the crowd that was continuing to grow in size. There was confusion and disappointment. But not everyone heard the message.

The crowd pushed forward.

The officer raised his loudhailer again. Troops in the back of the vehicles were struggling to see what was happening.

The Rastafarian again asked why the funeral had been banned.

Cas's response was, "I have warned you to disperse. You now have less than two minutes."

"And then what?" asked the Rastafarian, self-appointed as the spokesman for the mass of humanity now only about 30 metres from the Hippos.

"We will force you to go," said the now obviously nervous officer.

He was struggling to communicate with the man on the ground in front of him and his superior officer on the radio who wanted to know what was going on. Cas asked for reinforcements, saying the crowd was about 5,000 strong and refusing to disperse.

The Rastafarian, a Bible clutched in one hand, bent down and picked up a fairly large stone. He looked up at the white and obviously tense police officer and said, defiantly: "We have done nothing. You have guns. We have only a few stones like this. They cannot harm you in your armoured vehicle."

Again the crowd edged forward. Confusion was beginning to turn to anger. Anger at being delayed this way.

It was hot. They wanted to be at the funeral to bury and honour their dead, not stand in the sun and argue with a soldier. It was the speeches of their leaders they wanted. Not this.

Cas warned his troops to get ready. Jimmy stood with the rest, feeling shaky and rested his semi-automatic rifle on the side of the Hippo. The engine was still running, the fumes still filling the air. All the men stood, their weapons pointing at the crowd.

Again Cas warned the crowd to disperse. Again the message was lost on the vast majority and they pressed forward.

"Get ready to fire a warning shot," Cas said to a constable next to him.

The young man cocked his weapon, the others following suit as they took their cue from him. Cas was watching the Rastafarian and did not notice.

The crowd continued to edge closer. Voices rising in anger at this delay.

"You have had five minutes. This is your last chance to disperse," Cas shouted.

The Rastafarian raised the arm with the stone still clutched in his hand, apparently hoping to stop the crowd surging forward. They were now about 20 metres from the Hippo.

The soldiers were concerned as they clutched their rifles. Some looked nervously at their officer who was talking hurriedly into the radio. Others aimed their weapons in a show of bravado, trying to hide their fear. Even if the crowd only had stones, they were vastly outnumbered.

Cas said quietly, as he changed his mind, to the constable: "Load some tearsmoke. Wait for my command.

Perhaps that will scare them away"

No-one else heard him.

Jimmy and the troops were worried. Many had aimed their rifles at the crowd – almost in a show of bravado.

Why was that Rastafarian fellow waving that stone around?

Why was the crowd getting bigger and closer, refusing to disperse?

Why were they getting louder and, it appeared, more aggressive?

"Fire," shouted Cas to the constable.

The dozing driver was startled, his foot slipping from the clutch and the vehicle jerked forward. Before the soldier with his tearsmoke grenade could even lift his weapon, a ragged volley broke out as troops were thrown against each other, trigger fingers clenching instinctively.

Hendrik bumped Jimmy as they all fell to one side like dominoes being tumbled in that childish game, causing him to pull his trigger. In front of him he saw the Rastafarian pitch backwards, his stone and Bible falling from his hand as the bullet entered his chest.

Jimmy stood stunned. In shock at the inescapable fact that he had just killed a man. He felt sick. He felt as if he was floating, removed from the situation. Besides the shock of shooting someone, Jimmy was still feeling that weird deafness which follows a volley of shots. A feeling of detachment, helped by the dull ringing in his ears from the noise of the rifles firing right next to him and a dry mouth. Like being in a bad dream.

***

About 200 metres away, in some knee-high scrub bush to the right of the stand-off and fairly well hidden from view, Arthur, who was shepherding Nancy and Sam away from the area, watched the developing situation and stopped dead in shock as he heard, first, the shots, then the screams.

Instinctively, Arthur pulled Nancy and Sam to the

ground. Peering through the bushes, Arthur saw the crowd turn and run. But many in front had already fallen. Being side on, he had the Hippos to his left and the huge, swarming crowd to his right.

A pall of white-grey cordite smoke hung momentarily over the Hippos as Arthur saw some people in the forefront of the crowd fall to the ground.

First it was the Rastafarian with the distinctive red, yellow and green headscarf. Next was a youngster, about 12 or 13, who was pushing a bike and at the edge of the crowd nearest Arthur and Nancy. The boy had already turned away from the Hippo and was pushed forward about two metres, as if he had been kicked in the back, such was the impact of the shots that struck him. He arched like a tightly drawn bow before crumbling into an untidy heap, sprawled over his bike.

In a few moments more people turned and ran. More people fell as bullets hit them from behind. Some were shot from the front as they stood, shocked and stunned by what was going on.

Suddenly it was silent. All over in seconds. A deathly, foreboding quiet descended on the killing field as the shooting stopped.

This was followed by the muffled scurrying of many feet as people continued to flee and then, slowly, the rising sound of the cries of the injured. There were wails, sobs and cries of pain. Many continued to run away. Some went back to help those who were hurt.

From the Hippos, there was not a movement or a sound.

Cas, the most visible, stood with his mouth hanging open - as if unable to believe what had happened. The radio microphone dangled from one hand, the loudhailer from the other. Around him was heavy breathing, as if everyone in the Hippos had just run a tough race.

The men were frozen, staring ahead as if cast in stone.

Then, above the sounds from the strewn bodies ahead of the Hippo, came the rumble and roar of more vehicles. Over the rise behind them came two more Hippos and a

Landrover carrying the officer in charge of township patrols for the day. The vehicles pulled to a stop near the stationary Hippos.

The captain, as if awoken from a spell, slowly got out of the Hippo as his troops, too, seemed to come to life.

Ahead of them some bodies squirmed, some lay still, limbs widespread as if they were rag dolls discarded by a child. There were a few moans and whimpers. The rest of the crowd had disappeared as if spirited away.

The senior officer, a colonel, asked Cas what had happened.

"Why the bloody hell did you use live rounds and not tearsmoke?" he demanded.

Cas, still in shock, responded, "I did. I mean, we loaded some but ... then there were just shots. Lots of shots as everyone fired."

The colonel quickly summed up the situation. It looked bad.

"Okay. I'll radio for medical help. Get your men, in the meantime, to leave in my two Hippos. They must go back to base."

He then turned to his junior officer. "Get your men to put stones at the bodies, put some in their hands. Put some in the Hippos. It must look as if they attacked first and we fired in self defence."

He turned away. "The commissioner will never believe this, South Africa won't. Hell, the world will never believe this was done," he muttered as he settled back into his Landrover to radio - first his report to headquarters and then summonsing emergency medical aid teams.

***

To one side, Arthur and Nancy watched in horror as the white troops moved among the dead and wounded. They stared, dumbstruck as they saw the colonel return with some petrol bombs which he distributed haphazardly - even breaking one against the Hippo's side so it was soaked in petrol.

As the troops spread wider and closer to them, Arthur whispered to Nancy: "We have to get out of here. Get Sam to crawl backwards with us. If we get to that wall behind us we will be okay."

About 40 metres away was a low wall, behind it some streets and houses. They could lose themselves in there quite easily from anyone chasing them. Slowly, the three slithered backwards over the rough ground. As they got to the wall, Sam screamed. He had cut his knee on a broken beer bottle.

Arthur looked back, saw some troops looking and pointing in their direction.

"Run," he shouted to Nancy as she clambered over the wall and he grabbed Sam, lifting him over. "See you at home."

As he climbed onto the wall, he heard the colonel shout: "Stop them. They might have seen what we have done."

Suddenly Arthur's trousers snagged on a jagged brick, halting his progress. He heard a crack and then, almost immediately, a sharp sound as a bullet hit the wall near his shoulder. He could not work out which sounds had come first. Using all his force, he ripped his trouser leg and cut his leg as he fell to the ground over the wall and out of sight of the now running troops. Gathering himself, he sprinted after Nancy and Sam who had just disappeared into the warren of streets and haphazard buildings that made up the outskirts of Langa. As he ran he heard the sirens of the approaching first aid vehicles.

There were no more shots.

7

THE STREETS OF LANGA

It was strange. The usually bustling Langa was quiet - almost like a ghost town in an old Western movie.

Arthur jogged to catch up to Nancy and Sam. The youngster was limping, favouring his cut leg, while Arthur, too, was limping, having cut and bruised his knees while getting his snagged trouser leg free and then falling over the wall - spurred on by the shot fired at him. Not an elegant tumble, he thought, but effective.

As he drew closer to Nancy and Sam, he noticed there were not too many people on the streets. Usually there were kids playing soccer with an old tennis ball, some make-up games of cricket, away from the dust of the soccer games, with an old tomato box as wickets. Watching the kids play would be the older teenagers and the out-of-work 20-somethings, idly smoking, trading drugs, or just soaking up the sun.

In the doorways of the small houses would be the housewives, mothers of sucking babies or toddlers or grandmothers.

But today, as he jogged closer to his companions, Arthur saw only the occasional face at a window and some teenagers in the doorway.

"Hey, wait for me," he called to Nancy as he got closer.

She stopped, turned and gasped as she saw his torn trouser leg, blood on his exposed knee and his hobbling gait.

"Were you shot? Are you OK? Oh, Arthur ..." her voice broke into a sob.

"Naah, I'm fine, just a scratch. How's Sam's leg?"

She smiled weakly. "Just a scratch, too. You know how boys are."

Arthur turned to Sam. "Hey, brave boy. Well done on walking and running away with that cut. Let me look."

Sam proudly showed off the cut in the fleshy part of his

leg just above the knee.

"It's nothing that a bandage cannot fix," said Arthur as he tore a piece off his torn trouser leg - more to keep dust out of Sam's wound and to appease the boy's ego than to help the cut.

"There we go, you should be able to walk now," he said minutes later and was pleased to note that, after a tentative step, Sam walked normally. Holding his hands and swinging their arms to keep Sam happy, the three walked down the dusty road back towards Arthur's house.

"That was scary," Nancy said softly to Arthur as they walked. "I never expected to see such callous brutality. I mean, I saw soldiers in Ovamboland and they did attack and shoot … in our villages. They even killed my grandfather, but he was trying to protect me and his home," her voice tailed off and she shuddered with the memory as they walked along.

"Well, we have to do something. We cannot let this go unnoticed," said Arthur.

"Surely people will know and will tell the story?" asked Nancy.

"Well," replied Arthur, "There'll be talk and the townships will know. But if you look at the newspapers, there is very little about what actually goes on here. The whites do not get the full story of the brutal ways of the police."

He stopped in his tracks as he saw a telephone booth, a rare sight in the area, on the opposite corner as they approached a four-way crossing.

"I've got to tell the papers," he said walking firmly towards the booth, taking change out of his pocket.

Looking up the Herald's number, dialling and depositing the right money, he asked for the news editor. A woman answered. He told her there'd been a shooting. When she asked his name, he got cold feet and hung up.

"That's not the way," said Nancy, "You have to tell them."

Arthur called again. This time a man answered.

"Hello, I'm at a phone box in Langa. I called earlier. We saw the shooting. The police just opened fire for no reason. Then we saw them moving the bodies. Those that were running away when the shooting started."

The voice on the other side asked him where he was. He replied, "Hendricks Street is where my house is. Will you send a reporter? I'm Arthur Shipalana, I want to tell you what happened."

He was told a reporter and a photographer would be there as soon as they could before he hung up and they walked towards the house, all holding hands again.

"Well done," said Nancy squeezing his hand.

"I'm not too sure," responded Arthur. "If the Herald uses my name, the police will find me. My life, if I survive the grilling, will not be worth living."

"Maybe they won't use your name, or you can make up a name," Nancy suggested.

"We'll see."

A short while later they were home and cleaned up their wounds. The cleaning up and addition of a plaster seemed to perk Sam up and he went to play with a tennis ball in the yard with Arthur and Nancy watching.

***

Lost.

That was the only word for it. Clive decided to deviate off his route into the Langa area as he saw police vehicles up ahead, hoping to find a short cut to Maduna Road. Now, thanks to a large absence of street names signs, he was blundering north west, Jamie reading out the occasional street name that had not been removed or defaced.

"All we need is for the cops to ask what we're doing here. What do we say? 'Looking for the spot where you shot lots of people' and they're going to say 'Oh yes, just over the rise. Come we'll show you'. Not bloody likely."

Jamie winced as the car hit a bump. "Yes, maybe they'll chase us off but that's no need to drive like a rally ace!

"Anyway, best we don't make contact out here. They might be a bit touchy."

Clive smiled. "A bit touchy? Understatement of note,

Jamie.

"One of my neighbours is a policeman and he's hugely stressed. Says they've been working 18 to 20 hours a day and the pressure out there when patrolling the townships is incredible. He said even though they know they have more weapons and firepower than any potential threat the townships might throw at them, their fear is petrol bombs."

"Petrol bombs?" Jamie asked.

"Yes, these Hippos they're using are actually anti-mine personnel carriers designed for use on the border in the bush and desert, not urban stuff. So, they've got armoured sides and floor and are open to the sky. Anyone, with a fairly good aim, could throw a Molotov Cocktail in and the guys inside are in trouble."

Clive stopped at the next intersection, trying to guess which way to go.

"Not many people about," he said "Usually there are kids all over." With a shrug he turned left.

"Ah, Hendricks Street," said Jamie as he looked at his road map trying to plot where they were.

Clive brought the car to a stop and leant across to check the map too. As the two newsmen pored over the map, there was a loud thud as something landed on the roof of the car. Clive swore as he ducked instinctively, hitting his cheek on Jamie's elbow as the reporter raised his arms to cover his face. Both thought they were under attack and being stoned. After all white men in the township were an unusual sight, unless they were government officials who were not popular. As they looked at each other, there was knock on the left rear side window.

They turned and standing there was a young black man, holding a little boy by the hand. Jamie got out of the car.

The man spoke first, greeting Jamie in Afrikaans.

"No, no," replied the reporter. "No need for that, we're English-speaking. We're from the Herald."

"Ah," responded the man, "Well, this guy has something to say, and he'll do it now."

He looked down at the boy who hesitatingly said, "Sorry about my ball hitting your car."

Clive, who had also got out of the car, said, "It's better than a rock."

The boy looked puzzled, looked up at the man holding his hand who nodded and then the boy walked. off back to the house where the car had stopped.

"Are you here to see me? I'm Arthur Shipalana," said the man, holding out his hand.

Jamie shook it and, looking towards Clive, said: "To see you? Why? We're lost, trying to get to Maduna Road."

Now it was Arthur's turn to be perplexed. "Oh, I … I uh, called. I phoned the newspaper and said I had a story." He stopped, uncertain of whether he should continue.

Clive took over. "Maybe, but we're looking for Maduna Road, there's been a shooting there?"

Arthur's face lit up. "That's why I called. We saw it, saw the police shooting people. They were unarmed. We saw it all. It happened over there," He turned and pointed up the road. "It's about a kilometre away."

Clive looked at Jamie and made a quick decision. "You stay here and interview him, I'll be back. I'm going up the road to see what I can photograph."

"You'll pass a phone box at the crossing," said Arthur. "Go straight on. Stop after about 200 metres and go up the slight rise to your right. There's a wall there. It's just over that. But be careful, they could still be there."

As Clive drove off, Jamie got ready for what he felt was definitely going to be a front page story. An eye witness account of a police shooting.

It was to be much more.

8

THE AFTERMATH

The sight that Clive saw when he peeked over the wall shocked the seasoned photographer to the core.

The broad picture showed two Police Hippos were parked across the road to his left. Another pair with a Landrover was behind them. Policemen swarmed about and it was what they were doing that stunned the photographer as he fitted a long telephoto lens to his camera.

He saw an officer issuing instructions and men dragging bodies of black people lying along the road and in the scrub alongside it closer to the two Hippos in the road.

Clive lifted the camera and got a shot of a policeman picking up a woman's body. He watched through the lens, snapping occasionally, as the man carried his load towards the vehicles.

"That looks heroic," muttered Clive to himself.

Then the policeman stopped about 10 metres from the Hippos and just dropped the body into the road, near a discarded bicycle. The woman's legs and arms splaying awkwardly like a rag doll. Dust rose and settled as Clive took picture after picture.

"Should have brought the motordrive," he said.

As he changed film, Clive saw more policemen placing stones near the bodies. Others, to his amazement, took pangas out of the back of the Landrover and put these long, lethal knives on the ground near the bodies of younger men.

"This is crap. I can't believe it," Clive got a few more shots off. He even got some of policemen attacking the Hippos with stones to make marks on the paintwork. He watched as one, in vain, tried to crack the bullet-proof glass of one windscreen by pounding at with a rock as he stood on the engine cover. "The man looks stupid, but it makes good pictures," Clive thought.

Just then, some emergency vehicles came over the hill. Two ambulances and a Volvo estate car with its lights flashing. The police officer shouted some commands which Clive could not hear from his vantage point about 200 metres away with the approaching vehicles' engines not helping. But the policemen stopped moving bodies and stones and trotted over to assemble near their vehicles. He saw Des Hughes the paramedic chief walk over to the senior police officer, a colonel it appeared through the long lens. The officer pointed to the bodies and Des sent medics to go through the people lying on the ground. Clive counted 21 or 22. Some were lying too close to each other to be sure.

He took a few more pictures as bodies were carried away on stretchers to the waiting ambulances.

Interestingly, it appeared there were no wounded - only dead people.

***

Sitting in the shade outside Arthur's home, Jamie gratefully accepted a mug of coffee and watched as the young African man seemed to protect the slender woman and child. He ushered them through to the back while he and Jamie took seats at the front door.

"So," said Jamie as he got his note book and recorder ready, "tell me about yourself".

"No recording, please," asked Arthur. "If the Security Police get their hands on that, they'll trace my voice. It's not that I don't trust you, but ..."

Jamie readily agreed. "Well, as long as we know who you are and can verify that, we don't need to use your name in the paper. But my editor will want to know you're real. OK?"

"No worry about that. Ok. I'm Arthur Shipalana, aged 25, just turned 25 a few days ago. I was studying a BA in political science at Fort Hare University but about two years ago my parents died in a taxi smash. My father was working for Volkswagen, a senior line worker, and he was helping pay my fees. My sister, Miriam, who is 19, is studying teaching in Grahamstown. I thought she's got more chance of work with teaching than a political science graduate. So I started at VW so she could study."

Jamie listened intently. "A noble gesture. What happened next?"

"Well, with all the growing unrest and strikes, we were put on short time at the car plant, so I work maybe two or three days a week."

"And," asked Jamie, "that woman and child you were with? The one whose ball hit our car?"

"Yes, they're refugees. Came here from South West. Nancy's an Ovambo. Had some trouble in her life and Sam is her little boy. I don't know too much about them but she's looking for work and has some money. So she lives here too."

Jamie sensed a secondary story but that could wait. "So, tell me what you saw this morning."

Arthur settled into his chair, took a swig of his coffee and began his tale while Jamie wrote furiously.

"Nancy, Sam and I were walking to the shops. Then we saw the police vehicles in front of us. One man got out when they stopped and told us we could not walk there - Maduna Road where we were going. I knew about the crowd coming and he told us to go away. So we took another route, but as we came over the rise we saw the vehicles, the same ones I think, in front of a crowd of our people - about 2,000 maybe more.

"We were in the bush and long grass about 200 metres away when suddenly there were shots. I had been watching the crowd and all I saw was a Rasta guy in front, and a child on a bike to the side. The crowd were moving slowly forward, bunching up on those in front who had stopped.

"The shots were sudden and for no reason. The Rasta guy fell, the kid with the bike fell. Others dropped were they were and the front part of the crowd turned to run but behind them, people were still pushing forward. Only stopping after the first few shots. But it was too late. The

39

ones in front were shot where they were. It was horrible." He trailed off as Jamie still scribbled furiously, wishing his shorthand was better.

Arthur took another sip of his now cooling coffee and continued. "It all happened so quickly. We were stunned. We just stayed where we were, crouching and watching.

"I think it was planned by the police because they used live ammunition.

"That procession could have been stopped using teargas like they usually did but this time they used live ammunition. I think it was a conscious decision. They shot those people with live ammunition, even while they were running, so many were shot in the back while they were running away."

Jamie looked up at Arthur and saw the pain in his eyes.

"Then more police arrived, within minutes. And we saw the man in charge get other policemen to put stones and even petrol bombs next to the bodies. It is wrong, they, the people, did nothing wrong. They were just shot and killed for no reason.

"Then as we crawled away to the wall I told your photographer about, Sam hurt his knee and the police heard his cry. They chased us as we were getting over the wall. Shots were fired, but we got away," again he paused.

Jamie was dumbfounded.

"Amazing," he thought to himself. "An eyewitness account - brilliant!"

Just then Nancy joined them.

"Where's Sam?" Arthur asked.

"Oh, he's asleep. I think the excitement this morning was just too much."

She sat down, looked shyly at Jamie and then said to Arthur: "Have you told the story? There's something I want to say too."

Jamie sat forward, interested in a corroboration angle.

"Yes, he knows what happened," Arthur said.

"Not everything, nor do you." the young woman said, looking distressed. "Remember when that soldier spoke to us in the road before the shooting?" she asked Arthur.

"Yes," he replied, "You were crying. You said he reminded you of something in your past."

Jamie watched and listened, wondering where this was going.

"Well, he reminded me of my past, of a soldier in South West, in Ovamboland," she paused, gulping for air.

"Oh, well, they all look the same in uniform," said Arthur.

"No, it was the eyes. He is the same as the man who attacked our village with his other soldiers. The man who killed my father. Just shot him in front of me as he tried to keep me safe. Then the man, who looked like the soldier today, a lot like him but meaner, he raped me."

Arthur and Jamie were stunned.

"I couldn't tell you earlier, I felt dirty, used."

Arthur moved to comfort her. "It's not your fault," he replied, realising as he spoke that his words were of little comfort.

Nancy moved slightly away. "That's not all," she said, "He would have killed me too but another soldier stopped him and looked after me. Not long afterwards I discovered I was pregnant. Sam is that man's son. I hate the man, the one who raped me, but I love Sam."

She turned to the bemused reporter. "You must tell that story too."

9

LANGA AND MORE AFTERMATH

Nancy Nujomba's story was spellbinding and harrowing. And Jamie was quite keen to hear it - as they waited for Clive to return.

"The day of the rape in 1977 was another quiet day in our village. Not many men were about as the younger ones had either run away and joined SWAPO or run away to hide from the SA soldiers who would think they were SWAPO anyway. The older men, like my father, looked after the few cows and goats we had and did repairs around the place.

"So a hot, dusty day, like any other. I was cooking and could hear engines in the distance but thought nothing of it. The army vehicles were always passing by.

"But then there was a loud bang. An explosion nearby and then some shots. Just like those we heard this morning. Women were shouting and screaming for their children to come back to the huts. My father made me go inside and he stood at the door to our hut as soldiers approached, their guns ready and shouting at us to come out of the huts.

"There were only a few of them, about 10, there were more in the distance. Most walked passed our hut, it was nearest to the entrance of our village. I stood looking over my father's shoulder in the darkness inside. One soldier saw my dad and stopped. He had orange hair and blue, blue eyes.

"I think he saw me behind my father. My father tried to block the door to hide me. I walked backwards into the hut, watching all the time. The soldier walked up to my father, his gun ready. My father said, 'There's just me here'."

"The soldier paused, looked at him and then looked in the direction the other soldiers had gone, further into the village. He looked back at the hut and I took another step back. That was my mistake. I stepped on the cooking pot

I'd left on the floor and it banged into another one, making a loud clattering noise.

"The soldier asked 'No-one here?' and moved even closer, trying to look over my father's shoulder and into the hut. I don't think he saw me, but then he pushed my father with his gun and my father fell back into the hut. I screamed. I could not help it. That was my father he hit." She paused, sobbing quietly at the memories she was recalling.

Jamie wrote furiously while Arthur moved to hold her hand. Regaining her composure, she spoke on.

"It was horrible. He saw me and smiled this ugly smile, almost a snarl, like a hyena.

"Aha, a girl," he said and stepped into the darkness of the hut. My father stood up trying to push the man out of the hut. He then hit my father again, with his gun, swearing at him.

"Just then there was some shooting from inside the village. The soldier stopped, seeming uncertain. My father stood up and walked to me, to shield me, I think. I looked at him but could not see his eyes. It was too dark.

"Suddenly there was this bang and my father tumbled forward, spray from him hitting me in the face and on my body. It was his blood. I saw it later. He fell to the floor. The soldier pushed him to one side. I stood still, too scared to move. Then he stepped over my father, grabbed me and tore my dress off. Then, then, he ..."

She stopped and sobbed again. It was quiet, just the sound of her sobbing.

"Then another soldier came in. It was afterwards. He hit the man who attacked me and then called for help and someone to look after me. He was a good man, I'll never forget his face, or that of the man who attacked me. And that policeman today? The one who spoke to us on the road? He looked a lot like him, like his brother."

Just then, Clive's car came around the corner and skidded to a stop.

"Come on Jamie," he shouted out the window, not even switching the engine off. "We have to get back to the office.

I have good stuff here." He waved his camera as Jamie said a hurried goodbye, promising to make contact again and giving Arthur his direct line extension and his home number.

"I need to speak to you again. Call me when you can later today or tomorrow and we can make a plan to get together and talk further. We have to tell your story. But we need to be cautious too, extremely careful. We don't want the police finding out who you are."

He ran to the car and Clive drove off in a cloud of dust.

***

Arthur waited until the car had gone from view, then he turned and hugged his friend.

"Are you OK?" he asked, his voice heavy with care and affection.

"Yes," she replied. "I have more to tell you, let's have some coffee."

As Arthur made more coffee, she checked on Sam, who was still asleep, and then returned to the front of the house. They sat, a few minutes later, in a companionable silence, sipping their coffee. Arthur waited for her to continue.

Just then, with a roar of engine noise, two police Hippos came speeding down the road and skidded to a stop. An officer stood up in the first one, looked at the two and shouted: "Have you been here all day? Have you seen any white people in the township? Have you had trouble with crowds passing by? Did you hear shooting?" The questions tumbled one into another.

Arthur stood up and looked dutifully obedient as he replied, almost scuffing his feet in the dust in subservience, which he knew would impress the police officer. "No sir, nothing. We've been here all day, waiting for my sister to come home and to look after the house because there are many hooligans about and they will steal things."

The officer asked again: "Are you sure? We are looking for two white men who were here in a silver Cortina. They are reporters from the paper."

Arthur looked puzzled and asked what a reporter looks like, to make them different from other white people.

The officer swore at this man's stupidity and commanded his convoy to continue.

Arthur looked at Nancy and winked.

"You did that so well, even I believed you," she said. "I hope the reporters got out safely."

As Arthur settled down again and sipped his coffee, she told him, as briefly as she could, about her decision to leave South West Africa after Sam was born in 1978.

"There were more and more soldiers in the area, both South African and the SWAPO as well as Cubans and it was hard to have a normal life. With my father dead, I had no close family. My brother had gone to Angola and I hadn't heard from him since he'd left in 1974.

"Then there was a truck carrying army equipment that stopped near our village with a flat tyre. Sam was a year old. Myself, Sam and a friend got a ride south with the truck. Almost all the way to Windhoek where my friend had a relative who worked on the railways. We stayed with him for about three months. I got some part-time domestic work and things were going well for a while.

"But her cousin was a drinker and one night he tried to get into my bed while drunk. I refused him and he hit me.

"The next day I took Sam and we caught a train to Johannesburg. On the train I met some people who let me live with them in Soweto and then, again after a few months, I met a woman from Langa who told me there was more chance of work here. And you know the rest, meeting me at the bus stop near the station after visiting your sister and then offering Sam and me a place to stay."

Arthur was impressed.

"That's quite an epic story. But today's been epic as well."

Just then they heard Sam cry from the shack at the back.

"He's awake, time for a late lunch."

As they picked up their chairs and started moving to the

back of the property, Arthur saw a dark blue car with two white men in it coast to a stop at the top of Hendricks Road. One was talking on a radio, the other had binoculars aimed at Arthur.

10

THE STORY OF THE YEAR

Organised chaos seemed to rule in the newsroom. Phones were ringing, reporters answering, photographers hovering, the atmosphere tense and busy.

Daniel, having debriefed Jamie and Clive and sent them to write and process film, wondered what had happened to John and Mark. They'd been gone about three hours and not a word.

The news editor's job, at this time, was extremely pressurised. Not only did he have to have his finger on the pulse of the newsroom and attempt to maintain some order and calmness, but there were the calls from other newspapers, radio and TV to contend with. From the BBC world service to the newspaper in nearby East London and radio reporters expecting an instant on-the-phone interview, the calls were a continual stream - tying up one of the newsdesk phones.

More ominous were the calls from the police. Most were from the PR officer, Carl Strydom, who expected the newspaper to give him first look at all the reports so he could vet them and add suitable police comment. The last one, about two minutes ago and from which his mind was still reeling, had come from his old rival, Frans Jonker.

"Hello, Daniel, or should I say *Lieutenant* Jacobs? We need to have a little chat, you and me."

"Really?" responded Daniel, suddenly alert as he recognised the security policeman's voice.

"Ja, you have some information we need to have too."

"Well, we're dealing with Carl, Colonel Strydom. I suggest you speak to him."

"Whoa," said Frans. "It's about what you are going to publish. Well, not exactly. It's more about where you get your information. See, we know your teams have spoken to two people who claim to have witnessed what happened in Maduna Road, am I right?"

Daniel was stunned.

Clive and Jamie had been back about an hour. They must have left Arthur and the woman about 45 minutes before that and driven straight to the office. Only he, June, Jamie and Clive knew what information they had got from Arthur. He hadn't even got around to telling Jake yet.

"Really?" he said to Frans, his mind racing; trying to work out how Frans and his cronies knew.

"Yes, really. We have sources you don't know about. Anyway, two things we, and you, need to be aware of. Firstly, your sources are lying. They didn't see a thing. They are just publicity seekers and want to harm the image of the police.

"Secondly, and for that very reason, we need to have their address and whereabouts. A little chat to put them right is called for here," Frans said, a high-pitched giggle following his last words.

Daniel waited for the sick giggling to stop. "OK. Two things you need to be aware of. Firstly, we check our sources and verify, as far as is humanly possible under these circumstances, what they tell us.

"Secondly, I am not compelled to give you any information about our sources. And, at the same time, I am neither confirming nor denying we spoke to two people who claim to have seen the shooting. You say you want to find out who they are? Ask someone else. You want to know what they saw. Read tomorrow's Herald." Daniel was angry as he slammed the phone down.

Telling June he needed to speak to Jake, he marched off to the editor's office.

"Ah, Dan, just the man I want to speak to," said Jake, briefly looking up from his computer where he had been pounding on the keyboard with his stubby index fingers, able to bash out around 60 words a minute, before continuing his keyboard assault. "See, I'm doing an editorial on police brutality and the inequality of the battle in the townships. What news? Is there a firm death toll yet?"

"Yes, 22. And we have an eyewitness report verifying

everything we suspected. It's indisputable that about 16 police in the two Hippos opened fire on an unarmed crowd heading for the funerals. They were seemingly unprovoked, the marchers peaceful.

"We have interviewed two eyewitnesses. Jamie is writing it up now. Clive has photographs of the bodies still on the road and of the police apparently placing stones around the corpses."

Jake had stopped typing and swivelled to give his news editor his full attention.

"Are you serious?"

"Yes, we have all of that. We have to run it past the authorities though. And here's the catch. The security police know about our sources."

"What! How could they?" Jake looked perplexed.

"I don't know. Also, I've not heard from John and Mark who went to Uitenhage. John was convinced he could track down the Cradock Four and I also told them to go to the hospital and check what's happening there. Anyway, I'll keep you posted," Daniel said as he turned and left the office.

***

Back at his desk, he called the local emergency paramedic unit and asked to be patched through to Des Hughes by radio-phone.

"Hughes," came the slightly distorted reply.

"Hi Des, Dan at the Herald here. Where are you?"

"At the provincial hospital in Uitenhage, bringing in bodies from Maduna Road. Listen I can't really talk."

Daniel cut in. "Have you seen Mark Daly perhaps?"

A pause, then, "Yes he's here, hold on."

"Hello, Dan?" came Mark's voice.

"Hi, yes. What's going on, why have you guys not reported in?"

"Well, not much. I have some pics here at the hospital. There are lots of police trying to block me. Got some of bodies and the ambulances. And medics all over the place, it's busy."

"And John? What's he got?"

Another pause, more radio crackle and lots of background noise which, with the hubbub in the newsroom, made it hard for Daniel to hear Mark.

"I'm not too sure," responded Mark. "I dropped him near Kwanobuhle as he said he knew where Goniwe and his guys were and haven't seen him since. But I'm meant to pick him up there on my way back."

Daniel thought for a moment. "OK, when you think you have enough there, head back to Kwano and get John. If he's not there, come back and process the pics."

Putting the phone down, he turned to June.

"Any news from John?"

"No, not a word. That cop Jonker phoned back, wants you to call. And Carl called too. And the BBC again, offering cash for a report. What must I do?"

Just then Shaun came up to the desk.

"Hell, Dan, it's busy out there. I've been told the squad involved in the shooting are at Algoa Park, being debriefed. I also hear that the cops have made quite a few arrests and they knew we had a team there. They are looking for a silver Cortina. That's Clive's car, isn't it? I understand they know we interviewed some people in the area and are suitably pissed off that we sent a team in without their prior approval and knowledge."

"Bloody hell, since when do we have to let the police know everything we do?" asked Daniel. "Well, finish writing what you have and head out to Algoa Park and see what you can pick up."

Daniel mentally worked out the timing. Algoa Park, the nearest white suburb in Port Elizabeth to the Uitenhage townships was about 30 minutes away. That would, with about an hour snooping about there and the return trip, have Shaun back at about 6pm. Good enough.

As he turned to Monica, who had also approached the desk with a draft of her background piece for him to check over, June said, "There's a call for you, it's Frans Jonker again."

Daniel told Monica to leave her story on the desk and took the call.

"Hello?"

"Hello indeed. I take it things are all running smoothly Daniel. Your reporters are back from the field and the story of the year is going to hog the front page and, no doubt, boost tomorrow's sales?"

"Well," responded Daniel, "Things are going well, not that it's any of your concern. And I have work to do, so if this is not important ..."

"Oh but it is," interrupted Frans, the giggle starting again. "See? We've made some arrests, held some people who were in the area without permission. Some of them you might want to know about. We even had to pick up some white church ministers and escort them away. Cannot understand what good they thought they could possibly do there. This has bugger all to do with them and their kind. Interfering busybodies, the lot of them.

"Anyway, best of luck with your story once Carl has approved it. Just thought I'd check how you're doing. Oh, by the way, your Mr Temba might be late reporting in. Let's say he's been unavoidably detained."

The phone went dead.

11

SCARE TACTICS

The first thing Daniel did was to call Carl Strydom.

"Aaah, Dan the man, I was wondering when you'd call. Got some reports you want to send over?"

"Eventually," said Daniel. "But, first things first. Can you confirm for me that my reporter John Temba is being held by the police? I need to know where he is, why he's being held, what charges, if any, and whether we can have access to him?"

It was Carl's turn to pause. "Really? That's news to me. Must be the security guys. I'll get back to you soonest," said the Colonel, sounding concerned.

That was one thing about Carl that Daniel, and most of the news media in the region appreciated. The PR was a rare guy among the usual motley crew of police officers. He seemed to actually like some of the journalists he dealt with. Most of the other officers, it seemed to Daniel through his dealings with them over the years, saw the Press, and the English newspapers in particular, as an unnecessary evil determined to destroy the Nationalist government.

The head of the security police in the region, Colonel Nico van Rensburg, had once said to Daniel: "We know you guys want to bring us down. Why do you always side with the blacks?" The truth of the matter was, Daniel told him at the time, the newspaper was not taking sides, merely reporting rights and wrongs and letting the public decide for themselves.

As he got up to tell Jake the latest instalment, his phone rang again. It was Carl. "Yes, Dan, I can confirm John was picked up in the Kwanobuhle area. The security branch had a team tracking Goniwe and his friends from Cradock as they were expected at the funeral. And we had information they were going to meet others at a certain spot in Kwanobuhle, and that's where it went wrong.

"Another team swooped and detained a group of black

men at that place. But they were too soon. Goniwe's car hadn't even arrived. Your John was one of them. He's at the Algoa Park unit. I'm led to believe he has been questioned but is free to go soon. Can I help with anything further?"

"Yes, there is actually something you can do, Carl. Shaun Riley is on his way there now. Can you see that he gets a message to pick up John and bring him back to the office? That would be much appreciated."

Daniel then told Jake the latest and set about proofing stories before the evening news conference. Reporter shifts were due to change but most seemed happy to stay on and see the story through. After all, this was an historic day.

***

About three hours earlier, John, driving with Mark towards the hospital, saw some men he knew near Langa.

"Hey, Mark. Stop. Drop me here. I can get stuff from these guys about Goniwe and Fort Calata and the others. You can pick me up on your way back."

John got out of the car, aware that the group were watching suspiciously. They did not trust the white man behind the wheel, it seemed.

"Hey," John called as he approached and the car sped off. "It's me, John from the Herald." Two of the men recognised him as he got closer and greetings were exchanged.

"Hey, brother, saw you at the meeting last night," one said.

The other chipped in: "Yes, you're OK. Apparently Matthew knows you, you know Matthew Goniwe, from Cradock."

John was impressed that Goniwe, the school teacher from the rural town who was actually trying to get the Spear of the Nation, as the ANC's armed wing was known, to play a more active role, cited him.

"Yes, we did study together way back," the reporter

said. "Anyway, that's why I'm here, why my colleague dropped me. I'm hoping to catch up with Matthew. I know he was due to speak at the funeral and it would be good to get his comments on the shootings."

The group of men were suddenly silent.

"Yes, we've just heard some details. This is sad," said one of the elder men.

Another chipped in: "Yes. The police were definitely wrong this time, just using bullets and no teargas. This is just the incentive the youngsters need. The spark. It will be hard to control their anger. I feel lots of trouble coming."

John listened and waited his turn.

Another older man said: "This is going to be hard for our leaders. The ANC want an armed struggle but we must be properly prepared, right from grassroots level. People like Goniwe, Champion Galela and others now have to prove their leadership skills. I know Matthew wants the Spear of the Nation to be active. But we must wait, be patient. The right time will come. Our leaders on Robben Island, Mandela and Ray Mhlaba, must give guidance too." The rest nodded in assent.

John grabbed his moment. "Yes, this is where we, the media, can help too. We need to expose what the people feel, how they are suffering. I know our bosses are facing restrictions and censorship from the authorities but they are sensitive to the people's needs. I need to speak to Matthew, is he coming soon?"

"Yes," the older man answered, "that's why we are here. We understand he is coming this way and will speak to us before he has meetings with other area leaders later. I hear he is very angry."

Every time a car went past, the men looked up in anticipation, expecting Goniwe and his lieutenants. Not that there was a lot of traffic on this particular stretch of road. Even the occasional police Hippo, on route to somewhere more important, would slow down before speeding off again.

Then a dark blue Ford Granada, with two white men in it cruised past. The two men staring at the group before accelerating away.

"Bad news. Those are security branch guys," said John. "I've seen them around. I bet they're looking for Matthew."

The older man in the group looked at his watch and then said: "Well, Matthew's late by about 20 minutes. I say let's wait another 10 then we go."

The group concurred with John who decided it was worth his while to wait, too. After all, an interview with Goniwe would be good copy for the newspaper, especially his comments on the shooting. And he was in the spot where Mark was meant to meet him, so he sat down on the grass with some of the men while others stood smoking. They chatted aimlessly, passing the time and enjoying the sunshine.

Suddenly, two police Hippos, followed by the blue Granada appeared. The Hippos stopped on either side of the group even before the sitting men could get to their feet. Armed policemen jumped from the vehicles and the group of men were surrounded. The two men from the Granada strolled over, walked up to John and one of them said, "Mr Matthew Goniwe, nice to meet you."

"I'm not Goniwe, I'm John. You know me, I'm a ..."

His words were cut short as the bigger of the two men backhanded him through the face, the force of the blow causing the reporter to stumble.

"No backchat, kaffir," warned the man, kicking at John's legs so he fell to the ground. Two of the younger men in the group moved to intervene but froze as the policemen nearest them levelled their automatic rifles.

"He's right, he's not Goniwe," said the older man. "Goniwe's not here."

"And who do you think you are, Nelson bloody Mandela?" The policeman who had struck John turned angrily to the man.

"Enough," commanded the other man from the Granada. "They're resisting arrest. Let's take them in. The guy on the ground and that old man."

Armed policemen grabbed the old man by the arms and pushed him towards the nearest Hippo. The big policeman took another kick at John, the toe of his shoe just missing John's left eye as he turned his head. "Ja, resisting arrest, Mr Goniwe? This will teach you."

Before he could kick again, the other man stopped him and indicated to another two to pick up John and take him to the Hippo. He turned to his colleague: "Jonker, I've told you before. Control yourself, man."

***

The ride in the Hippo was not pleasant, least of all for John and the old man. They'd been thrown to the hot metal floor. John's eye was already beginning to swell.

It was hard to tell if the bumpy ride was causing the policemen's feet to slip and occasionally kick the two captives. But, during the 20-minute ride back to Algoa Park, John reckons he was kicked about 40 times, most of them with force and most on his body. Only one, obviously a miskick, hit him on the head, causing his left ear to bleed and, eventually, swell. The old man, he noticed, got off lightly by comparison.

When the vehicles arrived at the police base in Algoa Park, Frans Jonker and his senior officer, Du Preez, were waiting. The two prisoners were hauled out of the vehicle and marched off, taken to different interrogation rooms.

John never saw the old man again.

In his room, furnished with a metal table and two metal folding chairs, John was made to sit in one chair while Du Preez sat opposite him and Frans lurked menacingly at John's right shoulder, just behind him.

"So," began Du Preez, "you say you're not Goniwe. Well, let me tell you something for nothing, you look a hell of a lot like him."

Frans interjected. "Yes, but all kaffirs, sorry, blacks look the same to me." And he struck John on the back of the head with his open hand. A slap strong enough to cause the reporter's teeth to rattle in his mouth.

Du Preez glared at Frans, then continued speaking to John. "Well, can you prove who you are?"

56

John licked his lips, swallowed and said, quickly, assuming he'd be hit again: "Yes, I am John Temba. I work for the Herald. My Press card is in my jacket pocket, the inside one. You can call my news editor, Daniel Jacobs. He'll vouch for me. And that man you brought in with me, he knows me too. Use your head and check before you beat me for no reason." His head rocked again as Jonker hit him again. This time with a clenched fist on the right temple.

"Hey, don't get cheeky here." Then he leant forward, thrust his hand into the jacket, pulling out a wallet which he tossed on to the table. Du Preez looked inside, found the Press card and read the details. "OK, so, sorry. We made a mistake, these things happen."

Just then a sergeant knocked and entered the room. "Sorry Captain. Colonel Strydom, the liaison officer, phoned. He's asking if we have a reporter named John here. He seemed quite agitated."

Du Preez sat up straight. "Yes, we do. Tell him it was a case of mistaken identity and we're letting him go now."

As the sergeant left the room, Du Preez turned back to John. "No hard feelings, hey? We made a mistake. But, be warned, we can make a similar mistake again, even with your high and mighty news editor. Jonker, take him to the gates and leave him there and, listen to me, don't hit him again."

12

PIECING IT ALL TOGETHER

Feeling decidedly unwell, John stood in the hot sun near the entrance to the police base. It had not been a good day, all in all. Particularly from the reporting point of view. He'd told the news editor he'd get an interview with Goniwe and, so far, all he had achieved was getting beaten up by the police.

The sun hurt his now swelling eye and his ears were still buzzing. His body was aching from the kicks he'd received and the dried blood from his ear injury was sticking to his neck and shirt collar. Swaying and with his eyes closed to stop the growing nausea, he vaguely heard vehicles come and go, ignoring the taunts from policemen in troop carriers. The sound of a harsh intake of breath jarred against the other sounds and he opened his eyes.

Standing in front of him staring at his battered face was Shaun Riley. "Jeez! What happened to you?" asked the reporter.

"Oh, it's a long story - apparently a case of mistaken identity," replied John, wincing at the pain the mere act of talking caused.

"Don't tell me the cops did that."

"Yes, they did. Some guy named Jonker. Said he thought I was Goniwe. Strange, that's who I was looking for to interview when the cops picked us up at Kwanobuhle," said John. "Myself and an older guy were brought here."

"Well, I have to go in and see what's happening, try for an official police comment. Here are the keys to my car. It's parked over there across the road. Get in and wait there for me," Shaun said as he strode into the base.

***

He must have nodded off, despite the pain, because a

sharp rap on the window against which his head was leaning woke him. And standing there looking concerned was Matthew Goniwe. John opened the door and got out of the car. "Are you OK? You look terrible," said the activist, concern etched on his face.

"Yes, I'll live. What the hell are doing here? The cops are looking for you."

"Well, that's not exactly news, they're always looking for me," said Goniwe.

"I heard you and old Saliso had been picked up, so we came to see what's going on," he indicated a slightly battered and dusty car parked about 50 metres away in which John could see three other men. "They won't expect me to come here, to the lion's den, so to speak," smiled Goniwe. "Anyway, we blend in with the crowd."

John realised the Cradock teacher was right. There was a taxi rank nearby with crowds milling, waiting for a ride. And, closer to the base gates, were more people, seemingly just hanging around but, surmised John, they were probably hoping to get news of friends or relatives who had been picked up by the police patrols, brought to the camp and then, in most instances, set free.

"So," he said, reverting to reporter mode, "What exactly happened today?"

Goniwe briefly told John what he knew. "Our understanding is that 22 people were killed, many shot in the back. We also know of several dozen wounded who have either been taken to hospital or treated at doctors' surgeries. It's appalling that the government forces just opened fire with live ammunition. No teargas, no rubber bullets, no nothing.

"They just shot to kill, as plain as that. We have spoken to people who were in the crowd and I'm happy to give the Press a statement. "As I warned last night, this is the beginning, just the beginning," he paused while John wrote.

"Together, today, we have learnt the meaning of sacrifice.

"Together we have learnt the lesson of history that

victory can only come through struggle.

"Together we must make the pledge that nothing will stop us until power is in the hands of the people.

"To the bereaved mothers and fathers, brothers and sisters, sons and daughters, we say - be comforted and be proud in the knowledge that you blessed the nation with heroes and heroines who laid down their lives so that we should all be masters of our destiny." Again he paused while John wrote furiously, continuing only when the journalist looked up.

"Those people who were shot were walking in peace. They're people who were coming to the funeral service at Kwanobuhle. It was a very traumatic thing that we faced here. It was not the first time that people crossed from Langa through town to Kwanobuhle. In the past they did it and there was no damage, no beatings. There was nothing and the police were always there. They would escort people here and there would be no incidents. I think the police saw that despite the shooting of teargas and the harassment of people, the resistance was growing.

"I think it was planning on their part to use live ammunition. That procession could have been stopped using teargas like they usually did but this time they used live ammunition. I think it was deliberate. They shot those people with live ammunition, even while they were running, so many were shot in the back while they were running away.

"The nature of this incident will send a shockwave around the world."

Goniwe looked up and saw some police officer in the base looking towards him and John. "I think I'd better go. I'll be in touch." Then he sauntered off, showing no haste, stopping to chat to some people at the taxi rank.

John noticed that the policeman seemed to have lost interest. Then he saw Shaun trotting towards him. "Let's go. I have a statement from the Minister of Law and Order in Pretoria. I spoke to him directly on the phone."

***

Back in the newsroom later, Shaun briefed Daniel.

"I spoke to the Minister at Union Buildings," he said proudly. "He told me that the police were forced to open fire on a crowd of people estimated at between 3,000 and 4,000. He said the crowd was armed with stones, sticks, petrol bombs and bricks and it was not until the crowd was about five metres from the police that the commanding officer fired a warning shot into the ground next to the leader.

"But this shot, he said his sources told him, had no effect and the crowd surrounded the police, who they claim were pelted with stones, sticks and other missiles, including petrol bombs."

"What!" interjected Daniel. "That totally flies in the face of our information. We even have pictures."

"Yes, I know," said Shaun, "He then said that the police had no alternative but to open fire, in self defence. Once the shooting commenced, he said the crowd retreated and firing immediately ceased. He said the official figures show 17 died and 19 were wounded."

"Write it up," said Daniel. "All we have is good and usable. Jake has said we must go with everything and not worry about the consequences. He's spoken to our lawyers."

As Shaun turned away he added, "Don't worry about official police comment from Carl, I'm on top of that."

The next few hours were spent putting the details of the day's events together. The eyewitness accounts, the pictures taken by Clive on Maduna Road, the pictures from Mark at the hospital, Goniwe's statement and John's beating would all be used in full. The police side would also be given due prominence, even though it only served to show their lies. They would not be told about the eyewitness accounts which contradicted the statement from the Law and Order Minister. And, as the regulations stated, any comment by the Minister of Law and Order was deemed to be the ultimate police comment.

As Jake had once said, "This silly law will be their own

undoing."

The rest of the evening was a case of all hands on deck with everyone doing their bit to ensure the first edition had the full story. When it went to press at midnight, Jake called Daniel and the other late workers into his office for a drink or two to mark a job well done.

13

MARCH 22 - THE MORNING AFTER

Daniel awoke, still in his work clothes minus his shoes and, somehow, one sock, on his sofa. The headache was splitting. Not only induced by the superb red wine they'd shared in Jake's office after the first edition went to press, but also due to the stress of the day and the long hours. But it was not that which woke him, it was a noise outside his house.

Blearily Daniel looked at his watch, only then aware that his music system was on repeat and *Satisfaction* by the Rolling Stones was still playing. It was just gone 5am. Three and a bit hours' sleep. "Perhaps it was the paper being delivered," he thought as he got tenderly to his feet.

As he opened the front door, the smell of human faeces was quite overpowering. A huge turd was on the door mat, covering the green Welcome written there. There were also the words *kaffir lover* scrawled in faeces on the door. Then Daniel saw his car door was open, the interior light burning. Stepping over the mess at the door, he walked gingerly to his car.

Stunned, he noticed the words *We're watching you* scratched into the paint on the roof, saw that both headlights had been smashed and a copy of the Herald, also reeking of faeces, lay on the front seat.

He rushed inside and phoned Clive, who lived four blocks away in the same suburb.

"Er ... hello?" Clive answered.

"Hey, Clive, is your house ok? Check outside. Check your car." Daniel waited as the photographer went to check.

He heard a muted "Oh, bloody hell."

Then Clive picked up the receiver.

"How'd you know? My car's tyres are slashed, headlights smashed. What the bloody hell is going on?"

"I think I know," replied Daniel. "Take some pics. I'll call the police and come over to you with them in a while."

An hour later, a showered and refreshed Daniel was giving details to the police sergeant who'd responded to the call. But it was not going well.

"I can give you a case number for insurance purposes. That's all. Must be a random incident, someone you've annoyed."

"Random?" asked a fuming Daniel. "How can it be random. Clive Brent down the road has had the same thing. I'll take you there now. It's not random, it's a vendetta against journalists. Someone is trying to warn us, or tell us something."

Just then the house phone rang. It was Jake, to say his car, too, had been vandalised with similar wording scratched into it. And he lived right on the other side of the city.

"That's too much of a coincidence to be random," Daniel said to the sergeant after ending the call.

"Well, sir, we'll put our report in. Let's go to this Clive guy. I'll give you a lift, your car doesn't smell too good."

***

Later that morning, in the newsroom, Jake, Daniel and Clive discovered they were not the only ones to fall foul of vandalism. Shaun, Jamie and Mark, among others, reported similar incidents while Monica said she'd had phone calls through the night - one every hour - but no conversation or threats, just breathing and the last call, just before 6am, ended with a funny, high-pitched giggle.

"And before you ask," she said, "I did not disconnect the phone because my mother's ill and my dad might have called."

"That's it," said Daniel, "I thought it was the security branch bastards. Frans Jonker has a funny giggle"

"Well," said a more cautious Jake, addressing the group at the newsdesk, "It's going to be hard to prove that it was him or them. I suggest we just keep calm, keep our wits about us and be alert at all times.

"Jamie," he turned to him, "What are the chances of getting hold of the couple who were our eye witnesses? Perhaps they've had trouble too. I know we haven't used their names but, as Dan said, the police seem to know about them."

"I spoke to Arthur yesterday evening and I've arranged to meet him in North End," Jamie said. He's taking a taxi into PE as he has some stuff to do. I'm going to meet him at the municipal offices near the taxi rank. There are always lots of people there, so we should be fine."

Daniel issued assignments for the day. Most of them follow up stories and reactions to the events of the day before.

Shaun was the first back at the desk to report.

"Well, Dan, it appears Carl is royally pissed off at us, and he's getting flak from his superiors in Pretoria."

"OK, I'll give him a call," said Daniel. But, before he could do that, June, who'd answered the other phone, said that the leader of the Progressive Federal Party, Van Zyl Slabbert wanted to speak to him. Daniel took the call, knowing the man would condemn the police actions from the day before.

"Dr Slabbert, hello," said Daniel.

"Good morning, Dan, terrible time. I have a statement I'd like to give you. It's going to the SABC too, and the Afrikaans press. Quite simply, while I and the PFP condemn the shootings, we urge a cooling off period. I'm aware of what the Minister has said but I'd strongly urge the state to take a measured approach and that both sides, the police and the people, calm down and let a proper and thorough investigation be carried out.

"Some of the PFP see the police as being a large part of the problem in the township unrest. Because of this, police involvement for the time being should be limited to the absolute minimum in the townships itself so that provocative action on either side can be avoided. At the same time, we recognise the vital importance of funerals as social and political outlets and, correspondingly, how incendiary the state prohibition of funerals can be.

"I feel, therefore, that it is of extreme importance that the people are allowed to hold funerals without interference and when convenient for those who wish to hold them."

He paused and Daniel quickly asked, "What do you see as the fundamental problem in the townships - excluding the police presence?"

"Well, one of the country's fundamental problems is unemployment and the resultant economic austerity in the townships. But perhaps more important is the breakdown of Government policy as far as black urbanisation, local government administration and education are concerned.

"The PFP is of the belief that this fundamental problem cannot be handled through police action alone. It is essentially a problem that cries out for political and social action. Just an unequivocal assurance about South African citizenship for blacks would go a long way to reduce the temperature and hostility in the urban flash points. Furthermore, all efforts must be made to establish communication between Government and community leaders in these townships. That's it, thanks."

They chatted a bit more and the call ended. Daniel typed up the statement then called Carl. It was not a pleasant call - to start off. The police liaison officer was, as Shaun had pointed out, highly annoyed.

"Dan, Dan, Dan. What have you guys done, man? I've spent the past few months, since this trouble started, telling my bosses, the generals and so on, what good guys you on the Herald are. How you agree to show us everything, yet remain impartial and write the truth. I'm actually on your side, you know.

"But this, today's story, that eyewitness stuff, which you did not pass on to me, that's big trouble. For me and you guys."

He paused and Daniel cut in. "Yes, well. If we had, would we have got permission to use it?"

Carl was surprisingly blunt. "No, probably not. But now, the big guns are out. The security branch, in particular, is very upset and will do their best to track these people down. Meanwhile, I've been told to play hardball with you.

My bum's on the line here, too."

"Sorry about that," replied Daniel. "But the security branch, I think, has already started their stuff. Several of us - Jake, Clive, Jamie, Mark and even Shaun have had our cars and houses vandalised. And Monica got some weird phone calls last night too. I think they were from Frans Jonker, the new man in the team."

Carl paused and then gave a slow and measured response. "Dan, that is serious. And that is a serious allegation. I think you should file an official complaint. But, be warned, it won't stop here."

Daniel and Carl agreed to meet later, after work, for a drink and an off-the-record chat. He looked around the newsroom, after ending the call.

"Where's John?" he asked June. "Has he called in? He was meant to be here at 9." Daniel was worried, very worried. Given what had happened to some of the team, John could be in serious trouble.

14

IN HIDING

John Temba did not make it home that night.

Slightly under the weather, after a few beers and some wine with the editor, he'd left the office at about 1am, heading for the taxi rank about a kilometre away. Sauntering down the city's deserted main street towards the rank at Russell Road, he was lost in thought, thinking about the stories and, despite the tragedy of the day's events, the warming camaraderie in the Herald newsroom.

He knew that later that morning it would be another busy day but he was buzzing and decided he'd head to an all-night and illicit bar he knew in the city's north end. But as he got closer to the taxi rank, he heard the distant sound of a gunshot and instinctively moved deeper into the shadows, straining his eyes to see what was happening.

Next the night was filled with the sound of police sirens and two patrol vans came speeding down Russell Road, turning left towards the north. They were followed about a minute later by a slower, lumbering Hippo. John walked quicker, crossing Russell Road and ignoring the sole taxi at the rank, where the driver seemed to be asleep at the wheel, determined to see what was happening.

As he approached the side street where the bar was situated, near the South African Breweries' offices and stores, he heard another shot and some shouts. The sounds came from that street. Suddenly, out of the shadows, an arm stretched out and grabbed John's shoulder.

"Hey! Where are you going?" rasped a voice and the heavy-set man pulled John into the doorway where he'd been hiding.

"What's going ..." started John.

"Shut up and keep still! Wait here and you'll be OK."

Just then some camouflage-clad policemen ran past, automatic rifles at the ready, heading up to the main street.

Behind them, an Afrikaans voice ordered: "Form a cordon. Don't let anyone in or out."

John and the man crouched, trying to force themselves deeper into the shadows of the recessed doorway. He looked up his new companion, who smelled of beer - although John was sure he did too. "What's going on?" he finally asked.

The man, whispered hoarsely: "The Civic Organisation was having a meeting at the tavern to discuss a consumer boycott. It started at 11.30pm, as that's not the time when the police would expect us to meet.

"Anyway, somehow they found out and Sipho Hashe was saying there must be an informer in PEBCO when the police shot teargas into the tavern. So Hashe, Galela and Godolozi have managed to escape. We arranged a robbery of the Breweries store as a diversion, but there are more cops than we expected. Now the rest of us are trapped here." He stopped as some policemen came down the narrow street, shining torches.

Just then, the door behind them opened, and a voice said, "quickly, get inside!" They scrambled in and as the door closed they heard policemen approach the alcove. In the dark, John and the two men walked quickly away from the door and then into a waiting elevator.

In the light of the elevator, John saw that the third man was Kusta Jack, the spokesman for PEBCO. Before he could say anything, the other man said: "Kusta, how'd you get here? And where are we?"

Kusta smiled. "After Sipho and others got into Molly's car, the caretaker of the building saw me and a few others running and let us in."

"Molly?" asked John. "Not Molly Blackburn?"

Kusta looked at him for the first time. "Aah, John, 'Mr Herald', how are you? Wow, what happened to your face? Yes, Molly of the PFP. She was helping us. Making sure we did not cross too many boundaries."

As the elevator rose slowly, John thought quickly. "Consumer boycott?" The Black Civic Organisation was opposed to white rule but he did not think they'd go this far.

Then, Molly Blackburn? A well-to-do white political activist and PFP councillor in the city, who was involved in investigating the underhanded dealings in the police force. She was not popular with the police and he knew she'd received numerous death threats.

His mind boggling at these surprise developments, he waited until the elevator reached the top floor where the caretaker lived in a small roof-top flat. Inside the man's front room sat a group of black men, drinking beer and chatting. There were warm greetings as they recognised the reporter. Most of them he knew from various political and civic organisations, most affiliated to the UDF or ANC. John, Kusta and a few others shared a shabby sofa. A beer was passed to John.

"Guess we'll have to just wait here until the cops go," said Kusta, swigging his beer from a quart bottle.

John looked at him. He was a charismatic man, just 27 years old and already a leader, having worked his way up through the ranks of student and youth organisations, and having suffered police harassment and detention. Now he was one of many frustrated black leaders in the townships demanding the integration of public institutions, the removal of troops from black townships, and the end of workplace discrimination.

He looked at John again. "See, the trouble and strife that goes on in our townships, as you are aware, is unknown to most white citizens of Port Elizabeth since the white-owned newspapers and news stations do not usually report these disturbances. Now, with the Langa shootings, things have reached a head.

"So, we have decided to launch an effective campaign to cripple the white-owned institutions of Port Elizabeth and undermine the legitimacy of apartheid. Several of our members have suggested the idea of a consumer boycott. We will propose that, instead of shopping at white shops and businesses in the city, black South Africans should be encouraged to shop within the townships."

He paused and John noticed that most of the men near them were nodding their heads in agreement.

"So, Molly advised us to wait a while and to be careful how we go about this. We understand Van Zyl Slabbert has called for a cooling off period. We will wait then. But, if the police do not change their tactics, we will boycott from July. Molly said this economic boycott would be the most effective weapon used yet. People will then be aware of how we feel." He stopped as a loud buzzer rang.

"Oh, here it comes," said the caretaker, "That's the front door - I better go check." And he left to take the elevator down 10 floors to street level. John looked at his watch - almost 2am. He hadn't slept for about 20 hours and was due back in the newsroom in a few hours.

Again Kusta spoke to the reporter. "So, my friend, we will need you and your people, like Daniel Jacobs, to keep quiet about this, for a while anyway. We don't want to play our hand too early."

"I won't tell anyone what you've told me tonight," promised the journalist as he finished his beer.

A while later the caretaker returned. "That was the police," he reported. "They wanted to search the premises. I did not let them in. I said I did not have the key for the front door so no-one could be in here except me." He waited for the laughter to die down.

"But, they are going to be around until 6am, the officer said, and will only leave when it's properly light outside. He said they'd arrested several people for the attempted robbery of the store and would come back at 8am to get a report from the store manager when he's at work."

With the caretaker's stock of beer now depleted, the group settled down for the rest of the wait, some dozing, others chatting softly in pairs. John closed his eyes, hoping to sleep, hoping not to wake with a headache.

***

At the police base at Algoa Park, Jimmy Jonker and his colleagues from the shooting in Langa had spent the late afternoon and evening being debriefed by senior officers. They were offered psychological or pastoral counselling

71

and were then told they'd be confined to barracks and put on light duty for the next two days.

Usually, light duty meant darts and beer which was often the case if they'd been on a particularly heavy schedule of patrols. But this time there was a strange mood hanging over the group. Admittedly there were some hard-core drinkers in the mess. But they were drinking with morose intent. As if the alcohol would dull the memory of the bodies being jerked like marionettes as they were struck by the bullets.

Of people turning to flee and still being hit.

Of the guilty feeling for many of them, knowing that they kept firing even though there was no need.

For a few, the staunch racist nationalists, there was the bravado, fuelled by the drinking. "Well, we really showed those black buggers who's boss here, didn't we?" commented one first team rugby player loudly who was part of the squad, looking at Jimmy as he entered the bar area, ordering a cool beer to quench his thirst.

Most of the men were there. And it appeared some had been there for some time, if the flushed faces and glazed eyes were any indication.

"Ja," added another brandy drinker sycophantically siding with the rugby star. "Now they know their place, and that is where they'll stay. These black folks are not equal to us, no matter how white they think they are."

Jimmy riled. "Come on, man," he said, "they didn't stand a chance. We should have used teargas and rubber bullets. The whole thing was a mistake. Nobody should have died." He turned to walk out, to sit on the balcony and be alone.

"Ja, typical," chirped the same man. "Always think you're better than us hey? Just because your brother's in the security branch and your dad was a politician, hey?

"Well, my friend," he said sarcastically, "if you think that, how come you shot first?"

Jimmy dropped his beer, the glass breaking on the thin carpet as he lunged at his tormentor. Angrily, and almost through a red mist of rage and frustration, he swung a clumsy blow at the man, who ducked, causing Jimmy to hit the big rugby player who was standing next to him. The man did not even flinch as the blow grazed his cheek. He merely grabbed Jimmy's arm and twisted viciously, causing him to fall to his knees.

And, before they knew what was happening, almost everyone there was swinging punches at each other. It was almost surreal, no shouting or swearing just the meaty sound of blows striking home and panting.

At that moment the psychologist and church minister who'd been involved in counselling both walked in. The minister stepped forward to stop the fighting. The other man pulled him back.

"Leave them. Let them get their frustration and anger out. Rather this than hiding their feelings."

Smiling, the minister turned and left the room, followed by the psychologist. "I suppose it makes sense," he said softly. "Luckily none of them are on duty tomorrow."

15

RUNNING SCARED

At 9am, Arthur Shipalana left his house, heading for the bus stop and then, from Uitenhage's white area, caught a train to Port Elizabeth which would get him close to his meeting spot with the reporter.

"I'll be back as soon as I can," he said to Nancy with concern. "I'm not too sure what it will be like out there today, so I suggest you and Sam just stay at home. Try to keep him in the yard. Who knows what the police will be like today? And, anyway, Miriam is coming home some time today, so it'll be nice if you guys are here. Together you can make dinner. I'll be home before 5pm." He smiled and stepped away as Nancy swung a mock blow at him. They hugged and he headed off, walking briskly towards the nearest bus stop.

The streets were busier today. People were gathered on street corners, talking about the shooting, reading the Herald and commenting on the story.

"Hey, Arthur," shouted one of his soccer buddies as he approached, "Who do you reckon these eyewitnesses are? Real people or someone made up by the newspaper?"

As he hadn't seen the paper, he had been worried he and Nancy would be easily identified. But, if his fellow midfielder, who he'd known since schooldays, could not tell the eyewitness was him, he felt safe.

"I haven't seen the paper. What did they say?" he asked, pausing next to the group of five guys, all men ranging in age from 18 to about 30 and unemployed.

"Well," said another man, "It could be you, it could be anyone of us. They say the guy works or worked at VW and is in his mid 20s."

"Whoever he is, the cops will be looking for him," offered another.

They said their farewells and Arthur walked on. At the bus stop there were queues of people - and the police.

Again there were two Hippos and policemen were walking down the queue, interrogating people. As each bus arrived, the driver was made to wait until the police had cleared enough people to board.

Arthur wondered if an hour would be enough time to make his meeting. His turn arrived and he was asked for identification and where he intended to travel to.

"Why Port Elizabeth?" the officer asked gruffly.

"I'm meeting someone at the station, a relative who's travelled down from Jo'burg."

"OK and where were you yesterday?"

"At home."

"Did you go to Maduna Road?"

"No."

The officer made a note of Arthur's details and let him board the bus. Twenty minutes later he was at the rail station and the whole process was repeated. Trains, however, do not wait for police and, fortunately for Arthur, the number of commuters wanting to go to Port Elizabeth at this time of the morning, well after rush hour, was relatively small and he made the first train.

***

As Jamie left the office for the short walk to the meeting place, he saw John arriving. "Hey, John, you're looking rough and, if I'm not mistaken, you're wearing the same stuff as yesterday," he paused and looked closely at his colleague.

"Yes, you are, that blood stain is there on your collar."

John replied honestly: "Well, I didn't get home last night. I was heading for the all-night tavern near Breweries when there was a police raid, something to do with a robbery, some of us hid in a man's flat. I was scared the cops might recognise me, so I just stayed there until it was clear to leave. I went to an old girlfriend's place to wash up but, yes, it's the same clothes."

"Well, Dan will be happy to see you, he was worried. We all had some hassles last night. Anyway, I have to go,"

Jamie said quickly before John could ask about details. "Dan and the guys will tell you all about it."

Jamie turned and headed off up the main street walking into the crowds, unaware he was being tailed by a security policeman. But John caught a glimpse of the man as he entered Newspaper House, the face being vaguely familiar. And it was only when he got upstairs that he remembered seeing the man at Algoa Park. He'd been talking to Frans Jonker prior to his interrogation.

"Dan," he said as he approached the newsdesk, "I think Jamie's being followed by the branch cops."

"OK," responded Daniel quickly, calling Mark over. "I want the two of you to drive quickly to the taxi rank. John, you know what the guy looks like. Mike I want a picture of him, long lens. Even better if you can get Jamie in the shot too. OK, off you go, be back soon."

Meanwhile Jamie and Arthur were on track for their rendezvous. Jamie checked his watch, noticed he was slightly ahead of time, and stopped to look in a clothing shop window. In the reflection he saw another man also looking at the window display. As he walked off, Jamie noticed that the same man also walked off.

"No way," Jamie muttered to himself, "this is like the movies."

He stopped suddenly and turned round. The man quickly went into the shop. Youngish, short dark hair, almost a military cut, and a cheapish, ill-fitting suit.

"Well, he could use a visit there," thought Jamie as he walked briskly off. He did not notice the man walk out of the shop and resume his steady pace about 50 metres behind the reporter.

***

At the station in North End, Arthur and a handful of passengers got off the train. The police presence was not as strong here, he noted, just a handful of cops standing idly at the only gate, watching passengers come and ago and making the odd ribald comment. He and another couple walked briskly towards to the taxi rank area, up the hill from the railway station which was near the railway line.

The area was typical of any near a major commuting area in the country. Hundreds of entrepreneurs had set up pavement stalls, ranging from quick fashionable hairdos and braiding or haircuts to cooked chicken and cheap clothing. Commuters, stallholders and passers-by mingled in a mass of humanity. Taxi touts were there too, loudly exhorting the benefits of their particular minibus, with drivers cramming more than the legal number of 15 passengers aboard, going from that rank to any destination north, west or south in record time.

And just up from there, in the main street, was the municipal office where people paid their electricity, water and rates, also surrounded by satellite fast food shops and clothing stores of a more formal nature. Here there were more people milling about, an ideal place to get lost in the crowd and go unnoticed. Being the municipal offices, there were people of all races hanging about, which also helped make the meeting between Jamie and Arthur less conspicuous.

As Arthur approached the area, he saw Jamie standing in a queue, chatting to some black folk also in line. "A neat cover," though Arthur and he approached the group who were chatting about football and Kaizer Chiefs, one of the country's top professional football teams.

As he got there, the conversation got a bit more heated as Jamie aired his views that while the club had won four major trophies in the previous season, they would not be league champions for the coming season. This, of course, led to an outcry from the club's loyal fans and, during the heated debate which followed, Arthur caught Jamie's eye and the two started walking off, heading north, away from the city centre.

The man in the cheap suit, followed unnoticed by Jamie. But he was seen by Mark and John who had just arrived and had double parked on the other side of the road, from where Mark had started taking photographs. As Jamie and Arthur approached and entered a café where they intended to have coffee and a chat, the man following them stopped walking and started talking into a walkie talkie he'd taken from his jacket pocket.

"This is going to be trouble," said Mark as he prepared to get out of the car. "John, park this somewhere," he instructed as he got out of his car and walked up the pavement, on the opposite side of the road, seeking a vantage point for more photographs. Fortunately for John, a parking bay became vacant just ahead of the photographer's double-parked car and he eased the car in, noting there was still 45 minutes' time left on the meter.

John rushed over the road and entered the coffee shop, brushing past the security policeman who was standing near the doorway, looking up the road, waiting for something or someone.

Inside the relative darkness of the shop he paused, seeking out his colleague and the black man among the cosmopolitan mix of customers and then saw them sitting at a table near the back of the shop and the kitchen. Quickly he pushed his way through the crowd toward them as he heard police sirens in the distance getting closer.

"Jamie, I think it's trap. Let me get your man out of here."

John grabbed Arthur by the shoulder and headed him towards the kitchen where, he assumed, there'd be a back door.

"See you back at the office," he said as they entered the kitchen. A split second later police vehicles screeched to a halt outside and armed policemen burst in, one shouting: "A drug raid! Stay exactly where you are!"

Across the road, Mark stopped taking pictures and watched open mouthed as Jamie and three other white men who'd been in the cafe were hauled out and lined up against the shop front. The man in the suit, who he'd been photographing seconds earlier, pointed to Jamie who was then bundled unceremoniously into the back of a police van.

Mark watched as other customers were brought out of the cafe while the other white men were allowed to go.

After about 15 minutes, the shop had been cleared. Even the kitchen staff was brought out, but there was no sign of John or Arthur. All were lined up and the security policeman looked at each group, shaking his head as he did not find the man he was looking for.

At that stage Mark realised John had his car keys and there was no sign of his colleague. He quickly crossed the road and went up to the van in which Jamie was sitting. The reporter's face lit up when he saw Mark.

"Mark! What's going on?" he asked quickly, adding as policemen started approaching, "They've gone to the office."

A police captain strode up to Mark. "Hey! What do you think you're doing? That's a prisoner. You can't speak to him." He pushed Mark away from the van.

"But, he's a colleague of mine," replied Mark, quickly showing his Press pass. "Why's he being held?"

"Suspected drug dealer," replied the officer, softening his approach somewhat. "We're taking him to Mount Road for questioning."

As the police contingent departed, Mark started his walk back to the office. "A strange, strange day," he muttered to himself.

FALSE ARREST

Jamie Nelson had to admit he was a bit scared.

Riding through the city in the back of a police van - visible to the passing public in his portable cage - was humiliating. Now he knew how some of the black guys he often saw being transported in such a way felt. And he could now begin to grasp their hatred for the police. Fortunately the ride to the Mount Road headquarters was relatively short.

"Well, I'll tell the guys there who I am and I should be on my way soon," he thought, still keen to get his interview with Arthur done. "Hell, I didn't even get to ask him where Nancy was. I hope she's okay. Her story was really intriguing," Jamie pondered as the van entered the compound gates.

Waiting to meet it at the main building were the man he'd seen earlier in the cheap suit and a large ginger-haired man, in a slightly better fitting suit.

"Well, Phillips," said the ginger-haired man, "This is the guy I want, you've done well, thanks."

As the man named Phillips walked off, the other officer turned to Jamie as the journalist was let out of the police van by the driver. "Hello Mr Nelson, we're honoured to have you visit. I'm Jonker, Frans Jonker. I'm with the security branch and, don't worry, you haven't been picked up for drugs. Come inside, we need to have a little chat." Jonker took Jamie firmly by the elbow and led him into the building.

"But, I'm a journalist, you know who I am, it appears," said Jamie, trying to stand his ground.

"Yes, yes, yes. And I know your boss Daniel Jacobs too. So no worries, Mr Nelson. Just a few questions and then you're on your way, I'll even take you back to Newspaper House myself," said Jonker, giggling as he added the last bit.

When inside a small office, Jonker sat Jamie down and poured some tea for them both - not even bothering to ask Jamie if he wanted a cup.

"So, let's see," he said as he settled down and took a sip himself. "I need to ask about your visit to Langa yesterday. See, we also want to speak to your eye witnesses. Their evidence will be crucial to our internal investigations and we need to sort out what exactly went wrong."

Jamie was surprised.

"What went wrong? Man, it's obvious what went wrong. The guy in charge used live rounds - a basic tragic error which cost many lives," Jamie was furious as he relived his interview with Arthur and Nancy in his mind and the very real anger they had shown.

"Cool it, man," said Jonker placatingly. "I agree we seem to have been wrong, but the guys on the vehicle say there was provocation. So, we need to hear it from the horses' mouths so to speak - from your witnesses, in fact."

Jamie paused, sipped the over-sweetened tea, and said: "Maybe. I need to speak to Jacobs first."

He had no intention of divulging the identities of either Arthur or Nancy and he knew even asking Daniel would result in a firm no. But, hopefully, he mused, this policeman would let him make the call.

"OK," Jonker said, much to the relief of Jamie, "Just sit tight, I'll be back." And he left the office, locking the door as he did so.

***

John Temba's route back to the Herald newsroom was circuitous but he reckoned it was better to be cautious - given recent developments. He and Arthur walked along Chapel Street, parallel to Main Street, then through the OK Bazaars department store and across the main street into Jetty Street near the harbour and railway station before going around City Hall and the old Post Office to enter Newspaper House via the back entrance.

Upstairs in the newsroom, Mark Daly was debriefing Jacobs on the morning's developments. "Aah, John," he said when the pair approached, "Hope you still have my car keys?"

The reporter fished the keys from his pocket and handed them to Mark. Then he turned to Arthur and introduced him to Daniel.

"Dan, this is Arthur Shipalana, Jamie's contact."

The news editor stood and shook Arthur's hand warmly. "Arthur Shipalana, good to meet you, you're a brave man."

Arthur looked embarrassed. "Well, I was only doing what I thought was right. What Nancy and I saw was just murder."

"Nancy?" asked Mark.

"Yes," Jacobs turned to the photographer.

"Arthur and his friend Nancy witnessed the shooting yesterday. They are the two witnesses we quoted in the paper today. They were walking nearby when they were told to leave the area."

Arthur took over. "We were about 200 yards away when they started shooting at the crowd of funeral goers ... just opened fire at an unarmed crowd. It was horrible, scary and very frightening."

Daniel said to Mark: "Well, Mark, go and get your car, I think we'll try to get Jamie back and he can speak to Arthur here. John, get Arthur some coffee and let him wait at Jamie's desk."

With that he turned to his phone to get hold of Carl Strydom. "Carl? It's Dan again," he said as the Colonel answered his direct line on the second ring.

"More problems?" asked the police officer.

"Yes, this time the security branch seems to have taken Jamie Nelson in. He was with a contact in North End, near the municipal offices. There was an apparent drugs raid on the cafe there and he was, according to some of my team who were there, the only one taken into custody. The arresting officer told Mark Daly Jamie was being taken to Mount Road for questioning. Thing is, Jamie was pointed out by someone we think was a security cop."

Carl answered speaking deliberately. "Again? Those guys just won't let up. I'll try to find out what's going on. See you later."

At that moment Monica Davis came up to the desk. "What's happened to Jamie?" she asked looking tearful.

"Nothing to worry about," he said calmly. "He's with police at Mount Road. He'll be back soon."

"But Mark Daly said he'd been arrested in a raid. A drug raid?"

"Obviously wrong then, isn't it? The last thing Jamie would do is get involved with drugs," said Daniel. "Now don't worry, it'll be fine."

On his way out to retrieve his car, Mark first stopped off at the darkroom upstairs. Making sure Clive Brent wasn't about. He picked up the darkroom phone and dialled. "Fransie? It's Mark, Mark Daly. I know the name of the newspaper's eyewitness and his girlfriend."

He hung up abruptly as Clive entered. "Hi, Clive, I was trying to get hold of you. Can I get a lift to my car in North End please?"

17

A SAFE HOUSE

Jamie looked up eagerly as Jonker re-entered the office, this time with Colonel Strydom in tow. He'd been alone for about 10 minutes but it had felt much longer.

"Mr Nelson," said the Colonel. "Sorry for this terrible inconvenience. But it appears to have been a case of mistaken identity. "I've spoken to Dan, your news editor, who was surprised to find you'd been arrested. Well, it appears our informant was wrong and, obviously, you're not the man we were looking for."

"Really?" said Jamie. "That's surprising, because this Jonker guy was asking me about the identity of our eyewitnesses quoted in the paper this morning, nothing about drugs."

Jonker giggled nervously, "yes, well I was just trying to put you at ease, you know, chat a bit. Anyway, I have the information I need to help with our internal investigation, thanks."

Both Carl and Jamie stared at the security policeman.

"What information?" asked Carl.

"Nothing too serious, Colonel, one of my contacts called to say he knows who the people are, that'll make our job easier."

"But, hold on a sec," said Carl. "What internal investigation? You're not part of that team."

Jonker hesitatingly said: "Well, no, not really. But Captain du Preez has been tasked to get some info and, well, I'm helping him."

Carl looked puzzled. "No, man, that doesn't sound right to me. Why would du Preez be part of it?"

"Hey, don't ask me, Colonel, I just follow orders," replied Jonker.

"I think we need to go speak to du Preez about this. I'm not too happy with this development," said Carl. "But first, we need to get Mr Nelson back to his office."

"It's OK, Colonel, I said I'd do that," said Jonker.

Jamie stood up, ready to depart, "I'm happy with that."

"Fine," said Carl, "I'll call Jacobs and let him know. Then I'll get hold of your Captain du Preez and find out what's going on with this internal investigation. Something just doesn't gel for me here."

In the car on the way to Newspaper House, Jonker tried to apologise yet again. Jamie, on the other hand, wanted to know just how much the police knew about Arthur and whether they did, in fact, know he was his source. Either way, it was best he told Daniel and Jake all he'd found out during the morning.

"It would be a good idea," he thought, "to find out whether the two could be moved from Uitenhage and perhaps housed somewhere in Port Elizabeth. Better safe than sorry."

"So, Nelson, I guess you think we're all bad guys, us security branch men? Well, that's not the case. We have the long-term interests of our country and its government at heart. And to achieve those aims, we need to ensure that the country's security - both here within our borders and abroad - is not compromised."

"You sound like an instruction manual," Jamie replied. "But, seriously, while I can understand your point of view - not that I agree with it - why does that have to entail killing people? Like Steve Biko? Or Robert Sobukwe? Or shooting innocent people like what happened yesterday and even 20 years ago at Sharpeville?"

"Oh well, that's the trouble with you liberals, you don't really see the danger that's facing us. In fact," Jonker added, warming to his topic. "Even some of us Afrikaners are slack about it. That's why people like us, the security branch, are so important. The real threat is the Communists. They are the people behind the trouble the blacks are now causing."

He rambled on but Jamie managed to zone out, thinking about Arthur, and made the occasional supportive grunt to keep Jonker talking. He knew one thing for sure. If the security branch got hold of Arthur and Nancy, their lives would be in danger. People like Jonker did not want to know what the Herald's eyewitnesses saw, they wanted no-one else to know or to be able to verify their accounts.

"We're here," said Jonker as he pulled up in Military Road near Newspaper House. "You can hop out here, I need to head back. Just remember though, we know what's going on."

***

After the debriefing with Daniel and Jake in the editor's office, it was decided Jamie and Arthur would fetch Nancy and Sam. Jake thought it would be best if they stayed in his home - a large rambling house on the Swartkops River just north of the city.

He had only recently moved there and, it was hoped with its two-bedroomed guest wing and enclosed garden, the three could live there unnoticed for a while until things quietened down.

"But," Jake pondered to himself as the others made plans, "will it ever die down? Once the security police decide something or someone is a threat they hardly fail in eliminating that perceived threat, even going beyond the law to achieve their goals."

He then said out loud, "I think we're going to have to look at getting them out of the country."

The room fell silent.

"Really?" said Daniel. "And how and when do you think we can achieve that? If the police know about Arthur and Nancy, they'll be searching for them and watching our every move. It's not going to be easy to just spirit them out of PE."

Jake replied: "No, it won't be. But first things first. Let's get them moved to my house. Get Arthur in here and let's discuss this. After all, his input is essential too. They need to leave Langa."

***

Arthur was surprised at the summary Jake gave him of their meeting. "Are we in danger? Really?"

"We don't know for sure," Daniel replied, "but given the branch's history of violence and assassinations, it is better we play it safe than be sorry later."

"OK. Well, I appreciate what you want to do," said Arthur, "but my sister's coming home from college today. So can we make it tomorrow morning?"

Jake paused for a while and then said. "Arthur, I'm not too sure. I don't trust these guys at all. They seem to have a mole who is giving them info, based on what Jamie's told us. So we don't know, right now, what they know.

"Jonker said to Jamie they knew who you are," he paused and then addressed them all decisively.

"Perhaps it's best that we get Nancy and her son to my house tonight. Then, if something does go wrong, it would be easier for you to get away on your own. I'll give you the address and phone number of a friend of ours in Uitenhage. He's not too far away from the townships. I'll speak to him later. If anything does go badly wrong overnight, then you can either try to make contact with him or go to his home. His name is Stephen and he'll make a plan to get you safely out of there."

Arthur thought for a minute or two, then said: "I accept your kind offer. Let's get Nancy and Sam out to your house this evening. I'll come tomorrow after sorting my sister Miriam out. I need to make sure she's safe. Perhaps she can stay with my aunt a few blocks away."

"Fine," said Jake. "Jamie can take my car and give you a lift home. Then you can pack up Nancy and Sam and he can take them to my house.

"Dan," he turned to his news editor, "don't tell anyone what's happening. Go back to the desk and carry on as usual. After the evening conference you can give me a lift home and we can decide there what we'll do next.

"Jamie, you and Arthur wait here for a while and then you can both walk out the front - as if going home - then walk round to my car and hit the road."

At the newsdesk. Mark and Clive were waiting for their late day assignments and reporters needed debriefing as Daniel got back on track. He was so busy, a few minutes later, that he did not see Jamie and Arthur walk out the door.

But Mark, who was standing chatting to Clive, did see them go.

18

MORE TROUBLE LOOMS

Jamie felt quite good driving the editor's Mercedes Benz out of the garage and then on to the freeway heading north. Arthur sat in the back because the slightly tinted rear windows would make him less obvious to passers by. They drove along the side of Algoa Bay, past railway lines and factories before turning off near the N2 motorway to head towards Uitenhage. It was at this point that a car started following them.

Or at least Jamie thought it was. It had been behind them for a while but turning off the freeway where he had was not the normal route people would take. And it was a dark blue Granada, of which there were many in the city as Ford had its South African headquarters there.

"Lie down on the floor," he instructed Arthur, "I think we're being followed. I'm going to head towards a friend's panel-beating workshop."

Ever observant, Jamie had noticed damage on the left front fender of the Merc when he got into the car at the staff garage, presumably where Jake had scraped against one of the awkwardly placed pillars. That would justify the detour. And if they weren't being followed, then at least he was doing the editor a favour.

He turned left, back towards the city, into a side road running behind the Livingstone Hospital. The Granada followed.

"Shit," muttered Jamie and as he accelerated the Granada dropped back. But Jamie had exceeded the speed limit and that could be the reason for the other car seemingly going slower.

He saw the *Crash Flash* sign ahead where his squash-playing friend Ian worked, and indicated he was going to turn in to the entrance. In the rear-view mirror he saw the Granada pull to the kerb. A man in a suit got out, talking into a walkie talkie.

"Bloody hell, they're onto us already," said Jamie as he stopped the car and got out.

"Stay put," he told Arthur as he walked back to the road and then up to the man with the walkie talkie.

He noticed the Granada had Johannesburg licence plates.

"Can I help you? You might be lost," he offered to the man as he approached.

The man immediately looked flustered. He spoke in Afrikaans: "Yes, well, not too sure, actually. I was looking for the Mount Road turn off. See, I'm a forensics police officer, I have been sent here from Johannesburg and I seem to have taken quite a few wrong turns."

"I assumed something like that," said Jamie, "I saw you using a walkie talkie."

"Yes, I was trying to get someone to give me directions."

Jamie wasn't too sure if he bought the man's story but he gave him directions from there back towards the Mount Road and watched him drive off before returning to the Merc. He saw Ian and Arthur looking at the damaged fender.

"And now?" he asked as he approached.

"Hi, just looking at the damage here, your colleague said it needed fixing," said Ian, with a smile.

"Yes," added Arthur, "I said you were worried about the car behind us, so we tried to look businesslike while you spoke to that guy. Was he a cop?"

"Yes, but I'm not sure if he was tailing us. He said he was lost."

Arthur paused, thought for a moment then said: "I'm not too sure. There was a car just like that one, could have been a Granada, but dark blue anyway, near our house in Langa yesterday when you and Clive were there."

Feeling he was being left out of all of this and not too sure of what was going on, Ian piped up, "so do you want a quote for the car repair, Jamie?"

"Yes, please, can you post it to me at the Herald? Thanks man, see you later."

He and Arthur then drove off, both watching for the Granada or any other car that seemed to be following them.

***

Just around the corner, the police officer stopped his car and got back on to the walkie talkie.

"Jonker, you were right. It is that reporter fellow. I'm not sure if he had the black man with him, he stopped at a panel beaters. Then he came up to me when I stopped. I gave him a cock and bull story about being lost. So, he's just driven off. Back in the direction he came from, want me to follow again?"

"No," replied Jonker. "We know the car and he obviously knows yours now. We'll keep watch near Langa and hopefully pick him up again. Come back to the office."

Jamie, looking in his rear-view mirror, saw the Granada parked as they drove off. It did not turn to follow them. "I think the best thing is I drop you at the taxi rank at the township entrance," he said to Arthur.

"Then you get home, get Nancy and Sam sorted out and I'll meet you all at the taxi rank on the Uitenhage side. Let's say in two hours' time?"

"Yes, that should be fine. So that's about 7pm?"

"It'll be getting dark but just look out for this car."

"OK. I might not be there, depends on what we can sort out with Miriam," said Arthur.

As they crested the rise on the small hill on the main route between Port Elizabeth and Uitenhage, they saw smoke hanging over the township area. Police helicopters were flying about and it looked a scene from a war movie. Some of the smoke was thick and black, hanging like funereal palls over the area.

"That's from tyres," explained Arthur. "The people burn tyres in street blockades, to stop police patrols. The rubber gives that thick, bad-smelling smoke, and it really hampers the police. "Trouble is, all the homes nearby will smell for days."

Jamie pulled the car to one side as a convoy of police vehicles – Hippos, Landrovers and the usual patrol vehicles came screaming past, sirens wailing on the lead vehicle. "Looks like it's going to be busy there tonight," he said, looking towards the townships.

"Yes," said Arthur. "Talking burning tyres. You know the people are unhappy with the black councillors, who they see as sell outs.

"Well, I've also heard rumours that those old car tyres will be used for *necklacing*. The plan is to fill them with petrol and put them around informers or traitors and set them alight - a horrible, horrible way to die."

Jamie shivered at the image his brain created of a person being burnt to death. It's like self-immolation, a practice used by some Buddhists and Hindus to protest or to strive for martyrdom. The big difference, he thought, was that the Buddhists and Hindus planned for it. The informers or traitors Arthur spoke about would not be that prepared.

After being dropped by Jamie, Arthur walked over to the crowds at the taxi rank. The crowd there was not filled with its usual, late-evening bonhomie. The mood was sullen. A sense of anger, frustration and despair permeated the atmosphere.

In the distance a police Hippo stood, its crew of armed policemen lounging next to the vehicle, seemingly careful to keep their distance, their weapons pointed down.

"Hey, brother," one friskily built man in his 20s walked up to Arthur. "Where've you been? Been chummy with the whites have you? I saw you get out of that posh car." As he got closer his overcoat swung open, showing a sharpened machete, known locally as a panga, hanging from his belt.

Arthur stood rooted to the spot. He noticed others, also wearing overcoats, turn and walk towards him, forming an aggressive semi-circle between him and the taxi rank. This type of aggression and armed presence was unusual in a public area - and so close to the police.

"I... I've been in Port Elizabeth. And I got a lift from that white man. Why? What's wrong with that?"

"Are you an impimpi?" the first man, obviously the

group's leader, asked belligerently, moving his right hand to the panga's worn handle.

"No!" Arthur denied strongly. "That man was not a cop, he's a reporter, works for the Herald."

"Oh, so giving the Press stories, are you?" The man advanced again, now close enough for Arthur to smell his alcohol-tainted breath.

Arthur realised there was going to be no easy way out of this. This man and his cronies were spoiling for a fight. And, if it came to that, Arthur reckoned the police would keep their distance and let the blacks fight it out among themselves.

"No! Not that either! I was just getting a lift, I need to get home to my sister, she's come back from training college."

Arthur was caught short as someone lunged into his back, pushing him to the ground.

His assailant fell on top of him, mumbling: "Hey Art. My friend. Where, where have you been?"

The panga gang stepped back, watching as the man spilt liquor from his cheap bottle of wine all over himself and Arthur, cursing as he did so. "Another drunk? What's going on?"

Arthur twisted on the ground, shifting the man's weight so he could get up on his hands and knees and look at the wine spiller. He was surprised to see it was one of his former neighbours, and an erstwhile VW colleague, Nathan Mala, who had left the area about three years ago to move to Johannesburg.

"Nathan! What's up with you, buddy?" he asked.

"Ar ... Arthur. Man, it's all going silly here," Nathan said, sitting up and trying, badly, to set his bottle on the ground where it fell over, spilling the rest of the wine. Oh, well, there's more there."

Arthur looked up at the panga man. "What is going on?"

"Oh, yes, you've been in the big city all day, haven't you?"

He offered Arthur a hand up, speaking as he did so. "After yesterday's shooting, we decided we've had enough of these town councillors the white government has appointed. These puppets. And we want the police out of our areas. They just come here and kill. Anyway, we had a street meeting near the municipal bottle store in Umgeni Road. The store was open but the police then came and said they wanted to close it.

"We formed a barrier, a human barrier, while some got tyres and set them alight. We then raided the store and helped ourselves. This is the start of the revolution, we vigilantes will sort it all out," he patted Arthur on the shoulder and walked away. Nathan appeared to have fallen asleep.

Arthur realised it could be a dangerous night and he hurried to the rank, grabbing the first minibus that was headed towards his home.

It was not an easy trip. The roads were littered with bricks, rocks and tyres. Even supermarket trolleys, wheelbarrows and huge chunks of pre-cast concrete were scattered about.

The minibus had to inch its way through the debris - taking twice as long as it usually did to cover the distance. They passed mobs of youths in the streets some of them, now that they were deeper into the area, blatantly carrying knives, pangas and sticks.

At his stop, at the telephone booth where he'd made his call to the Herald only yesterday, Arthur noticed that the glass panels had been shattered and receiver ripped from the booth. He trotted the short distance home.

Although it wasn't quite twilight, there was an air of foreboding about and a kind of stillness. Whereas people normally met over their fences to chat about the day's events, most had retreated indoors. The smoke palls seemed to be growing and that, Arthur realised, was the main reason why the township felt gloomy. Most noticeable among the usual background noise of traffic on the freeway and passing trains in the other direction was the *thwup thwup* of helicopters as they flew about the area. Arthur saw at least three matt green Alouette helicopters and the bright yellow police chopper flying about.

At the door of their house he was met by a nervous-looking Nancy while, in the background, he saw his sister Miriam playing with Sam on the front room floor. He could smell meat cooking and it was a welcoming smell.

"Arthur! I've been worried about you," said Nancy as she accepted his warm hug. Then she pulled back, wrinkling her nose. "You smell of cheap wine, have you been drinking?"

"No, a drunk friend of mine fell on me at the taxi rank. Apparently they broke into the bottle store and helped themselves. I've been with that reporter, Jamie Nelson. It's been a busy and scary day. I'll tell you later."

He walked over to his sister, who looked up smiling from the floor where she had Sam occupying her lap. Arthur knelt and embraced her, kissed her cheek and, at the same time, patted Sam on the head. "Great to see you again, sis. You're looking well."

They chatted while Nancy prepared food and when he walked over to her she whispered: "Arthur, I was really worried, just before Miriam arrived two policemen - I think they were Zulus, not Xhosa - came looking for you. Well, I think it was you. They said they said they wanted to see the man who lived here and used to work for Volkswagen. They seemed quite furtive and kept looking around as if they, too, were scared."

"Yes, there have been some Zulu policemen down here, I heard. They're the tough guys from Natal who were brought in because there was the worry that the Xhosa guys would be too soft on their own people. What did you tell them?"

"Oh, I lied," she said, almost proudly. "I said you'd been away for a few days and your sister was coming to keep me company. They seemed happy with that and then left. But I'm worried. What if they come back or are still watching the house?"

"Well, we'll have to just deal with that. I want to move you and Sam to a safe house in a white area that the newspaper boss has offered. But I'll also have to sort Miriam out. I don't think anyone should be here for the next few nights."

19

DEATH BY FIRE

As a result of Arthur's bleak announcement and the war-like scenes and noises outside, the hurried dinner was a quiet, sombre affair. A loud knock at the door made them all jump. Miriam was the one who went to open the door. Nancy was holding Sam protectively while Arthur moved to one side, ready to flee if it was the policemen again.

But, of all people, it was Nathan Mala, appearing even more drunk and clutching two litre bottles of cheap wine.

"Mizz ... Mirr ... Miriam!? How good to see you ... is Arthur here?" and he stumbled past her, spying Arthur and brandishing his booty. Look, buddy, wine to replace my bottle you knocked over."

"Nancy," said Arthur softly. "Get some coffee going, then go pack your stuff. I'll sort him out."

He turned to Nathan as Miriam took Sam under control while his mother made the coffee. "Come," said Arthur to his friend. "Let's sit and discuss what's happened today."

He guided Nathan to one of the three chairs in the small room, managing to relieve him of one of the two bottles before it was dropped to the floor. Nathan sighed as he slumped into his seat.

"What a day, what a day." He looked over at Arthur, focussing sharply. "Hey," he said, smiling, "I'm not that pissed. Really. If you check that bottle you're holding, it's probably 80 per cent lemonade." And with that he took a deep swig from the other bottle, and gagged.

"No, this one is, maybe you do have the real, unadulterated wine. No bother, the coffee will be good though," and he turned and grinned at Nancy.

"Nathan," said Arthur sternly, "what the hell is going on? You knock me over at the taxi rank, spill wine on me, then arrive here pretending to be drunk. Why?"

Nathan smiled yet again, and then leant forward

confidentially.

"Well, would you believe I'm a journalist now, I'm a correspondent for the BBC, based in Jo'burg? Anyway, after the news broke about the shooting and we saw the Herald's story with the eyewitness account, the BBC flew me down here this morning with two facets to my brief: Get a colour story from the inside and track down the eyewitnesses. Easy huh?"

Arthur was surprised, and stunned. Did Nathan know he was the eyewitness? And if so, how? While some of the police seemed to think so, the Herald's people were trying to ensure his safety.

"So why are you here?" he asked.

"I was at the mass meeting, saw the bottle store raid and thought, if I pretend to be drunk, I can kind of wander anywhere and get an idea of the mood. I have and it's decidedly ugly. I have some great stuff but don't know, now, how to get the story out. All the phone booths have been trashed.

"And, by the way, when I saw you at the taxi rank I knew you were in trouble. Those panga guys had already slashed someone earlier - just because he gave them backchat.

"You seemed to be heading that way, so I knocked you over. The bad news is those guys said earlier that they're going to hunt down some of the councillors and give them justice. What does that mean? Any idea?"

Arthur replied cautiously: "Well, I've heard rumours from the vigilantes and street committees that they intend to make an example of the councillors, like Ben Kinikini by necklacing them to death. It will be a terrible death. Not even Kinikini deserves that."

"No," agreed Nathan. "A horrific concept and brutal. That would get all the world's media interest focussed on SA. Already the Langa shooting is headline news everywhere, I'm told."

The two sat, lost in their thoughts at this potentially terrible twist to the unrest and fighting. Then Nancy entered the room, with Sam in tow and a suitcase in hand.

"Right, I'm ready. What's next?"

"Well, we need to get to the taxi rank near Uitenhage and then you guys will be picked up by Jamie Nelson, the reporter, in a silver Mercedes. He'll take you to Bluewater Bay, the editor's house. I'll join you tomorrow after I've sorted out a safe place for Miriam. I do not think this house is safe if the police know who you and I are?"

"Know you?" asked Nathan. "What do you mean?"

"We're the eyewitnesses the Herald quoted," said Arthur deciding, on the spur of the moment, to trust Nathan. He really had no choice. "Now it appears, somehow, they've found out who we are - the security branch. So it's not safe to be here, if they find our house."

"Well, the bad news," said Nathan, "is they might have, I'm sorry to say. I was pretending to be drunk because there were some guys in a dark blue Ford cruising the area. Two white guys and two black guys. The black guys were Zulus."

Nancy gasped and said: "Did the one have a scar on his left cheek? If so, they were here earlier."

Nathan paused, then said: "I really cannot be certain. It was dark in the car, even when they stopped and questioned me. I could not see the faces of the two in the back clearly. But I heard the one say, in Zulu, that I look like him. I had no idea at the time who him is or was. But now ... well, Arthur, you and I are of similar build, age and general appearance. So maybe he thought I was you. It's starting to make sense."

Arthur looked at Nancy and Sam. He was now extremely concerned for their welfare but he was trying his best not to show it. The last thing they needed now was for Sam to get worked up. At the moment, he was quite placidly fiddling with his tennis ball, seemingly unconcerned with the tone of the conversation.

"I have an idea," said Miriam. "Let's assume they are not too sure what Nancy looks like. Why don't Nathan and I dress warmly, scarves and so on and walk out of here to his house? If the police are watching, they'll follow us. So, you Nancy and Sam wait a bit then go out over the back fence."

Arthur and Nathan looked at each other.

"Yes, it could work," they agreed.

"I'll meet you guys at Nathan's house in about 45 minutes," said Arthur.

***

Less than 10 minutes later Arthur, Nancy and Sam had left by the backdoor, scaled the small fence and were heading for the taxi rank. No-one seemed to notice them as they emerged from the neighbour's yard and walked hand in hand down the road, like any other young family. The suitcase Nancy had packed was small enough not to attract any undue attention. Just beyond the taxi rank, Arthur easily spotted the shiny Merc, parked among some dustier and older cars.

He said a quick goodbye to Nancy who, surprisingly, grabbed him in a warm embrace before walking off with Sam. She didn't look back and Arthur did not see the tears in her eyes.

***

An hour later, Nathan and Arthur were enjoying a glass of cheap wine. Nathan and Miriam had had an easy walk to the house. There was no obvious sign of the Granada although Nathan said he thought he'd seen it in the distance. But the mobs roaming the streets made things difficult.

"Yes, the situation out there is worrying," Arthur said, while Miriam and Nathan's mother spoke in the other room.

"I think there's going to be lots of trouble tonight - even deaths."

"I agree. I was thinking about that," responded Nathan. "My suggestion is Miriam spends the night here, she can use my bed and you and I go back to your house. It's not safe to leave your house unattended. We need to guard it. My neighbour has two sons who are good guys. I'll ask them to keep an eye on my mom and Miriam. Anyway, this

99

is a quieter area, further from the major township roads, so they should be okay."

By 8pm, Nathan and Arthur were making their way back to the Shipalana home. An almost apocalyptic atmosphere ruled outdoors. It was dark and difficult to see where sky stopped and smoke started. A strong stench of burning rubber permeated the air becoming one with the surrounding noise. From the clatter of the occasional helicopter with its bright searchlight sweeping the area - highlighting the palls of black smoke - and the rumble of Hippos, to the shouts, screams and occasional shots out of the darkness in the distance.

The mood was heavy and ugly.

Sticking to as many back roads as they could, Arthur and Nathan made good progress, managing to avoid the angry mobs or police patrols. Until they got closer to the busy areas. Here things were really kicking off. As they approached a strip of shops, Nathan grabbed Arthur and pulled him to one side as rocks came flying in their direction.

"Hell! What's going on?" he shouted in surprise.

"Look behind us, that's what's going on," said Nathan.

Arthur turned and saw two Hippos. They paused at the intersection before they drove off - away from the crowd followed by a hail of stones, rocks and bottles as youths ran after them. Ahead of the two men, tyres burned in the street.

Suddenly there was a loud, bloodthirsty roar from the crowd.

"Oh no! I know what's going to happen," said Arthur.

They were outside the Kinikini Funeral Parlour, the undertaking business run by the disliked town councillor. Arthur knew that Ben Kinikini's sons lived in the flat above the business. And so, too, did the baying crowd. Many residents in the area suspected that the Kinikinis used the mortuary as a torture chamber where they beat and sometimes, according to rumours, killed anti-government sympathisers.

Now, fuelled by blood, lust and alcohol pilfered from the

raided bottle stores, the crowd sought justice for these supposed wrongs. Standing on the fringe of the mob, their backs to a boarded shop window, Nathan and Arthur watched in horror.

The crowd surged closer to the building.

Shots rang out from the first floor windows and two people fell, wounded or fatally shot, they could not tell.

More stones and rocks were thrown including petrol bombs, crudely made Molotov cocktails. Two went through the now shattered windows and flames could be seen rising as the curtain caught alight.

The crowd surged again, Arthur and Nathan being swept along with them.

Suddenly the crowd's roaring got louder. Standing on tip-toe, Arthur saw the double doors to the hearse parking garage open. A hearse, its engine over-revving and its headlights on full beam, tried to force its way through the crowd. But to no avail. Its windows shattered and front tyres punctured by slashing pangas, the vehicle stuttered to a halt and stalled. Four men were pulled from the vehicle.

Panga blades gleamed in the lights as they swung up and then down, their colour changing from silver to red.

The crowd pulled back a bit.

Arthur, his toes now cramping, saw the senior Kinikini being held by two men. On the ground lay three, maybe four bodies. As he watched, he saw another two men force a tyre over Kinikini's head and pull it down over his arms.

The old man fell to his knees.

Another man then leant towards Kinikini and hurriedly stepped back as flames leapt from the tyre.

Even as the volume of the crowd's chanting and shouting grew, both Nathan and Arthur could hear the man's tortured, pain-filled screams. Flames now engulfing his upper body, Kinikini rose to his feet and staggered towards the building. He stumbled as the crowd gave way and the flames took hold, burning his hair and flesh.

Everyone stood still. Except for one man who swung his panga viciously at the moving man's head, silencing the screams.

The crowd stood, this time almost silent, as they watched the body burn.

More shots rang out and one of Kinikini's sons ran from the mortuary entrance, firing wildly and screaming in fury. He made about ten metres before he too was chopped down.

Nathan and Arthur slipped away as the bodies on the ground were set alight.

20

A NIGHT OF TERROR

With the stench of burning rubber and the sickly pork-like smell of seared flesh in their nostrils, Nathan and Arthur slipped down an unlit alley between two buildings just seconds before they heard the sirens of approaching emergency vehicles and the clatter of the police helicopter.

"Someone in the crowd or nearby must be working with the cops, or maybe there was still somebody in the Kinikini flats," said Nathan as he paused, shock etched on his face. They had only progressed about 100 metres and could still hear the shouts of the crowd.

"I cannot believe what I just saw - that's a barbaric way to kill. And the mood of that killing crowd? Man, that's ugly and I think it will get worse."

"Sadly, I think you're right," said Arthur. "That's all the Kinikini men wiped out in a few minutes. I hope, for her sake, Mrs Kinikini wasn't in the flats. I'm sure some of the ring leaders are inside now, looting the place. We've got to get away from here. The police will think we're part of the mob."

The two ran down the alley, only to find the end blocked by a high fence.

"There's no way over," said Nathan, looking up, "guess we'll have to go back."

Arthur looked to one side. "Hold on, there's a small gate here, perhaps we can get through."

He knelt and peered in the darkness at the rusty lock, noticing it was broken and the gate's bolt could be slipped back.

"Here is where we can get through," he told Nathan as he squeezed through the narrow opening. Nathan followed.

They brushed their clothes off and then peered around. It seemed to be a backyard for the shopping complex and they were only about 75 metres from the back of the funeral parlour.

"Not a good place to be," muttered Nathan and he pulled Arthur into the overhang of the building as the police helicopter swooped lower, its spotlight sweeping the area. Fortunately, it was aiming for the other side where the riot and burning had taken place.

Suddenly a back door opened nearby and a man tumbled out, crying out and falling to the ground about ten metres away.

A growling, huge Alsatian half-breed was attached, by its mouth, to the man's thigh, blood running down its mouth. The man had a panga in his hand but was unable to get a clean blow at the dog. He saw Nathan and Arthur.

"Help me," he cried. "This beast is going to kill me." His voice trailed off as the dog let go of his thigh and stepped back. As the man sat up and feebly swung his panga, the dog launched itself at the man's chest. Its front legs and chest hit the man just as the panga hit its face on the left side, damaging the dog's eye and causing it to yelp with pain.

The man fell back, knocked over by the dog's weight, and dropped his panga at the same time. As the dog tried to bite his throat, the man lifted his arm and the dog firmly bit it, causing his victim to scream in pain.

As Nathan instinctively reached for the panga to fight the dog off, a woman in her 50s or 60s came running through the door, part of her dress on fire. Arthur recognised her as Mrs Kinikini.

He grabbed her and rolled her on the ground, covering her body with his to kill the flames, as he'd been taught in safety training at VW.

"Hey! Hey!" Mrs Kinikini shouted as they rolled on the concrete paving. But the fire was doused and they sat up, Arthur grinning ruefully at her.

He then heard another yelp from the dog as Nathan hit it with the flat of the panga on its muzzle and it let go of the badly bleeding man who stood up and ran awkwardly back through the door, which he slammed shut behind him. But not before the dog managed to squeeze itself in. The three outside heard more growls and screams.

At that time the sirens were even louder as the ambulances pulled to a stop outside the front of the building. Shots rang out. Some coming from the front and one, maybe two, from inside the mortuary.

"We must get you away from here," Arthur said urgently to Mrs Kinikini who was just sitting slumped against the wall, in a dazed state.

"Nathan, help me get her up," shouted Arthur.

In one of the sweeps of the helicopter's searchlight he'd seen another gate, about 30 metres away which, hopefully, led to another street running parallel to the front of the building. Together the two men lifted the woman to her feet and half carried, half dragged her to the other gate. Fortunately, it was also unlocked and they managed to swing it open and get through, just as the back door burst open yet again and the same man who'd been bitten by the dog fell through, this time far worse for wear.

As he fell to the ground, a policeman followed and fired a single shot into him. He jerked and then lay still. As he looked up to see if anyone else was in the yard, the helicopter dropped quite low and its searchlight shone at the policeman, blinding him and making him turn and re-enter the building.

***

Struggling with a half-comatose Mrs Kinikini, Arthur and Nathan worked their way down the road, hoping to get away from all the noise and action. But that was not easy. Groups of youngsters ran in all directions. Drunks stood swaying on street corners. Police Hippos, with their distinctive diesel rumble, could be heard travelling around, luckily none on this road.

Two men stepped in front of Arthur and Nathan, forcing them to stop.

"Is she hurt?" said one.

In the gloom, Arthur could just make out their dark

green paramedic uniforms. Relieved, he said: "Yes, I think she was in a fire. She has burns on her back and her legs."

One of the paramedics said: "OK, we'll take her from here. Our ambulance is in the next road."

He paused, looked at the woman, and said: "Ma Kinikini? It's Wellington. I'm one of little Ben's friends. I'll help you."

As he supported the woman, the other man turned to Arthur and Nathan.

"We've found the burnt bodies of her sons and one hardly recognisable body. Can't find her husband though."

"That's him," answered Arthur. "The badly burnt body. They put a tyre round him and set him alight."

The two walked off, leaving the paramedics to their task.

"Well, Arthur, guess we better get ourselves to your house, if it's not too late," said a still traumatised Nathan.

"That's enough killing for one night and I don't even think it's 10 o'clock yet," replied Arthur, linking arms with his old friend so they could support each other as they walked. Two blocks away, things were quieter. The police helicopter had flown off, the crowds were sparser but there was still activity. Most street corners had been blocked by burning tyres and makeshift barricades to impede the police patrols. Every so often a panga-wielding man would approach Arthur and Nathan, see they were local and, after a few words, let them go.

"Hey, I've just noticed. Most of these guys who are stopping us are wearing white scarves made of rags or torn shirts on their heads. Is that the local vigilante force?" Arthur shrugged. "I've no idea. First time I've seen it too. Anyway, they seem to be the friendly ones so we'll keep a look out for others and be careful."

As they turned the next corner, into Hendricks Road, they stopped in their tracks. Two Hippos and the blue Ford Granada were parked at the Shipalana house - or what was left of it. Smoke and flames could be seen on one of the two almost intact walls. The rest was burnt and ruined.

Without thinking, Arthur shouted out and started running

towards his home. Nathan, quicker than his friend, tackled him. As they fell, Nathan saw their approach had been noticed by the policemen standing about 50 metres away.

They got to their feet to run off as shots rung out. Arthur heard one hit the ground near him. Stones shot up and stung his leg.

He heard another shot and a grunt and, out of the corner of his eye, saw Nathan's head explode as his friend was struck by the bullet from behind. The body took two more jerky steps before falling.

Arthur ran for his life.

21

DUCKING AND DIVING

After vomiting and dry-retching several times, Arthur sat with his head between his knees. He'd run about a kilometre after Nathan was shot, more bullets whizzing past him until he'd turned a corner. But fear and adrenalin kept him going beyond that until his legs eventually collapsed.

The image of Nathan's head being ripped apart as the bullet exited was etched on his mind. There was even blood spatter on his jacket, he just noticed and he puked yet again, just sour bile this time. A few minutes passed until his heart slowed to an almost normal rhythm.

He thought back to the good days when he and Nathan were youngsters, growing up together, dreaming of becoming football stars, having girlfriends or being famous.

Good times, indeed. Now the man, who suddenly came back into his life a few hours ago, was dead - killed during the third act of kindness he'd shown in that short time.

"Incredible," Arthur thought, "I've been saved from a possible panga attack, then Nathan offered refuge to Miriam and then, finally, stopped me from running into the police at his house - losing his life, unnecessarily, in the process."

Somehow, he had to let Daniel Jacobs know. He could contact the BBC and tell them.

Arthur looked around, trying to ascertain where he'd ended up after his frantic run. He was just off Maduna Road - about 500 metres from where the shooting had taken place. "Was that only yesterday?" he said to himself, his voice and throat raw from the retching.

At the site of the shooting there were small fires burning and people gathered, quite peacefully, their shadows jumping and moving in the flames, even though they were all standing still. It looked like a prayer vigil.

Arthur got tiredly to his feet and walked over. Some white priests were indeed praying. A crowd of about 50 people had gathered in a circle, their heads bowed in prayer. As Arthur sidled up, one priest looked up, caught his eye and walked slowly over.

"Can I help you? You look worn out," he enquired softly, concern showing in his warm eyes as he gazed intently at Arthur.

Shocked at the emotion he felt, Arthur blinked furiously as tears sprang to his eyes. Offering him a handkerchief, the man said: "I'm George Irvine, a Methodist minister. What can I do to help you? What has happened to upset you so much?"

Arthur, sobbing and speaking haltingly, told the calm, grey-haired man the whole story, right from witnessing the shooting the previous day to the necklacing of Ben Kinikini and the shooting of Nathan Mala less than an hour ago. He also included snippets about the newspaper and the security police.

George looked shocked. "My dear man, Arthur is it? I must say that is a lot to have to endure in such a short time. I know both Dan Jacobs and Jake Swarts personally. If they said they'll look after you, they will. Now, where are you going to stay tonight?"

Arthur told him about the safe house idea and that Jamie Riley had already taken his friend, Nancy, and her son there. And that he was meant to join them the next day.

"OK, that's no problem, I can drive you to Jake's house in a few minutes. I must just take my leave from my colleagues."

With that, George turned to the nearest priest to briefly explain his reason for leaving. He then called a black priest over and asked him to get details about Nathan's address from Arthur so he could break the news about the fatal shooting and let Miriam know that her brother was safe and being taken to the safe house.

A few minutes later, Arthur was in George's car as the minister drove him to safety.

***

At Jake's river-facing Bluewater Bay home, Jake, Jamie and Daniel sat chatting while Nancy and Sam watched TV and Jake's wife Beth made some snacks. Daniel had briefly met the two. And the woman Nancy had looked vaguely familiar to him. But it was 10.30pm and it had been an exhausting day for everyone.

The men sipped whiskies and beer and discussed what to do next.

"Well, we have Nancy and Sam which is good. I'm assuming Arthur will arrive some time tomorrow morning - all being well," said Jake, savouring his 12-year-old Dalmore single malt.

"I hope so," responded Daniel, "The last time I checked with the newsroom, it was kicking off in Langa. Reports of several shootings, looting and burning have come in."

Jamie, the beer drinker, chipped in. "When I left with Nancy and Sam, it was fairly quiet, but there seemed to be an air of anticipation and the people at the taxi rank where I waited all seemed anxious. It was not a good feeling."

"Yes, we might have to have staff working longer shifts." said Jake. "I have arranged for Clive and Shaun to go up in a private aircraft tomorrow at first light and fly over the area. We should get some good shots of the extent of the damage," said Daniel.

At that moment Beth entered the room. "Jake," she said, "there's been a car cruising up and down the road. It slows down at our driveway then drives off again. It's been four times now."

"It's not a dark blue Ford, is it?" asked Jamie.

"I'm not too sure, it's dark but I have no idea what type of car it is," said Beth. "Why?"

"Oh, it's been following us during the day, we think it's the security police."

Jake stood up. "There's one way to find out," he said firmly, "Let's go outside and flag them down."

The three put down their drinks and walked out into the

coolish night air. At the entrance to the house's driveway were two tall Poplar trees. They stood near the trees and waited.

The night was quiet, just the distant hum of traffic on the Port Elizabeth-Grahamstown road and the lapping of the river against a jetty across the road. It was peaceful and far removed from the anguish and death of the Langa township about 25 kilometres away.

The sound of a low revving car engine could be heard approaching, slowly, from the sea side of the road. When they saw the headlights on the road, Jake and Daniel stepped out into the road while Jamie waited on the sidewalk, effectively blocking the car's passage.

As the car - a dark blue Granada - stopped, Jake strode up to the driver's side window. "Are you lost? Can I help? I could not help notice that you've gone up and down this road a few times," he said innocently.

A man stuck his head out and said, "Yes, you can, actually, I'm looking for number 64."

"Well, sorry to say you're on the wrong road. There's no 64 here. There is on Silversands Drive, however, which is parallel to this. Keep heading straight on, go right up the hill and then right again. It'll be on the left hand side."

The man thanked Jake and drove off. But he did not turn right as instructed, just continued up the road.

"Strange," said the editor, shaking his head.

"Not really," said Jamie, "I'm pretty sure that was the man Arthur and I saw near Livingstone Hospital. He said he was looking for the Mount Road Police Station."

He turned to Daniel, "That's the guy who said he was a forensics officer, sent down from Pretoria. Also that could be the same Granada that we saw in Langa yesterday."

"OK. So we know the security police are following us. We know they have inside information. But we don't know who the mole is. I assume it's not one of us. So I suggest we think about planting a false story in the newsroom tomorrow," Daniel said. "Let's go back inside and chat about it quickly before I give Jamie here a lift home."

22

A FALSE TRAIL

While Nancy put Sam to bed, with Beth in close attendance, Jake held a council of war with his news editor and Jamie.

"Right, do we have any suspects?" he asked pouring himself another whisky then offering the bottle to Daniel.

Refusing the drink, Daniel replied: "Not really. I suppose, however, if you look at lifestyles, Shaun Riley spends a lot of time with the police. But that's his job.

"Then Mark Daly fishes a lot - surf angling and deep sea - and he has some mates who are cops. Two of them in the security branch, brothers named Paul and David.

David owns a ski boat and Mark goes out with him quite often. He's in the security branch, not too sure what he does though. I do know his brother spends a lot of time in Grahamstown, monitoring student behaviour at Rhodes University."

Jamie intervened, "Yes, but I have friend who plays rugby and that doesn't make me a fan of the game."

"Jamie has a point," Jake said. "Personally, I'd be surprised if it's someone in the newsroom. What about works or advertising?"

"No," said Daniel. "The information got out too quickly. Sadly it has to be someone on our floor. In our newsroom, in fact."

He paused. "Well, Shaun and Clive won't be in tomorrow morning so we can do a test on Mark. How about we say, when Mark's at the desk, that Jamie is going to take Arthur and Nancy to the airport at noon, to fly them to Jo'burg. Then, we send him out on a job with Monica Davis and she can let us know if anything untoward happens regarding Mark's behaviour."

Jake thought as he sipped his whisky.

"Yes, it's a possibility."

Just then, there was a knock on the door. Jake went to the door and returned with a bedraggled and exhausted-looking Arthur and George.

"Arthur! Are you OK? Man, you look buggered - sorry, George," said Jamie, smiling at the minister.

While Jake poured a drink for George, an offer which Arthur declined, Daniel and Jamie looked concernedly at their new contact, noting the blood on his jacket, some on his face, the cuts to his trouser leg and the haunted look in his eyes.

"It's been a hell of a night," said Arthur tiredly. "Sometimes I think, if I hadn't have made contact with you, things would be OK and my friend Nathan would still be alive."

"Nathan?" enquired Daniel.

"Oh, yes, you don't know. He is, or was, a friend of mine. We grew up together. Then a few years back, he went up to Jo'burg.

"Anyway, I literally bumped into him today after Jamie dropped me near the taxi rank. He's now a reporter for the BBC and they sent him down to cover the story and find the Herald's eyewitnesses for their own story. He didn't know it was me. Anyway, we saw all kinds of horrible things tonight. Even a necklacing."

He looked at Jamie who had paled significantly. "Yes, just like I told you.

"Then, walking back to my house, we saw it had been set alight. There were some police there and they started shooting at us. As we ran off, a bullet hit Nathan and ... and he's dead."

He paused, sniffed and swallowed and said: "I'm sorry. I'm so sorry that this all happened. Mr Jacobs, can you please get hold of the BBC and tell them? Tell them he's been shot, please. But is Nancy here? I need to see her and tell her what happened."

Daniel, who knew the house quite well, took Arthur off after he had thanked George for his help and the lift. As the two left the room, George included Jamie in the quiet conversation he'd been having with Jake.

"I understand you guys might have an informant in the newsroom. Jake was telling me about your plan. Well, it just so happens I'm going to be at the airport tomorrow to meet Desmond Tutu who's flying in. He arrives from Cape Town at about 1.30. So, I suggest you all keep to your plan and I'll be outside the airport from about noon, so I can keep a lookout if you want?"

The idea seemed totally plausible and they readily agreed.

"Look, I don't want you to do anything or intervene. Just keep an eye out for extraordinary police activity and, obviously, for Mark. If he shows, then we know he's our leak," said Jake.

When Daniel returned, the assistance of the minister was explained.

"Oh, Tutu's arriving tomorrow? That's great, he always makes good copy. Will we be able to speak to him? I mean, seeing as Jamie here will be at the airport."

"You never miss an opportunity, do you?" smiled George. "I'll try to arrange an exclusive but I cannot guarantee that the other media won't be around too."

With that settled, Daniel and Jamie left for home as did George. They were all tired after a long day.

***

In the guest suite, Sam was already asleep. It was almost midnight and Arthur had sat on the edge of the bed, explaining what had happened to Nancy. She held his hand as he talked, tears occasionally springing to her eyes as she listened. When he'd finished, she leant over and hugged him warmly.

"Right, time for you to have a bath and then get some sleep," she said, getting up and moving through to the en suite bathroom to run the water. Arthur looked around and noticed there was only the double bed and a small two-seater sofa. Sam was asleep in the single bed in the adjoining room.

Arthur walked through to the bathroom. "Two things,

Nancy," he said as she looked up from where she'd been turning off the taps. "Firstly, there's only one bed and, secondly, I have nothing to sleep in."

She smiled. "Well," she said shyly, "we will just have to make do. It is, after all, an emergency. Beth has provided pyjamas for us. Your sleep shorts are there on the cabinet. Now get undressed and have a bath."

She left the bathroom, closing the door behind her. Arthur found the hot bath water surprisingly soothing. As he lay there soaking he looked around.

"This is way better than we have in Langa," he thought, looking at the gleaming ceiling high white tiles, the toilet and basin cabinet with the huge mirror behind it. "Oh, well, one day."

The next thing he knew was a distant banging and Nancy calling him. He'd fallen asleep in the now tepid water and she was calling his name as she banged on the bathroom door.

"Arthur ... Arthur! Are you asleep? Get out, the water must be cold."

He dried himself quickly, put on the sleep shorts and, by the time he'd entered the bedroom, she was in the bed, sitting upright against the fluffed up pillows. A beside lamp was burning, the room softly lit. Arthur slipped into the bed, marvelling at the cool sheets against his skin. He lay down, trying to keep some distance between them. She moved down the bed, switched off the light on her side table.

Both were asleep almost instantly.

23

MARCH 23 - THE TRAP BAITED

While Saturday was not a usual working day for the Herald, Daniel had some staff on duty given the severity of the situation with ongoing unrest and international focus on South Africa and the Eastern Cape growing.

Shaun and Clive were at the airport waiting for their flight over Langa and Uitenhage while he, Jamie, Monica and Mark were in the newsroom. It was 9.30am.

Daniel had already made contact with the BBC and broken the news about Nathan's death. Neither the corporation's Johannesburg bureau nor London had been informed yet, by the police, of the man's fatal shooting. That was earlier, before the staff arrived.

As planned Jamie, at the morning round table meeting, announced: "Right, with Jake's help, we've arranged for Arthur, Nancy and Sam to fly to Johannesburg. I'll be taking them to the airport at noon."

"Good stuff," said Daniel, "you might as well hang about there for a while then. I understand Desmond Tutu is arriving at about 1, so you can try for an interview. If Clive and Shaun are back in time, I'll get Clive to join you there for pictures."

"Well, I can do that," said Mark.

"No," said Daniel, "I need you and Monica to go to Mount Road police headquarters where Carl Strydom is holding a press conference. Apparently he is going to announce an investigation into the shootings. That's at 10.30. Then, from there, go to the University's Rag Day procession - they start from the Crusader grounds at about 11.30. We need a picture page for Monday. After all, there is a normal world out there. It's not all unrest and township mayhem.

"And before you guys head off, here's the sports photo diary for the weekend. You're down for tennis this afternoon and tomorrow, and Clive's assignments are there too, just so you know what he's doing."

Daniel turned to Jamie: "Before you go out, can you do a quick round of the usual crime and calamity calls? Just in case there's something for Mark to get. Mark? Just hang about here for five minutes while Monica gets ready and Jamie makes those calls."

While Mark sat at June's desk, Daniel called the Algoa Flying Club and found out that Clive and Shaun had yet to take off. He briefed Clive on the Tutu job, hung up and then turned to Mark. "So, what do you think of all this unrest?"

Mark looked up, putting his cameras away. "I don't know. I worry that the blacks are getting out of hand and, while I can see their point of view, they do seem intent on destabilising everything. Some of my mates in the police, the guys I fish with, reckon it is essential to curb the unrest now, even if it takes some deaths. They must know their place, they say."

"Yes, but what do you think? Who's right, who's wrong?" Daniel asked again.

"Hell, Dan, you know me, I don't take sides. I just do my job. And all of this has given us some great pictures. But I feel for the guys who have to patrol the townships. Those youngsters are quite scared."

Jamie came back to say nothing out of the ordinary had emerged from the checks, Just the usual Friday night road accidents and incidents which the Sunday staff would get the next day. A few minutes later, Monica was ready and she and Mark headed off.

"So, what did you tell Monica?" Daniel asked Jamie.

"Well, I told her to keep Mark in sight all the time. And to let me know if he does anything unusual. So, we'll see."

Daniel sat back and thought for a bit. "Yes, you're right. After all, maybe Mark's not the leak, we really don't know. Maybe it's not Shaun Riley either. We have no idea, do we? So, I guess you should head off to the airport in a while. Say, leave here at 11. I'm going to call Carl quickly, we were meant to meet for a drink last night and, well, things as you know got out of hand and we didn't. So, I need to apologise for that.

"Then I must meet Jake at 11.30 at his club to discuss what we do with our three key people. You know the number if you need me. I'll see you back here when you're done at the airport."

* * *

At the Mount Road police headquarters, Frans and Jimmy Jonker were chatting, standing outside the main building in the autumn sun. It was the first time the brothers had spoken for some time.

"So, Jimmy, I hear you were on one of the Hippos at the shooting. How was it?" asked Frans, puffing on a Lucky Strike.

"Horrible, to be honest. It was a mess. We did not have to shoot them. It all went horribly wrong. How did you know anyway?"

"It's our job to know," he said smiling. "I also know there's going to be an official internal inquiry, starting tomorrow, and all the guys who were there will be interviewed. Your name was on the list, so that's how I found out."

Jimmy, who was dressed in a tracksuit as he and the whole patrol had been put on stress leave for two weeks, looked at his brother. "You did border duty with Koevoet, so you've seen some bad things but, trust me, seeing people being shot in the back by a group of panicking policemen. That's not right and I have nightmares about it. How do you sleep?"

Frans smiled again and then said, wryly: "Well, you don't know all the things I've seen or done. At first, up in Angola and South West I had the worst nightmares you can imagine. I'd scream myself awake. We all had it.

"But, we knew we had a job to do, it was our duty to stop the Commies or the blacks trying to take over. The guys who did our motivational lectures assured us we were doing the right thing, saving South Africa for the safety of our future generations."

He paused.

"How do I sleep? Well. I know what I have done, am doing or will still do, will be for the good of our land. That gives me some peace. The rest? Brandy. The solace of many."

Jimmy looked at his brother closely and saw the haunted look in his eyes. He also noticed the tell-tale signs of heavy drinking by the ruddy veins on his nose and the slightly jaundiced yellow colour to the whites of the eyes. There was a discernible shake to the security policeman's hands as he lit yet another cigarette.

"Frans, I worry about you. And I know Dad does too. All of us are taking strain but, man, you don't seem to be coping."

"Don't you worry about me, I'm fine. A lot to do, a lot on my plate but I'll be OK. I'm getting long leave in April and May."

"Oh, that's nice, I'll be in the UK then. Why don't you take an overseas trip, come and visit?"

Frans paused, about to answer when he saw Mark Daly's car at the gates. "Yes, OK, we can talk about it. Must go. There's one of my newspaper contacts."

Jimmy looked on as his brother walked up to the car and leant in at the driver's side window. An attractive woman was sitting in the passenger seat and Jimmy smiled at her before turning away to the squash courts where he had a game booked.

At the car Frans said: "Hello Mark, what are you here for? The press conference?"

He looked past Mark at the woman who was watching him intently.

"Hey," she said pointing to her left, "there's another of you over there." But the track-suited Jonker was already walking away.

"Yes, that's my twin brother," said Frans.

Mark interrupted. "Yes, we're here for that conference but I'd rather be at the airport, lots of comings and goings."

"Really," said Frans. "Anyone famous or important?"

"Tutu is arriving but I haven't got that job, Clive has it.

Oh and some people you know are leaving - even before you get to meet them."

Frans looked sharply at him. "My black friends?" he asked.

Monica interjected. "Come on, Mark, we must go. It's almost 10.30."

"Yes," said Frans. "You don't want to be late for the Colonel. Thanks Mark, see you later at the angling club?"

As they drove off Monica said: "Why'd you tell him that? He doesn't need to know."

Mark said: "Know about what? Tutu? Of course he should."

At the main building, Monica excused herself to use the toilet and rushed to find a phone to call Jamie.

24

DECEPTION AND ANGER

Daniel and Jake were sipping beers at the club. It had been decided that the best plan, for the safety of Arthur and his two charges, was to get them out of the Eastern Cape.

Jake said: "Earlier this morning, I was chatting to Steven Russell, our MD in Johannesburg, and he said he'd help with getting Arthur and company to safety. First up north and then, possibly, to England. He even spoke about arranging a book deal with his contacts in London, based on the events here and their eyewitness testimony. But that can wait. The first thing is their safety. It won't be easy as the security branch are after them too.

"But Steven has a safari lodge near the Kruger Park where they can go into hiding with you, I'm afraid, as their minder. This is mainly because you've been to that area recently. Gavin can temporarily run the news desk."

Jake paused and smiled as he saw the surprise on Daniel's face.

"What's wrong? Don't like safaris anymore?"

"No, it's just, well, I'm enjoying my job. I'm good at it and these are crucial news times. What about Jamie? He can go with them."

Jake smiled even more. "No, Dan, this all dovetails into a plan I had been working on for the past few weeks anyway. Yes, you are a good news editor and it's great to have you on the team. But the job of bureau chief in London for the entire group is coming up in June. And you were one of the names put forward. You're what, almost thirty? Think about it. A year or three in London and you can virtually choose the paper you want to edit here in SA. You've no family ties here since your divorce and, frankly, this is a golden opportunity.

Before Daniel could reply, a waiter came to their table and said there was a call for the editor's guest. Daniel went to take the call and was back within five minutes.

"That was Jamie. Monica says Mark told that Jonker guy about his friends leaving for Jo'burg. The trap has been baited.

"And, yes, by the way. It's a yes to that bureau offer. I agree it's a great opportunity and thanks for your faith in me."

Jake responded by raising his glass in a toast and finishing his beer. "Well, then, let's get ourselves to the airport and see whether our man Jonker and his team will be there."

At about the same time, in a Cessna twin-engined aircraft, Clive and Shaun were flying low over Langa. Their pilot, Jess Jones, a former mercenary who'd seen action in the Congo, spoke through the headphones to his passengers. "Just look at that. It's like Brazzaville back in the day."

He swooped even lower, down to about 400 feet, so Clive could get pictures of the Kinikini Mortuary which had been torched during the night. Around it the shops and other buildings had also been burned to the ground. Police Hippos were still patrolling the area but being subjected to attacks from gangs of youths who put up roadblocks of burning tyres and shopping trolleys on street corners. Hippos would stop and be pelted with stones, rocks, Molotov cocktails or whatever the gangs had to hand. In the worst scenario, the police would seek an alternative route, usually down a narrower road where they could be blocked in, forcing the crew to abandon the vehicle.

"Yes," Clive agreed, "It's like a warzone."

As Jones prepared for one more swoop his intercom crackled and they heard the pilot of the police helicopter, which they had earlier seen in the distance, instructing them to gain height and leave the unrest area.

"OK guys, that's it I'm afraid. They know my registration details and I don't feel like a huge fine or whatever other penalties the cops might dream up."

As the Cessna turned for home, Shaun continued with his note making and rudimentary sketches so he could later map the area with the newspaper's graphic artist. Another voice, also distorted by static, came through on the radio.

Jess listened intently and then said: "That was the AFC, my base. The cops have lodged a complaint about my flying. I told them I was instructing a rookie who insisted on flying low.

"Anyway, it's home we go, we'll be there by 11. Oh and there's a message for you there from your news editor about pictures you have to take at the airport."

***

In their office in Mount Road, having recently moved from Strand Street, Frans Jonker and Arrie Du Preez were planning how to snatch the eyewitnesses.

"I reckon we can enter the airport on the pretence of a bomb scare and clear the building. Hopefully, in the chaos, we can get the guy and the woman. If we only get him, that's also OK," said Jonker.

Du Preez, the senior ranking of the two, was more circumspect. "No, none of the bull in a china shop type of thing. We must be more subtle. When they go through security, that's when we grab them. We can get one of our guys in as a security check official and he can then pull them out for questioning."

"Might work," conceded Jonker. "What if they are not travelling alone? Remember these are not people of the world. Someone from the paper will probably travel with them, like that Riley guy. Just to hold their hands and make sure they don't get lost."

Du Preez replied: "Well, that makes no difference. Chances are that if we take the guy for instance, the others won't get on the plane. It's less hassle and public fuss this way. So that will be the plan. We'll get one of the airport policemen to be the security guy and you and I can wait backstage and take them when they are escorted off for a body search."

He paused, and then added: "So it's just the two of us.

No fuss, OK?"

As they made ready to leave, Jake and Daniel were arriving at the airport. It was 11.30 and Jamie was already in the terminal building. Jake waited at his car, parked where he could get a clear view of the car park entry gates and the terminal building entrance while Daniel went inside.

He saw Jamie sitting, backlit, near the window, talking to a black man who looked a lot like Arthur. As he got closer, Daniel realised it wasn't.

"Hi," he said approaching the pair. The other man looked at him suspiciously and Jamie spoke.

"Wellington, this is my boss, Dan. Dan this is Wellington. He's the gardener for Monica's parents up the road in Walmer. "I popped in and borrowed him for a while. My theory is, we sit here and if the cops come in, they'll see us and make their move."

"Yes," agreed Daniel, "and if you see them and don't go through boarding, hopefully they'll assume you did spot them and changed your mind. You guys stay here. I'm going to sit in the coffee shop where I can see the road and the door, so I'll notice if they arrive."

As he moved off, the two security policemen turned their car into the airport entrance.

Du Preez, who was the passenger, said to Jonker: "Look, they know you more than me. I'll get out and see if they are there. You just double park and wait for me. I'll be back in a sec."

Jonker dropped him at the door and moved to a nearby space on a yellow line. Within seconds an official came and asked him to move along but was satisfied when Jonker showed his police ID.

Entering the terminal, Du Preez looked around and saw what looked like Jamie and another person in conversation near the windows. Moving to one side so he could get a better view, he stepped right into Daniel's line of vision just as the news editor was returning to his table with his coffee.

Du Preez, satisfied that the man he was looking at was

Jamie, turned on his heel and left, not even glancing into the coffee shop. Hurriedly putting down his coffee and giving a quick thumbs up to Jamie, Daniel strode quickly to the door.

Outside, Du Preez walked up to the unmarked car where Jonker had got out to remove his suit jacket. He did not see Du Preez approach as he folded his jacket and put it on the back seat. Nor did he see Daniel who had spotted Clive standing on the other side of the road. Daniel pointed and Clive, guessing correctly, took some long distance pictures of Du Preez and Jonker as the two conversed.

Daniel turned quickly and re-entered the building as Jonker looked in his direction. "Damn, I hope he didn't spot me," said Daniel to himself as he hurried up to Jamie and Wellington.

Just then an airport announcement was made, calling for boarding of the South African Airways flight to Johannesburg. As usual, it was a busy flight and queues formed at the security gate.

"Great," said Daniel, summing up the situation. "Let's join the queue, we can always walk off at the last moment."

As the three joined the slow moving line, Clive and Shaun entered the building. They were not noticed by the two security policemen as they moved off in their car - heading for a demarcated police parking area. They did not see Jonker and Du Preez rush from the car into the airport charge office but Jake did as he left his car about 20 metres way and strolled over.

As he entered the office, he saw Jonker and Du Preez leave through another door accompanied by another policeman.

"Bugger," said Jake and he turned to enter the terminal building.

The door the policemen had used took them straight into the security area where passengers were being checked. Du Preez and the other man moved to the checkpoint where the official was replaced by the policeman. They turned to Jonker and moved with him towards another smaller cubicle, where body searches were carried out. Jonker took one last look at the passengers and, as he did so, Jamie and his companion were at the front of the line.

Jamie recognised Jonker just as the policeman saw him and instinctively pulled Wellington out of the line.

"Bloody hell!" swore Jonker. "They've seen us."

And without waiting for Du Preez he ran off, back through the charge office and to the terminal entrance, where he was just in time to see Jamie and the black man meet Jake and walk off towards the parking area. Out of the corner of his eye, just as he was about to approach them, Jonker saw Clive and Shaun. Clive was taking a picture of him.

He stormed over. "What the bloody hell are you all doing here and why are you taking pictures of me?" demanded Jonker.

"It's a public area," responded Clive.

"Yes," interjected Daniel, approaching from behind. He'd stayed back in the terminal to see what would happen and was now joining Clive and Shaun. "He has done nothing wrong. But, tell me, why are you here?"

"None of your bloody business," shouted the infuriated police man as he grabbed for Clive's camera. Clive stepped back and, before anyone could move, Jonker swung a haymaker which connected with Clive's right cheek. Clive stumbled, tripped on the kerb and fell to the ground.

"I've had enough of your bloody interference," screamed Jonker and he swung wildly as Daniel tried to grab his arms.

"Hey man, stay calm," urged Daniel.

But the incensed man was difficult to hold and he stepped free, turning on Daniel with his fists raised. He swung wildly and missed as Daniel ducked. Jonker lost his balance and stepped forward again, cursing as he did so.

"I'm going to have you buggers for resisting arrest," he said, grabbing for his pistol which was in a holster at the small of his back.

"What? You have to be kidding," said Clive as he got

back to his feet, checking to see if his camera was damaged as he took another shot of Jonker, this time a close up of the man's enraged face.

As Jonker struggled to free the gun from its holster, Du Preez ran up and grabbed him by the shoulder, swinging Jonker around and away from the journalists. The gun was now free and, as Du Preez grabbed for Jonker's arm, the man pulled the trigger. The shot hit the cement paving and ricocheted, striking Jonker on his right calf. Surprised, Jonker dropped his weapon and fell to his knees clutching his now bleeding leg.

"What the hell are you doing? Are you crazy?" shouted Du Preez as a small crowd began to gather. Now weeping with pain, Jonker looked back at Daniel, Clive and Shaun. "You bastards, I'll get you, just you wait and see."

25

MARCH 26 - TRAITOR FORCES

Monday morning was a quieter affair in the Herald newsroom. The morning paper had been a blockbuster yet again. Clive Brent's aerial shots made the front page along with a wrap of the weekend's incidents and the interview with Tutu.

The airport incident and the shot being fired, written in the third person, made a short page five story. It had to be reported, the paper felt, as the incident had been witnessed by other people. It included the fact that police were investigating an 'accidental discharge of a firearm in a public place', a comment from the weekend duty liaison officer when pressed about the incident at the airport.

His comment also included a vague reference to a security policeman being injured during an 'investigation related incident' at the airport. This resulted in wry chuckles from Daniel, Jamie, Shaun and John as they met to discuss the day's plan of action concerning the unrest.

Monica was at St John's Church attending a press conference held by Irvine, Evans and Tutu which had been called for 9.30am, 30 minutes earlier.

Mark, in the meantime, had been summoned to the editor's office for a private meeting which was due to start at noon, when the photographer's shift began. John said he was hoping to have a meeting with Kusta Jack and other community leaders about the ongoing violence.

"It appears there are some vigilante groups which are backed by the police in a covert way. These, the leaders understand, are causing most of the trouble by burning houses and looting. What's more, I think Matthew Goniwe will be there, according to my sources," said John.

Shaun said the police inquiry, announced on the Saturday, was due to start at noon.

"Carl told me this morning we could attend and take pictures but some sessions, if sensitive, would be closed to us."

"OK," said Daniel, "you and Clive can go to that. John, go to your meeting and Jamie, you and I will have a chat after conference about what follow ups you can do."

Daniel spent the next 30 minutes briefing other staff on their assignments for the day and then getting ready for the conference which involved all the departmental heads - news, features, business and sport - meeting the editor to discuss the next edition.

The phone rang. It was Carl Strydom for Daniel.

"Hello, Dan. Man, you guys know how to make my life a misery. This story about the firearm incident at the airport. Who told you about that? It appears your information is wrong."

"Really? What is the real story then?"

"Well, my sources tell me the security branch were following a tip-off that someone needed for an investigation was preparing to leave the city. So, two men were sent to apprehend this person and, in the ensuing scuffle, a shot was inadvertently fired, injuring one of the police officers. The person they were after made good his escape. There was no involvement with the media beyond one of the officers requesting that no pictures were taken during this official action, which is, as you know, the law."

Daniel was gobsmacked. "So, that's the official story? Well, I was there. Lieutenant Jonker of the security branch - I know we didn't name him in our story - was shot in the right calf. And it was, as we reported, during a scuffle with another man.

"What we did not report was that the other man is Captain Arrie du Preez, Jonker's superior officer. Jonker had lost his cool and was trying to draw his weapon, after my photographer Clive Brent had indeed taken his picture.

"Let me point out, this was not an official act of duty by Jonker. He had caused Clive to fall by trying to grab his camera. We could charge him with assault. Do yourself a favour and speak to either Jonker or Du Preez, preferably both as I don't trust Jonker. One of them should confirm this."

Carl replied: "Strange, but I have to take you at your word. OK, I'll check it out and get back to you later. It will be after the inquiry. By the way, Jonker is in hospital. His leg muscle was damaged during that shot. He'll be there for a day or two."

"Shame. Anyway, why not meet this evening for that drink we still have to have?" asked Daniel. "Say, 7pm at the Anchor?"

Carl agreed and ended the call.

***

Bay Hardware, in North end, was where Kusta Jack worked as a salesman and where, thanks to its sympathetic white owner, Rory Riordan, a fearless human rights campaigner, Jack could host a clandestine meeting to discuss the situation in the townships.

Huddled in the storeroom when John arrived were Jack, Molly Blackburn, Matthew Goniwe from Cradock and Sipho Hashe, Champion Galela and Qaqawuli Godolozi all from PEBCO.

"Comrade John," said Jack in greeting. "You are welcome. We welcome you as a brother and as a representative of the newspaper that fights our corner too. However, comrade, I must advise you that, while you can attend you cannot use any information we discuss at this meeting."

Molly Blackburn spoke up: "Yes, I agree wholeheartedly. We want to discuss two things though. While John can get further information about the vigilantes and use that as a basis for further interviews and stories, we do not want him divulging anything about the impending consumer boycott.

"That, I'm afraid to say," she added, turning to face John, "is still highly confidential. If any word leaks out, the whole idea is dead in the water."

There was a murmur of assent from around the group. John readily agreed. After all, it was the vigilantes and the problem they potentially posed, that was of importance right now. "That is fair. Why don't you discuss the vigilante issue first? Then I will leave."

Goniwe addressed the group. "Comrades, from information we have gathered here, in Uitenhage and even Cradock over the past few weeks, it seems exceedingly clear that the apartheid forces are intent on destabilising civil society in our townships.

"So, what they have is this. They've brought in some Zulu policemen from Natal and we all know the Zulu and Xhosa do not get on. These Zulus have been training up those among our own people, Xhosa like you and me, who support the regime as it now is. Then, these people are being bussed in to where there is trouble, like Langa last week,

"What they are doing is they are taking these traitors and making them instant constables, then they are deployed to ferment trouble. And because our own vigilantes, who are there to protect our people and their property, wear white scarves to be identified, these constables, too, are wearing white scarves."

He paused and John quickly interjected. "Interesting. But how can I prove this? How will our readers believe what I say?"

The group sat quietly and then Jack answered. "Well, the simple answer is we get one or two of them so you can interview them."

"Great idea," replied John, "but I will need them to give me some information which only they and the police would know. With that I would have a story."

Goniwe, Jack and the PEBCO three got into a huddle while John and Blackburn waited.

"You know this is the continuation of the 1976 education troubles. You know, too, that this won't end until the government changes its unjust laws which have been with us for decades. But I mustn't soapbox my political ideals to you. I assume you know that Archbishop Tutu is here, meeting with Bishop Evans and George Irvine?"

"Yes, we do, we have a reporter there now."

"Good. And did you know that Allan Boesak is coming to the city too? He arrives this evening."

Now that he did not know. John knew that Boesak, an ordained church minister and president of the World Alliance of Reformed Churches, was an outspoken critic and opponent of the National Party's policies. The liberation theologian, as he was dubbed, had played a major anti-apartheid activist role as a patron of the UDF from 1983. John recalled reports of how, at a World Alliance of Reformed Churches meeting in Canada, Boesak had introduced a motion requesting that apartheid be declared a heresy contrary to both the Gospel and the Reformed tradition. The alliance adopted the Declaration on Racism and suspended South Africa's white Dutch Reformed Church.

"Great, thanks for that," he said to Blackburn. "Will we be able to interview him?"

"Yes," she answered. "He'll be staying with George Irvine tonight at the manse in Central. It's a secret visit, we hope. Allan is driving up. I'll fix it with them this afternoon and then call you at the Herald. Shall we say 3pm?"

John was then aware that the murmured conversation among the others had stopped.

Galata spoke. "OK, comrade, we will try to do what you ask. As soon as we have captured one or two, we will let Kusta know and he, in turn, will tell you."

John agreed, and then added: "However, we will put it to the police today, off the record, that we suspect this. My news editor will do it. If they give us a comment, we will use it. Can I then quote any of you?"

Jack replied, "Yes, quote me."

But Blackburn again interjected. "No, that's not safe. If it comes from a white mouth, it will be more believable right now. And safer for the person being quoted. I'll be quoted and I'll get George Irvine and Bruce Evans to support me with statements. They know of this emerging situation, too. That should do it."

After some chit chat, John rushed back to the office - another potential scoop at hand.

***

Meanwhile Monica Davis was listening to the church leaders make hard-hitting statements about the unrest, police brutality, human rights and the tragic loss of human life. To her mind, Tutu's best quote was, 'I come to you armed with only my Bible because I am a Christian leader and not a politician, though there are some who insist that I am really a politician who is trying very hard to be a bishop'.

He also said it was interesting how the government always blamed unrest in the community on agitation, and he asked whether a person with a toothache needs to be told whether he was in pain.

Bishop Evans re-iterated Van Zyl Slabbert's remark that it was 'of extreme importance that the people be allowed to hold funerals without interference and when convenient for those who wish to hold them', adding that many people in the townships were Christian and burials were all part of their faith.

George admitted that funerals had been hijacked and had become, in many instances, platforms for political rallies. But, he had hastened to add, "the government had to carry responsibility for this for banning meetings and many of the black leaders. As a result, funerals are just about the only way the masses can be addressed - short of speaking in churches where we try not to be too political, on buses and at taxi ranks."

He also announced that the three of them, plus Allan Boesak who was expected to arrive that evening, would be holding a march and commemorative service on the site of the shooting on Thursday of that week. A delegation of ministers was going to attempt to attend the police inquiry at noon.

As the conference ended, George asked Monica to remain behind. When they were alone, he asked about Arthur.

"Well, you know he's now fine, thanks to you. But we are concerned about future activities by the police to track them down."

"Yes," replied George, "I was at Jake's home last night and heard the chat about a possible mole. Has he been caught? I was delayed in getting to the airport, so I don't know what happened there. I saw the short story about the gun being fired during some disturbance. I take it that was the trap you had set?"

Monica confirmed this and then was surprised when George said: "Look, I'll help anyway I can. And I'm sure I can call on Allan and Desmond too. Get Jake or Dan to make contact."

26

APRIL 13 - PORT ELIZABETH

Things were moving slowly towards getting Arthur, Nancy and Sam out of Port Elizabeth and Dan into his London posting.

While the police inquiry, not surprisingly, had resulted in a finding that no-one was accountable for the deaths, based on its available information and was, therefore, postponed to a later date, the mood in the township had calmed. This was, in no small part, due to the efforts of the clergy and even the UDF who all called for tolerance and patience.

For their part, the police and the government allowed the funeral of the 22 killed to go ahead on a Saturday. And today was the day. As a result, the Herald again had staff working on a Saturday Daniel had decided that Clive and John would attend.

Jake and Daniel had also decided, during the fuss that the funeral would no doubt create, to move their three charges to a house in Walmer, near the township. All three had complained of cabin fever and, with an almost constant vigil by the security police on journalists' homes, it was a better option. Monica Davis's parents were semi-retired and had offered accommodation gladly to Arthur, Nancy and Sam.

They were expected at noon - about the same time as the funeral would start. So, at 11.30am, Daniel arrived at the Swarts's house in a borrowed minibus. After saying their farewells, they left for the other side of the city. Nancy and Beth had established a friendship and she was sad to be leaving.

In the meantime, Daniel's car was being driven aimlessly about the city's western shopping areas, diligently followed by his assigned security branch tail. And in Kwanobuhle, where the funeral was being held at the intended destination of the marchers the previous month, around 80,000 people were either inside the stadium or still trying to get in.

Among those already inside was John armed with a camera while Clive was on the outside in the event of any trouble. Members of UDF had assumed gatekeeper duties and refused entry to members of competing organisations.

Next to Clive was Des Hughes, with some of his emergency vehicles and teams parked nearby, also in the event of trouble. "Surprisingly," Des said to Clive, "it's quite peaceful. We've just had a few scratches and cuts to deal with, and some drunks. But no undue force involving the police who have only had to manhandle a few people away. If only every day was like this."

He stopped as a loud cheer went up from the thousands still outside. A motorcade had stopped about 100 metres from the gate. Alighting from the cars and immediately recognisable were Desmond Tutu in red, and Allan Boesak in a formal suit.

It was for them the crowd cheered. The presence of Bishop Evans, Rev Irvine and other church leaders did not attract too much attention. Nor did the small group of men, assumed to be minders, who walked with them.

Clive focused his zoom lens, took some shots of the leaders and then aimed at the others. "Wow! There are two guys who seem to be prisoners," he remarked as Des tried to focus his binoculars. "They're being escorted by the other three. I wonder what's going on."

Des, ever the paramedic, said: "Well, they don't seem hurt although I can see one has swelling around his eye. Strange indeed."

***

Packed tighter than sardines in a can was how John summed up the situation on the stands. Sweating profusely in the midday heat and from being tightly pressed together, the crowd were uncomfortable.

A loud, distorted voice over the public address was

urging calm. The 22 coffins were lined up on the field on makeshift trestle tables, with a guard of honour in attendance. Nearby, in the middle of the field, a platform stage had been erected with a canvas covering to shield the yet-to-arrive dignitaries.

As the loud roar went up from outside, the master of ceremonies announced the arrival of the church leaders and the crowd struggled to its feet causing more discomfort to almost everyone.

John struggled for a clear view as a praise singer led Tutu, Boesak and their party in. He noticed a group of five men with them, who then detached themselves from the group near the platform where they stood among the overflow crowd which had taken over some of the playing area. But his attention was quickly drawn away as the bright yellow police helicopter clattered overhead, dropping in altitude as a TV camera was visible from it.

"Damn, SABC TV gets all the perks," John said to himself ruefully.

The previous day Daniel had intended using Jess Jones for a flyover but had been told, in no uncertain terms, that the townships would be a no-go area for the duration of the funeral.

The crowd struggled to settle down as the preliminary speakers began their talks, all non-political at this stage and John sat back for a long afternoon in the sun. John felt himself nodding off every so often, jostled awake by his neighbours. But he was awake to makes notes when Boesak spoke.

Boesak was harsh in his criticism of the apartheid government: "I do not think God wants this government to continue ruling South Africa because it does not know what it is doing. Whenever you have a government of force also in power by coercion, and whenever you have a government not of the consent of the people things like the shootings of March 21 are bound to happen."

Tutu was even more so. He asked: "Do you doubt you will be free? Do you want to be oppressed?"

The crowd, in unison, responded, "No!"

"We do not need agitators to tell us that ours is an inferior system of education," he said, referring to one of the black population's major gripes. We also do not need agitators to remind us that we live in ghettoes while others live in affluent quarters. The greatest agitator in the country is apartheid."

Then, rejecting racial hostility from either side, he asserted that 'black people are not against whites but against injustice, oppression and exploitation'.

The Archbishop then made reference to the police order to eliminate petrol bombers as an example of how cheap black life was to the state. "But I disapprove of all forms of violence, being a man of God and peace. And this includes the violence within the townships between rival groups. Let us not use the methods of the enemy because only the enemy rejoices when we set our opponents on fire. I cannot approve of these methods, even though I know you do it out of anger. But let us not undermine our cause. Let us use methods which we will be proud of when we look back after attaining our liberation."

He sat to tumultuous applause.

But it was the next step that took everyone by surprise.

Jack and Goniwe stepped on the platform to be welcomed by Tutu and wildly acclaimed by the crowd.

"Comrades," Goniwe said, urging silence so he could speak.

"Comrades, while we have gathered here to mourn, we must not forget the wrongs that have been done in the past few weeks. The senseless killings by the authorities must not go unremembered.

"They must not go unchallenged.

"They must not go unavenged."

The crowd roared, anger swelling.

"But," said Goniwe holding his arms up for silence and getting it almost immediately now that he had their attention, "now is not the time. Our time will come. Freedom will be ours!"

He waited, again, for silence. "Let me tell you, comrades, that the apartheid forces have another weapon.

They are infiltrating our ranks and sowing dissension. They have put spies among us. Not only the Zulu policemen.

"No," he said as the noise rose again. "Not only have the Zulus but some of our own have been turned."

The rumbling roar rose again. Without waiting, he beckoned into the crowd near the platform and the two prisoners Clive had seen earlier were bundled on to the stage. They cowered at Goniwe's feet.

The crowd went silent.

"These men, these cowards, they are two of the traitors."

The crowd's roar rose in decibels. Goniwe held up his arms again. Silence was almost immediate. "Comrades," he said softly. "We will deal with these traitors. They will get what they deserve. But not now. Now they have another use for us."

John wondered, as the noise rose and ebbed in waves, if these were the men Jack and Galata had promised he would get to interview.

***

In Port Elizabeth, Frans Jonker was driving through Walmer on his way to his favourite drinking hole, the Humewood Hotel, on the city's idyllic beachfront. While still off duty with his leg wound, Jonker had kept in touch with goings on and daily received reports on the activities of the journalists. Despite almost 24-hour monitoring of their homes, no sign had been seen of the eye witnesses he so desperately wanted to get his hands on.

"Just imagine," he said to the empty car, "if I get them, I'll definitely be up for promotion. Now that would be great, to be Du Preez's boss."

Deep in thought, he almost collided with a mini bus at an intersection near the airport.

The driver of the vehicle was not looking his way. After all, Jonker had shot the stop street. But he did see that it was Daniel driving and that he had two passengers. One of them was a woman sitting in the front where the side windows were not tinted. She looked vaguely familiar so Jonker decided to follow at a distance.

"Could it be?" he wondered. "No, that was impossible."

He followed for about 200 metres until the vehicle ahead turned right into a street parallel to the township, but separated by a wide field with tall trees. Jonker then drove on to his destination, now desperately needing that first drink of the day. At least he knew the eyewitnesses were still in the city area. He'd find them.

MAY 7 - UNNECESSARY TRAGEDY

Civil disobedience was the order of the day in most parts of the country now as other regions followed Port Elizabeth's lead. A consumer boycott, called the previous month, had almost crippled some white-owned businesses and the government's decision to call in Defence Force troops to help the police in patrolling the unrest-hit townships was having an effect too.

Not least of all on the Herald's newsroom staff.

Night news editor Gavin Patterson had been called up to do duty as had Jamie Nelson and Shaun Riley. This left Daniel working a double shift along with some of his staff, John and Clive included. The long hours were taking their toll and tempers were often short.

Sitting in Jake's office that morning after conference, Daniel said: "We're really stretched, Jake. I'm not sure how much longer some of us can go on. Clive's a bundle of nerves after witnessing some necklacing in Walmer Township and John's come in twice now very badly hung over. I also know he's having a few drinks in the afternoon which is showing in the quality - or lack of quality - of his typing."

"Yes, it's tough for lots of us, I know," comforted Jake. "But, look on the bright side. Gavin's back in two weeks and you're off at the end of the month with Arthur and company to the Eastern Transvaal before heading overseas to London."

Daniel paused, thought, and then said: "So, I assume Gavin will take over as news editor? Who'll do nights then?"

"Aah, don't worry about that. The deputy news editor of the Cape Times has applied for a transfer here as his parents live just outside the city. So he'll do the night desk and, yes, Gavin will take your role. Anyway, it seems quiet today. Why don't you take a break, go see how Arthur's doing and come back at about 4? We can cope until then."

"Yes, I'll do that, thanks. John's off to the airport later to speak to his boycott contacts. I understand they are looking at easing the boycott. So, I'll probably meet him there at 3 and then come back. OK?"

Jake agreed, leaving court reporter Simon Ngiki to man the news desk for the day.

***

At the single men's quarters at the Mount Road barracks, Sgt Frans Jonker and his now civilian brother Jimmy were arguing.

"Frans, man, you're a disgrace. Drunk already and it's only 11.30," fumed Jimmy at his twin.

"Yes, well, what's it to you," slurred Frans as he knocked back a tumbler of neat brandy and smirked at his brother. "You're a soft civvie now. One bit of shooting in Langa in March and you get given two weeks to rest and recuperate. I get shot in the leg in the line of duty and that's the only reason I had two weeks off."

Jimmy smiled inwardly, noting that his brother had ignored the fact that the wound was almost self inflicted.

"Anyway, I came to tell you I'm off next week - for London. And that Dad is worried about you and your drinking. Remember, he's got mates high up in the police and, if they've noticed your drinking enough to tell him, then you've got a problem."

"Rubbish," said Frans. "They don't know the pressure I'm under with Du Preez on holiday, the things I've seen and the long shifts I've worked since being back."

Then he got up, swaying slightly but quickly correcting himself, shrugged into his crumpled suit jacket and made to leave the room. "Oh, enjoy England. And send me your address. I might still pop over later when my holiday starts." With that he turned and left the room, leaving the door open.

Downstairs at the security branch ops room, Frans saw that trouble seemed to be brewing in Walmer township, with residents burning tyres and disrupting traffic on the main road between the city's airport and the residential areas. His shift only started at 2pm so he reckoned he had time to drive over - on his way to the Humewood for a liquid lunch - and see how bad it really was.

His hardened drinking over the past few months had increased his tolerance for liquor and Frans managed to behave relatively soberly as he signed out a car, drove to the gates and chatted to the constable on duty there. As he drove, he listened to the news on the radio.

"More trouble everywhere," he said to himself. "Will these buggers never learn that they do not have the power or intelligence to run their own country and that they need us whites?"

As he drove the white police Cortina onto Cape Road, Frans could see the pall of smoke hanging over Walmer, near the airport. At the same time the news reader announced that several flights to and from Port Elizabeth and Cape Town were being affected by adverse conditions.

"Coward," he swore at the radio and said: "Where are your balls, SABC? Why not blame the blacks for it so people know."

Getting closer to the area, he heard the police radio dispatcher warn all vehicles that the situation at Walmer was escalating and that all caution had to be applied. Driving, Frans remembered the suburban street he'd seen Daniel turn into a few weeks back and decided he could go down that road to check out the troubles and miss the blocked roads on the way to the beachfront. And, if he was really lucky, he might catch a glimpse of the black man and woman he wanted to find.

***

In Walmer Township the atmosphere was decidedly edgy. Mobs were roaming the streets, the stench of burning rubber was everywhere. Some police and army patrols had managed to breach the burning barricades and tearsmoke was being fired at the crowds in an effort to disperse them. The plan was to clear an area so fire engines could safely enter and douse the flames.

At a primary school nearby, teachers decided to prematurely end the school day. Among the children being sent home was Sam Nujomba, a temporary attendee at the school where Linda Davis was a benefactor. He and a group of friends headed south towards the township's outskirts, playing soccer with an old tennis ball - ignoring the smoke and noise which was about two blocks away.

"Hey Sam," called one boy, "why don't you come play at my house?"

Sam thought for a moment before replying. "No, I have to go home but you can come to where I live."

The two broke away from the rest of the group and headed towards the white areas.

"Wow," said Sam, "I've never seen so much smoke before. I didn't know there were that many tyres here to burn."

Laughing, his friend pointed his hands as if holding a gun at Sam and shouted: "Hey, trouble maker. Put your hands up and stop burning tyres! I will shoot you if you don't let me arrest you."

"Oh Mr white policeman sir, please don't do that. I have a family to feed and look after," said Sam, pretending to be serious.

As his friend lowered his hands, Sam turned and ran off quickly, shouting over his shoulder, "Silly policeman, you are too trusting."

The boy gave chase as Sam zig-zagged through trees towards the Davis's house. Lost in their game, they took no notice of the pall of smoke ahead of them, blown south west by the strengthening winds and starting to drift over the road ahead.

"Bang, bang. You're dead!" shouted Sam's friend as Sam ran into the smoke. At the last moment Sam looked to his right and saw a white Cortina heading straight for him.

It was the last thing he saw.

28

HEARTBREAK AND KIDNAP

As he drove down the street, Frans noticed that the thick, black and pungent smoke from the burning tyres was dropping as the wind speed fell. He accelerated into the smoke, hoping to get through it quickly when suddenly, seemingly out of nowhere, a child ran into the car, striking the left front fender. Instinctively he swerved and braked but, even in his slightly befuddled state, he knew it was too late.

The child was flung into the air by the speeding Cortina, landing on its roof and then sliding off the left side of the car as it juddered to a halt - two wheels on the verge and two still on the road.

Undoing his seatbelt he opened the door to get out of the car, leaving the engine running and the car bucked and stalled as he took his foot off the clutch. This sudden movement caused the door to swing closed again, striking him in the face and causing his nose to bleed and his eyes to water. He stumbled round the car to the crumpled body.

Even in the gloom caused by the smoke and through the tears in his eyes, Frans could see the child was badly injured. His left leg was twisted unnaturally and there was blood coming from his ears and mouth. He knelt next to the boy - about seven or eight years old, he guessed.

Suddenly another child emerged out of the smoke and screamed when he saw the white man kneeling over the body of his friend.

Frans looked up. "Quiet! Shut up and call an ambulance. Go to one of the houses there and get the people to phone," he instructed to the confused child.

The boy ran off towards the white-owned houses.

"Bloody hell, I'm in trouble now," he said to himself.

The boy on the ground was unconscious and convulsing slightly. Quickly Frans got up, opened the passenger door and took a half jack of brandy out of the pocket of his suit jacket lying on the front passenger seat. He cracked the seal and downed most of the contents in four gulps, coughing as he did so. Wiping his mouth he reached for the jacket and put it under the child's head.

"No use," he said quietly as he felt the broken skull move under his fingers.

He slumped to the ground, the bottle falling from his fingers. Holding his head in his hands, he furiously tried to think of a way out of this mess.

"OK, so the child ran into the car. I had a drink because I was shocked. Maybe that'll do it."

But he remembered his brother's harsh words about his drinking earlier and his comment that senior officers had noticed.

"Well, it's only a black kid, so who really cares?" he muttered softly, moving forward to check the child's condition and noticing that the rise and fall of the small chest had virtually stopped.

Next thing he knew, he was struck forcefully and knocked to the ground as a black woman, screaming wildly, flung herself past him and grabbed the child in her arms.

"Sam! Sam!" she cried, cradling the broken body in her arms. She stared down at the face, her vision blurred by tears streaming down her face as she wailed in heartfelt agony.

Cursing, Frans struggled to his feet. He looked down at the woman who ignored him as she cried.

"Bloody kaffir, you can't hit a white man like that," he said.

She looked up at him. "Sorry but my boy..." she paused, wiping the tears from her eyes and then froze as she focused on the white man's face.

She knew him.

That look in his eyes, the look of hatred and loathing she recalled instantly as her mind flashed back to 1977 and the humiliating rape near the body of her father in the family hut in hot and dusty South West Africa.

This was the man who had raped her.

And this was his child she was now holding.

Nancy screamed again and moved away on her haunches, dragging Sam's now lifeless body with her as he took a step towards her.

He was puzzled by her behaviour. Then he remembered. This was the women he saw in that minibus in April, being driven by Daniel. And, yes. It was her. The Ovambo woman he'd raped eight years ago was now crouched at his feet again.

Again she was scared. But this time there was a raw anger too.

"OK, so that's your boy. Well I'm sorry but he ran into my car while I was on police business." He stopped talking.

"Why," he thought to himself, "am I trying to explain what happened to this woman. "Not only that, but she could tell people about that incident on the Border. Can't have that."

Keeping his eyes fixed on the now silent woman, he scrabbled for his pistol in the holster at the small of his back, deciding he'd take her and the child away - at gunpoint if necessary.

A firm and harsh grip on his wrist stopped him and made him wince. "Don't you dare," said Daniel as he twisted the policeman's wrist, forcing him to turn.

As he turned Frans saw, out of the corner of his eye, a black man rushing to the woman. But his focus was entirely on Daniel and the pain in his wrist. "Let go, you bastard. You're interfering with a policeman trying to carry out his duty," he snarled at Daniel, almost nose to nose with the newspaper man.

"Oh am I?" said Daniel, tightening his hold. "And you're pissed. You're in no state to handle a firearm."

He watched as Arthur led Nancy away, carrying Sam, back to the Davis's house. Then it all fell into place for Daniel.

"It's her," he said, totally stunned at the coincidence. "Nancy is the woman you raped. I don't believe it."

Unthinkingly, he loosened his grip on Frans's wrist.

He broke free and viciously pushing him away, ran to his car and drove off before the stumbling Daniel could do a thing. But he only got as far the corner where he stopped as an ambulance and accompanying police vehicle, both with sirens blaring, cut him off. The police van had stopped in front of Frans's car.

Daniel signalled for the ambulance to stop and pointed out the Davis home where Nancy and Arthur were standing with Linda. Then he ran on to the police vehicles.

"This is the man," he said, gasping for breath. "This is the man who knocked the child over. He's drunk. He's trying to get away."

Acting quickly the policeman nearest the car leant in and took the keys out of the ignition.

"Hang on," he said. "I know you, you're in the security branch."

Jonker sat slumped over the wheel, not paying any attention, tears coursing down his face.

"Yes, he is," answered Daniel, "but that does not alter anything that happened here."

***

Two hours later, Daniel was back in the newsroom. He'd updated Jake on the latest developments. Monica Davis had been sent home to her parents and Beth Swarts was heading over to help console Nancy and assist with funeral plans.

Carl Strydom confirmed that Frans Jonker had admitted to driving the car while under the influence and that he'd struck Sam Nujomba. As a result, Frans was suspended from duty and confined to his quarters.

Daniel put his head down and started getting everything ready for the evening conference. "Where's John?" he asked Simon.

"Don't know, Dan. Haven't heard from him since he left for the airport. I'm sure he'll be back before your conference with an update."

"I hope so, time is tight and we need to know if he's got

anything," responded Daniel.

He had enough to do to keep himself busy and at 5.30 he went into the evening conference without hearing from John.

After 15 minutes, Simon interrupted to say John was on the phone and needed to speak to Daniel urgently. "Dan," an excited John said. "You're not going to believe this but it appears Hashe, Godolozi and Galela have been abducted!"

"What! How? Who?" asked Daniel.

"Well, it appears they came here because they were told a British embassy official interested in providing a cash donation to PEBCO had called Hashe at his home and said he'd be flying in today. So they arranged to meet me to discuss the boycott and to chat to this Embassy man. As usual, the airport was busy with lots of people milling about. We had just sat down to talk when Godolozi's driver came in to say there seemed to be more police about than usual and he was worried.

"The Cape Town flight had landed so the three waited to meet their contact while the driver went to check outside. In the doorway I brushed past that Jonker guy - you know, the security cop."

"Yes," said Daniel, "but he's suspended, I was told."

"Nope, definitely not," John cut him short. "Because he and two others went up to Hashe, Godolozi and Galela and took them away, through a side door and into the police charge office.

"This happened 10 minutes ago and there's still no sign of them."

"Stay there and keep watch," said Daniel, "I'll get someone out there."

***

Back outside, John was just in time to see Frans and the two other men take the Pebco three from the charge office and bundle them into the back of a waiting minibus. Quickly John ran across to where the Pebco driver was waiting at his car, an old Toyota Corolla.

"Hey, the cops have got them. Can you follow that bus and, when you get a chance, call me at the Herald?"

As the man left to follow the police and their prisoners, John had a bad feeling. "This is not going to work out well," he said to himself as he saw Clive drive up.

Running across, John jumped into the car. "Follow that Toyota and that blue minibus."

But that was easier said than done.

Clive managed to keep pace with both vehicles from the airport, down towards the freeway which ran from south to north, towards Grahamstown. But as they approached the Bluewater Bay interchange they were cut off by a heavy goods vehicle which swerved into the lane Clive was using, forcing him to brake. Once he'd passed the lorry Clive accelerated but, after racing along for about two kilometres, neither he nor John could see the two vehicles ahead.

"Damn, they must have turned off into Bluewater Bay," he muttered, doing an illegal U-turn through the grass on the central island and racing back. At the Bluewater Bay turn-off, John saw the old Toyota parked on the roadside.

Clive stopped and John ran over. "Hey," he said to the driver. "Where'd they go?"

"I don't know. They went into the garden of a house in Silversands Drive, number 64. They went straight into the garage and then the door was closed. I parked opposite and waited. But no-one's come out and there's no movement in the house."

Clive came up to them and said he'd investigate. He drove the 100 metres down the road to the house, parked on the drive and went up to the front door. He knocked several times but there was no response.

Walking round to the back of the property, he saw the garage was a drive-through type which led into a service lane behind the house. The rear doors were open and the minibus they'd been following stood inside.

It was empty.

29

MAY 8 - MURDER MOST FOUL

Another night of rioting, police action, killings and arrests ensured the Herald and other news media were kept busy. Unrest was spreading throughout the country. In Port Elizabeth, Daniel was having an interesting conversation with Carl. It was just gone 11am.

"Yes Carl, I'll say it again. That's what my reporter saw. At the airport, Jonker and others walked in and then took off with Galela and the two others in a minibus. We have another witness too."

"Well, I'm baffled, Dan," said Carl.

"As I told you yesterday, Jonker was put off duty and confined to his quarters. That was the official word. If it changed, no-one told me. If it hasn't, then he's in trouble."

"Oh, I must add," responded Daniel, "Galela, Hashe and Godolozi have not been seen by anyone since yesterday at the airport. They were at the airport to meet a man from the British Embassy. Well, we checked and the Embassy did not send anyone. We think it was a set up by the security branch to get the three. Also, we checked at the homes of all three and they did not go home at all. In fact, Hashe was meant to be at a church meeting and he did not arrive. So, something fishy's going on, that's for sure."

Carl sighed and then said, "I agree, but I cannot say anything to you - on or off the record - until I've done some checks. I'll call you later."

As he hung up, the other phone near Daniel rang and he picked it up swiftly.

"Dan?" It was Des Hughes.

"Man, strange stuff going on. We've just had a call that human remains, possibly of three men, were found on a farm near Cradock. It's an old deserted farm near a police outpost, Post Chalmers. They were burnt - so badly burnt that we will struggle to even tell if there are more than three - but three skulls were definitely found. It appears they were in a huge bonfire. Now, as you know, nobody voluntarily jumps into a huge fire."

"What? Are you saying they were murdered?" asked Daniel, furiously making notes.

"Well, that's my guess at this stage. We'll know more once the coroner's had a look at the remains properly. But as of now he says three men, African and possibly in their 20s or 30s. Time of death? He's not sure but the fire was not that old, maybe 12 hours even less. I'll call you when I have more."

"Coincidence?" thought Daniel. "Three men missing, all African and in their 20s and 30s.

"The same three men kidnapped the evening before by the security police?

"Three men found burnt to death on a farm near a disused police outpost in the countryside.

"The same three men?"

The farm, Daniel knew, belonged to the police despite the outpost not being in use. He knew that senior officers went there for teambuilding weekends - usually drink and barbecue weekends.

"No," he decided, "there was just too much going on for it to be a coincidence. Also, Jonker's involvement seems suspicious."

He started getting a team together to see if they could get a story together for the next edition. Although he knew a lot would depend on what the police released and what he could use from Carl's off the record comments when he got them.

***

Arthur had spent the night trying to comfort a heart-broken, confused and angry Nancy. Sam's body had been taken to a nearby mortuary.

Nancy's emotional state was a bit helter-skelterish. She alternated between grief for her son and then anger at the fact that the man who raped her was back in her life and in such an intrusive way.

"Why? Why? Why?" she kept asking.

Arthur could only hold her and whisper somewhat meaningless words of encouragement. But his anger was rising too. He felt an almost unreasonable anger against Frans and he wanted to avenge Sam's death. But smashing that cruel cop's face to bits was not the answer, despite his primitive feelings.

He also was now more determined to get himself and Nancy away, as the Herald people had suggested, to hopefully start a new life together. Daniel was going to visit them that evening to discuss leaving Port Elizabeth.

Linda had arranged that Sam's funeral would be held in two days' time after which he and Nancy were free to go.

"Nancy," he said to the distraught woman sobbing on his shoulder, "let's go for a walk. We can't stay here cooped up inside this room. We need, you need, some fresh air to clear your head."

"OK, Arthur, but not in that road where Sam..." she faltered.

"No, don't worry about that. There's a park down the road, we can go there. Mrs Davis said it's peaceful and quiet there. Victoria Park, it's about two kilometres away."

They left, taking Duke, the Davis's pet Labrador along for a walk.

***

Frans Jonker and his brother Jimmy were driving along, in Jimmy's car, from the city's beachfront area towards Mount Road.

"Bloody hell, Frans, I cannot believe you'd deliberately go against orders and go out when you were specifically told not to."

Word had got out that Frans had gone missing from his quarters and when the Jonker home was called that morning to check if he was there, Jimmy knew exactly where to look. The bar at the Humewood Hotel opened at 11 and he knew that's where his brother would be. So off he went, after telling the head of the Security Branch he'd get his brother back to Mount Road by lunchtime.

Frans was, indeed, in the bar when Jimmy got there at 11.30. He was slumped against the bar, intoxicated and chatting to the barman. He was the only person in the bar when Jimmy walked in quietly.

"So we put a sleeping drug in their coffee," he heard his brother say to the barman. "And when they all passed out, we just took them outside, shot them - it was the thing to do."

He paused as he lifted his tumbler of brandy shakily to his mouth, spilling some of the amber liquid on to his stained tracksuit top. He was wearing jeans, boots and the green and yellow top which had, besides the liquor, stains in a brownish red colour on it and smelled of wood smoke.

Silently Jimmy stood and surveyed his brother. What was he rambling about? As the drinker held out his now empty tumbler for a refill, he continued his rambling story, unaware of the third person in the room.

"Yes, so one by one we shot them. Charlie was with us and he'd made this big fire. So we threw the bodies on that. They took a while to even burn properly. Even with the diesel we poured on them. Man, we were up there the whole night. Drinking and eating."

The barman looked bemused. He knew Frans to be a police officer who was involved in some interesting stuff. He also knew him to be a heavy drinker who was a bit of a bragger and a show off. He stopped getting the next drink ready when Jimmy indicated to him not to pour it. Despite his drunken state, Frans saw the barman look beyond him and he turned on his barstool to see his brother walking towards him.

"Hey! It's Jimmy, have a drink with me."

But Jimmy just walked up and grabbed his brother firmly by the shoulder. "No thank you. We have an important meeting to go to and you need to get cleaned up. Pay your tab now."

Later, driving through Walmer towards Mount Road, he turned to his befuddled passenger. "So what was that you were talking about in the bar?"

Frans straightened himself and said: "Man, I've done the country a favour. I followed instructions, followed them to the letter. "We were told last week to get hold of the people who are organising this boycott and eliminate them. And tell me, what does *eliminate* mean? It means remove them from society. Kill them if needed.

"So, we set up this scam. Got one of our guys to pretend to be from the British Embassy and wanting to offer PEBCO funds. We reckoned this would get them to the airport. And it did, so we moved in and took them. Now they're dead and my job is done. OK, so I broke the rules and didn't stay in my room. I'm a naughty boy." He broke into his high-pitched trademark giggle.

Jimmy was worried. Was the pressure of the job getting to his brother? Was he telling the truth? As he turned at a traffic light, his passenger yelled: "That's them! That's them! Look! Stop!"

Frans was hitting the side window and pointing at a couple walking with a dog. "Hey man! I said stop! Those are the guys who saw the shooting in Langa. They need to be eliminated too."

But Jimmy was aware of traffic all around and could not stop, nor could he look at the couple. He drove on becoming more convinced that his brother had finally lost his marbles.

A couple walking a dog calmly on a busy street were sought by the security police? "Unlikely," he thought, and drove on while his brother ranted.

30

MAY 14 - THIEVES IN THE NIGHT

After the funeral of Sam Nujomba, there was little to keep Nancy and Arthur in Port Elizabeth. Nancy had come to terms with her grief but seemed to have withdrawn into herself, which was a worry for Arthur. But, at the same time, she was thriving in the company of Linda Davis, a caring, comforting woman.

The replacement for Daniel had arrived at the Herald and the hand over to the former Cape Times man and Patterson was well under way with Daniel playing a caretaker role and getting his stuff together for the move to the UK.

Meanwhile, the consumer boycott continued and arrests were the order of the day as the security police tried to round up community leaders.

And, surprisingly, Frans Jonker was back on duty.

"Yes, the evidence was that the little boy he hit with the car was not visible in the smoke," Shaun Riley told Daniel at the news desk, having just returned from the morning crime conference at police headquarters. "And what's more - and this will surprise you - Galeta, Hashe and Godolozi are still listed as missing. I asked those specific questions after the others had left.

"Carl said the case against Jonker had seemed shaky at the outset. And somehow the blood readings for the drunk driving charge had got lost, he told me. He said the investigations into the whereabouts of Hashe and company were ongoing. The police, of course, deny that they were kidnapped from the airport, despite our eyewitness accounts and reports. The official line, even now some two weeks later, is that they were questioned for a few hours and then released."

"Bloody cover up, if you ask me," answered Daniel. "And, the fact that Jonker's still on duty confirms Jamie's worry that he'd been hanging around Walmer. Twice now, since he and you returned from army duty, he thought he'd seen Jonker in a car near their street. Now we know it could be him."

Shaun agreed. "Well, look on the bright side. You, at least, will be out of this soon and in London where your biggest worries will be the cold weather and the warm beer, or maybe Peter Hain and the anti-apartheid guys."

"Yes, I'm sure I'll get used to it," smiled Daniel. "Guess I'll have to. We leave in a few days."

The rest of the day was pretty routine, with Daniel dividing his time between doing his job and getting ready for the impending trip. Sitting in the editor's office just before the end of the day, Daniel heard the plans for his departure, along with Nancy and Arthur. It seemed melodramatic but, given the fact that the security police were still looking for the pair, it did make sense.

"So," said Jake, "to recap. The three of you will get a ride with the big delivery van which does the East London run, leaving at 4am on Saturday. At the Daily Dispatch offices you'll be met by Andrew Jordan, the news editor, who will look after you until 10am when you fly to Nelspruit. There you'll be picked up by Herold, Russell's safari guide, and taken to his lodge for a few days. Hopefully by then things will have quietened down and you can leave on May 29 for Johannesburg - again from Nelspruit - and then fly that evening to London."

"Passports for Arthur and Nancy have been sorted," said Daniel. "We pulled some strings at Home Affairs to get them rushed through and June's fetching them tomorrow morning. Our bigger suitcases will be flown as cargo to the London office at the weekend where we'll collect them when we get there. I've arranged a flat in Bromley - an easy 25 minute commute to the city - for us for the first three months."

"Good, so all is in order. Enjoy your evening and remember your farewell party on Friday," said Jake in dismissal, turning back to the paperwork on his desk.

***

It was a dark, moonless and windy night. The typical Port Elizabeth wind howled through the tall trees in Walmer as two dark-clad figures approached the Davis's home.

"Careful, remember their dog could be in the backyard," whispered one hoarsely to his companion. "Get ready with that chunk of steak."

Drugged meat to distract and put watchdogs to sleep had become the normal practice for burglars looking for riches in the white suburbs. Some even drugged the meat enough to kill animals, which was how the trend was first picked up. Usually, it was enough to knock the animal out for a few hours. This dosage normally would be good for 10-15 minutes, which was all they needed. The pair approached through a neighbour's driveway, stopping to peer into a car parked there. It was empty.

Quietly, any noise disguised by the wind, they moved on towards the boundary wall. A low growl could be heard.

"Quick, the dog knows we're here," said the taller man softly but urgently, his balaclava muffling his voice. "Throw that meat over, away from the house."

They heard the thud as the huge chunk of meat landed followed by the dog's snuffling and contented growls as it started eating.

The pair waited.

After less than five minutes there was silence from the dog. The taller man peered over the head-height wall. He could just make out the shape of the dog lying on the lawn.

"All clear," he said and pulled himself onto the wall, turning to help the other man up before he jumped into the garden next door. As he landed, he was aware of a movement from the dog and he froze, every nerve taut and his ears straining. But the dog was just shifting its weight and then started snoring lightly. The man indicated for his companion to jump. The two crouched with their backs to the wall, surveying the house ahead of them.

A low light was burning in the main building, probably a toilet light, judging by the small window it was shining through.

"There, let's start there," said the tall man, indicating rooms towards the back of the house which were in total darkness.

The pair walked slowly and stealthily closer. As they approached they could see a door with small cottage pane frames which seemed to be between two rooms. The smaller man, wearing thick gloves, stuck a piece of adhesive paper over a pane nearest the door handle and then punched it swiftly. There was a slight cracking sound.

Taking a screwdriver from his coat pocket, he then pierced the paper near the centre and pulled it back, bring the broken glass with it and leaving a hole big enough for him to get his hand through.

The key was in the lock. He turned it and the door unlocked. Cautiously, he opened the door, it swung smoothly inwards - no squeak. The pair moved indoors, shutting the door behind them.

The room to the left was a sittingroom and the shorter man went in there, his empty kitbag at the ready. The taller man hesitated, watching as his companion took some bottles of wine from the rack and some CDs too, which he put into the bag, ripping a cover from a cushion on the sofa to stop the bottles rattling. He then moved on to other stuff in the room, selecting what he wanted, leaving the rest. The tall man moved on, deeper into the house.

It was a long passage. At least 10 metres long, he guessed. A frosted glass door about four metres away seemed to divide this section from the rest of the house. The door to his right was closed. It could have been a bedroom as the one ahead was a kitchenette and, opposite that, a bathroom. He moved forward and closed the glass door. Returning to the kitchen, he checked inside the fridge. Not much there, milk, fruit, eggs, butter and some cans of soft drink. The cupboards contained crockery, some cereal packs, sugar, coffee and tea, the usual stuff. A set of kitchen knives in a wooden block on the counter caught his eye, a long carving knife with a 15 centimetre blade was the one he selected as he moved back into the passage.

His companion was at the door, with two bags laden with stuff he'd taken. "Wait at the wall," said the taller man. "I want to check what and who is in the bedroom. If someone wakes up, then only one of us has to rush for the door."

The shorter man shrugged, seemingly unconcerned, and left the house quietly. As the tall man moved to open the bedroom door, putting his hand on the handle. He froze.

The handle was turning, the door was being opened from the other side. It was turning slowly, very slowly. Either the person on the other side knew he was there or the intention was not to disturb whoever else was also in the room. The door opened into the room. As it did so, the tall man stepped back, keeping the knife low and pointed to the floor.

He bumped into the soft form of a woman.

***

It was a dream that had woken Nancy. Well, not so much a dream but a nightmare.

She saw Sam being hit by a car and flung into the air. The driver's face, larger than life, was that of Jonker - her rapist and now her son's killer. She awoke with a start, checking that Arthur, lying on the other side of the bed, was not disturbed.

"In fact," she wondered to herself, "does he know it was his child he killed? Given his apparent dislike for all things black he'd probably not be that upset."

She heard a click outside, near the door. But the wind was blowing strongly, branches brushing occasionally against the windows. She strained her ears, trying to discern between inside sounds and the noise from outdoors.

There! Again she heard something, definitely from inside.

Should she wake Arthur? But he was sleeping so

soundly that she did not have the heart. Maybe it was her imagination. She listened intently, all noise and sounds amplified. No, it was all silent. She closed her eyes and turned on her side, ready to sleep.

Again, in her mind, she pictured Sam and Jonker, together this time. Now Jonker was carrying Sam's body towards her. She jerked awake.

There was a noise. A man's voice, very soft. Then the click of the door, definitely the door.

Softly, so as not to disturb Arthur, she got up and went to the door, pausing there with her hand on the handle.

31

MAY 14/15 - READY TO LEAVE

As he bumped into her, the tall man pulled the knife back, instinctively hoping not to cause injury. But, as he did so, he felt the woman reach for his face, trying to claw him with her nails.

At the same time the bedroom light came on, temporarily blinding the man who felt his balaclava being pulled off as he screwed up his eyes. The next thing he knew, he was being pushed back into the hallway by someone harder and stronger than the woman.

He dropped the knife and fell back, slightly winded by the charge into his upper body.

"It's him!" he heard the woman shout.

He opened his eyes and saw the black woman holding his torn balaclava.

Frans Jonker realised he had been identified. He pushed the black man away and ran for the outside door.

But Arthur was quick, desperate to protect Nancy. "Wait," he called, tackling the fleeing man who fell forward, his right hand thrust forward to steady himself.

Jonker's hand went through the broken window pane, cutting the palm and the fleshy part of the thumb.

"Bugger!" Jonker swore as he felt the pain and pulled his hand free, kicking at Arthur who clung to his left ankle.

The first kick hit Arthur on the temple, causing him to lose his grip as Jonker broke free and ran from the house. Outside he tripped over the still semi-drugged dog which had made its way back to the house. As he landed, twisting his left knee, Jonker slid forward and hit his face against the raised edge of the small veranda.

"Bugger!" he swore as he felt his cheek hit the brick and cut open. As he stumbled to his feet, the dog feebly barked and tried to bite Jonker's left calf - succeeding mainly in ripping the black jeans he was wearing and inflicting a minor flesh wound.

Jonker stumbled forward to the wall and, with the help of his companion, managed to climb over just as the quickly recovering dog barked loudly and ran to the wall, still slightly unsteady on its feet.

"Come on! Let's go," shouted Jonker's companion and half dragged his companion down the driveway and to the road. The pair half trotted, half ran to where their car was parked about 300 yards away. Shoving Jonker into the passenger seat, the other man slid behind the wheel and drive rapidly away.

"Well, that was a waste of bloody time," he said looking at Jonker. "What happened to you? Your balaclava's gone, your cheek's buggered and you're dripping blood from your left leg. This was meant to be a simple, faked burglary. I even stole some stuff to be planted in Shipalana's home in Uitenhage so he could get the blame. But, no. Mr Cleverpants here decides to check in the bedroom doesn't he? And what does he do? He succeeds in stuffing the whole thing up."

He exhaled with frustration as he drove rapidly back to Mount Road.

"Well, I'm sorry, Captain," Jonker said humbly as Arrie du Preez drove briskly and with angry determination.

"Sorry? Well, it's too little, too late this time. Jonker, I'm sorry but you will have to take indefinite leave, a suspension, if you like. To save face for you, I'll put it down as stress leave. Lots of the guys are doing that. You'll be off for three months on pay, but part of it will be your leave.

"And, before you argue," Du Preez quickly said, sensing that Jonker was about to speak, "my decision is final. As of now you're off duty. And, if anyone asks me, I have absolutely no idea how you got that bite on your leg, the cut to your face or what you were doing in Walmer."

Jonker slumped visibly in his seat as Du Preez drove through the night. But his brain was ticking over furiously, still planning and scheming how to eliminate Arthur and Nancy. This was not the end of it, he thought.

Not by a long shot.

***

Back at the Davis house, everyone was awake. While Linda tended to Arthur and Nancy who were both distraught, Mark Davis made tea and petted his now recovered dog. All of them were in the sitting room.

"So," said Mark, "you are absolutely certain that this intruder was this Jonker fellow. The security policeman who took Sam's life?"

"Oh Mark," Linda said to her husband, "don't be such a ninny. If Nancy says it was him, then it definitely was. Now, leave us alone."

"Yes, it was him," said a still shaken Nancy. "I've had enough of this, we need to get away from here."

"Well, that's the plan, you know it is," said Arthur, reaching for Nancy's hand.

"I know but it must be now. How long do we have to wait while this man makes everything terrible for us, for me?"

Linda interjected, "I know from Anne that Dan is having his leaving party in a few days, so it shouldn't be long."

"Talking about Dan, we should let him know about what happened here," said Arthur and he turned to Linda. "Can I call him when he gets to work?"

"Of course you can," she replied. "Now, it's almost 3am, let's get some sleep." And, with that, she got up and headed off to her room.

Arthur looked at Nancy. She seemed drained and still shocked. He helped her to her feet and took her to bed, where he held her, stroking her back softly, until she fell asleep.

***

The start of the working day was busy. Dan took the early call from Arthur about the incident in the night with the dog and Frans Jonker.

"Dan, I tell you man, we're worried. This Jonker guy. He's not right in the head. He really seems to have it in for us, well, Nancy especially," Arthur said after he'd given the details of the break in.

"Yes, I agree. It could be because you guys saw what happened at Langa. I thought that, at first, this was the reason. But now it's become more personal. Don't worry though, I'm taking this further."

He then told Arthur the plan was for the three of them to leave on Saturday morning and fly to the Eastern Transvaal for a few days before taking a flight to London.

"So, I'll come around after work today and we can discuss Saturday's plan of action."

Daniel then contacted Carl Strydom to inform him of the decision to lay a complaint of intimidation, assault and breaking and entering against Frans.

"I tell you, Carl, this man is not well," said Daniel.

"You're right," the colonel responded. "In fact, he's been booked off on stress leave for three months. I see this was as of yesterday, so your incident last night appears to have been off his own back. Anyway, I'll see that he's tracked down and formally charged."

But that did not happen.

On returning to Mount Road with du Preez in the early hours of the morning and after completing the necessary paperwork for stress leave and his annual holiday, Frans packed up his few personal belongings in his quarters and left. He did not go home to his parents' house as was his original intention. Instead he went to the flat of one of his drinking friends on the city's beachfront, where he'd spent many a night after one too many at the nearby pub. It was, for Frans, the perfect hiding place. Nobody, except his drinking buddies, would know where he was.

32

MAY 19 - LYING LOW IN THE LOWVELD

Flying into Hoedspruit on an SA Express turbo prop was an exhilarating experience. To the west the mighty and rugged Drakensberg mountains towered over the area. To the east of the airfield, the scrub-covered plains of the sub-tropical region teemed with elephant, buffalo and herds of Impala - all living the good life in private game reserves adjoining the world famous Kruger National Park.

It was in one of these private areas in Timbavati where Daniel, Arthur and Nancy were to spend a few days. They were met on disembarking by Herold, the game ranger from their lodge, with his drab olive green open Landrover. It was a two hour drive to Sumatra.

"Mr Russell is pleased to have you as our guests," Herold said as he drove. "We have arranged food and drinks for the four days you are scheduled to be with us. And, if you want, I can take you on a game drive this afternoon at 3pm.

"Trust me, there's nothing nicer in this world than standing on the banks of a river as the sun goes down, sipping a cool drink and watching buffalo, giraffe and so on drinking. Of course, we have to keep an eye open for hippo, crocs and the odd lion," Herold chuckled as Arthur looked nervous.

Sumatra was centred around a remote ranch-type house with smaller chalets, or rondavels, scattered around the main building. It was in these that the guests slept, the main building being for cooking and entertaining. Once they'd freshened up after their flight the three met at the main building for a light lunch at 1pm.

"Are we the only people here?" Daniel asked Herold and his wife who helped in the kitchen and kept the rondavels tidy.

"For now, yes. But Mr Russell and two other guests are arriving tomorrow. And then I understand you will leave with them on Wednesday morning for Johannesburg."

The Lowveld, mused Daniel, seemed so far away from the troubles of the Eastern Cape and the hustle and bustle of the newsroom at the Herald. But coming up was the new experience of life in London and working for the group's newspapers in South Africa - not just the Herald. Exciting times ahead.

However, right now, his priority was to look after Arthur and Nancy, the young couple dozing in the afternoon sun nearby. They'd been through a lot - the loss of her child, being shot at, attacked and hounded by the police. Now as they were on the verge of a new life, this could be the time to relax, recharge the batteries and prepare for what lay ahead.

"And," asked Arthur, "are we the only people in this area? I think I saw another lodge as we drove here."

"Yes, there is another lodge, another two in fact. But they are far flung and only the one you saw, Shabana Lodge, is close to us. It's owned by a German man who has close links with the army and police. I think he's a surveillance equipment supplier. I'm not sure, but an Air Force helicopter often brings men in suits, you know, the VIP type."

"Anyway, that's not our worry. Let's enjoy these few days," said Daniel. "I'm more than ready for a game drive later."

***

Just after 3pm the Landrover was ready to go. Passengers and refreshments were aboard, Herold had provided binoculars and had his radio tuned to the main camp's frequency.

"They tell me there's a pride of lion about five kilometres east of us, towards Kruger. But that's quite bushy. Then there's a leopard with a kill to our west. That's about 45 minutes away, but it's near a river which is good place for our drinks break. And there are normally some crocodiles and hippo there."

Heading west was the unanimous decision and the vehicle bumped along the dirt road, with Herold stopping occasionally to point out certain birds, identify buck in the distance or let his passengers marvel at the antics of a baby elephant with its herd about 50 metres from them - all seemingly oblivious of the Landrover and its fascinated spectators.

Eventually, as the sun seemed to draw closer to the horizon and the air started to chill, Herold said they were close to the leopard. For several minutes prior to that, the radio had been crackling and he had been chatting in his native tongue to other rangers. Arthur had said to Dan he could understand some of what they said but the distortion made it difficult for him to grasp the full meaning.

"Yes, the leopard has taken its kill into a tree, which is great for us. There are hyena about too, hoping for some scraps," Herold said as they slowed down and crawled along a secondary road.

In the distance they saw the lights of another vehicle, stationary on the side of the road. "That's the Shabana Lodge people, they're near the leopard. But it's OK, we can join them. We're allowed two vehicles at a sighting."

It was a magnificent sight. A fully-grown male leopard on a thick branch in the tree, about three metres up from the ground. In front of him, propped on smaller branches and held down by one of his paws was the carcass of a small Bushbuck. Unperturbed by the audience and the vehicles, the leopard was chewing on some meat stripped from the buck's shoulder.

In the other Landrover were five men and two women, besides the driver. They hardly glanced across as the second vehicle approached, so enthralled were they by the leopard and his kill. Camera lenses clicked as they took pictures. Daniels, Arthur and Nancy just stared in wonder at the leopard. Every so often, it lazily looked at them. In the growing darkness hyena could be heard calling to each other with their funny laugh call.

"They're about 30 metres away," said Herold quietly. "They won't come closer. But they know the leopard will come down after a while, maybe to get water but he will rest at the bottom of the tree. Hyena cannot climb so his kill is safe from them."

"So why are they here?" asked Nancy.

"Well, the leopard does not eat the entrails, he usually discards them by burying them nearby. We don't know if he's done this. So we wait and see, and so will the hyena."

They settled down, pulling their rugs closer as the air grew even colder and watched. After about 10 minutes the other Landrover started its engine and pulled away. As it turned, its headlights shone on Herold's vehicle.

A voice from the other vehicle called out in surprise: "Dan Jacobs? Is that you? What the hell are you doing here?"

Daniel froze. It was Colonel Derek Spies, a former head of the security police in the Eastern Cape. He had been promoted about two years ago to police headquarters in Pretoria. Dan waved but did not answer as the other Landrover accelerated away.

"Who was that?" asked Arthur. "He looked like a cop."

"Yes, nothing to worry about. He's now a general in Pretoria."

But even as they were having their evening beers at the river nearby, while Herold kept a watch out for dangerous animals, Daniel could not help wondering at this coincidence.

33

MAY 20 - A NEW MEETING

There was something incredibly calming about the South African bush, Daniel thought as he awoke early the next morning, hearing birds chirping outside his rondavel.

The night before, after the game drive, they'd sat around the fire, sipping wine and beer and chatting to Herold. There was even a bottle of Meerlust Rubicon, Daniel's favourite wine. Both Arthur and Nancy seemed envious of the ranger's uncluttered country life.

After Herold retired for the night, the three of them stayed on, until the wine was finished, and discussed the next move.

"Yes, it's a major step, going to the UK," said Daniel, "but, quite honestly, I think it is for the best."

"I agree. There's not much to keep Nancy or me here and I'm worried, very worried, about security police action against us," Arthur responded. "What I've seen in the past few weeks has convinced me they'd stop at nothing to silence us." He paused and took Nancy's hand in his before continuing. Even that cop driving into young Sam, that was not an accident. I think it was done to scare us off."

He held Nancy's hand tighter as she stifled a sob. Wiping her eyes, she said: "What will we do in England? It's a strange country. Will we fit in? I'm scared."

Daniel, feeling a bit less confident than he sounded, tried to reassure her: "Of course, it's very cosmopolitan. I was there a few years back and the area we're going to will be fine. Remember, the main part of the trip is to keep you safe and to tell your story, so the world will know what happened. That, plus the ongoing struggle, will help bring about change here even though there are those who are set against that ever happening."

***

At 11am that morning, the sound of an aircraft disturbed the tranquillity of Sumatra lodge. The trio were sitting sipping coffee, having turned down the offer of a morning game drive to relax and take things easy for a change.

"Aah, that's Mr Russell arriving," said Herold, walking out to the veranda. "His friend has this twin-engined Cessna and likes to be flown in, I guess he can afford it. Anyway, I'm off to pick them up, the airfield's about a kilometre away from here. We drove past it last night, but I'm not sure if you even noticed."

He smiled, turned and walked off. A few minutes later the Landrover left in a small cloud of dust.

"Well," said Daniel, "now we get to meet the boss and find out more about what he has planned for us."

He sat back, lost in thought as Arthur and Nancy spoke quietly to each other. Firstly, would Steve Russell speak about the possible book deal Jake had mentioned a few months ago? Daniel hoped not, feeling this would intimidate Arthur and Nancy. Beyond that, he hoped Steve would make the pair feel safer and more confident about going to London. He knew that through his contacts in the UK capital he had looked at setting up possible jobs for the pair. Hopefully there'd be some news on that front. After all, he did have contacts as was proved by the speed at which their passports and travel documents were arranged.

For his part, Daniel was happy to be going to the UK and to face a new job. Running the London bureau for the group of newspapers was a top job and was, as Jake had pointed out, a necessary stepping stone to eventually becoming an editor of a South African newspaper. So, Daniel reckoned, he'd have three years in the UK and Europe, then return home to a deputy editor post and an editor a year or two after that. By the time he was 40, his career could be made if everything went according to plan.

The return of the Landrover stopped his daydreaming in the warm sunshine and, leaving Arthur and Nancy sitting on the veranda, he went to greet the newcomers. He immediately spotted the tall, imposing figure of Steve

Russell standing on the Landrover as he passed bags down to Herold. The managing director's silver-grey hair glinted in the sunlight. He saw Daniel approach and waved a greeting as he continued to help Herold.

Daniel turned his attention to the other two newcomers. One was a woman but she was partly behind the vehicle and he could not see her properly. Just a glimpse of a slim leg, a pert behind and long auburn hair. The other was a stocky but well-built man in his 50s or 60s with a confident nature and a sweating bald head. His pale skin made Daniel think perhaps he was from Europe.

"Hello, and welcome," he said as he walked up and held out his hand.

"Aah, hello indeed. You're the journalist Steve told us about? I'm Erik Pedersen," the man grasped Daniel's hand firmly.

"And this is my daughter, Adair, a journalist, too." He turned to welcome the woman as she approached them.

Daniel was immediately struck by her green eyes and pale skin contrasting with the auburn hair.

She smiled and took his hand too. "Pleased to meet you."

A slight Scandinavian accent, Daniel noted. Not as strong as her father's but unmistakable.

"You're from Denmark aren't you?" he asked, including both of them.

Before either could answer, Steve approached. "Stop being an inquisitive reporter and take us to the beer. It's hot here, too hot to stand and natter."

As they turned and walked to the house, Adair said softly to Daniel: "Yes, Copenhagen area. But I live in London now. My dad's still in Denmark where he is a publisher and runs an international news agency. That's who I work for in London."

On the veranda introductions were made while Daniel fetched cool beers and some soft drinks from the fridge. Talk went around the troubles in the country, what Arthur and Nancy had witnessed and how they were on the run. Daniel was totally taken by the Danish girl and found it hard to concentrate on the talk.

As they broke for lunch, Nancy and Adair went off together, seemingly comfortable in each other's company.

Steve caught Daniel's attention. "Hey Dan, I think we'll let the others go for an early game drive with Herold while you and I chat about the next few days, OK?"

"Yes, there's a lot to sort out," agreed Daniel.

"I'd like to chat too but I also want to see the animals and the leopard Herold told us about," Erik interjected. "Anyway, there's time enough to catch up. Steve, don't forget to tell Dan about my offer."

The light lunch of cold meats, salads and fruit, with more beer and soft drinks was a pleasant and light-hearted affair. Conversation flowed around the table and Daniel found himself wondering about two things - Erik Pedersen's offer and whether he and his daughter would meet up in London.

"It would be nice."

"What would?" Adair asked, surprising Daniel who did not realise he'd spoken out loud.

"Oh, the game drive, if you see the leopard," he said.

34

MAY 21 - UP AND AWAY!

That afternoon Daniel and Steve sat in the shade of the veranda and spoke about the next step while the Pedersens had set off on their afternoon game drive. Nancy and Arthur were relaxing in their bungalows. Herold estimated they'd be away about two hours, depending on game sightings.

Steve started the conversation. "Well, I must tell you I am pleased with what you've done regarding Arthur and Nancy. Spiriting them out of the country and then having them tell their story will be a great news coup for the group. In fact, it will make front pages in many countries. However, as you've realised and experienced, this is not without its dangers. We also have information that the security police have got wind of the fact that you intend to leave tomorrow. So you are actually going tonight.

"Erik's plane will be back before 5 and will take you directly to Jo'burg where the three of you will board a British Airways flight and not an SAA flight as originally planned. You'll be in London by 8am tomorrow." He paused to sip his beer while Daniel took this in.

"OK, that's fine. Last night, by the way, we bumped into some guys at the leopard sighting. One of them was General Spies, formerly the top security cop in Port Elizabeth and now at headquarters in Pretoria. It's probably nothing but he did recognise me," Daniel said. "He's with that German guy at Shabana Lodge."

Steve replied tentatively, thinking as he spoke: "Well, let's hope so, but I do not believe in coincidence. Word is out in PE that you have left the city and are heading for London, that's obvious. But somehow the police found out that Arthur and Nancy have gone too. Did Spies see them?"

"Well, it was dark, after 8. He would have seen that Herold had three passengers. The staff here and at

Shabana Lodge probably communicate with each other, so they know there are guests at Sumatra. But no, I don't think he would even have been able to tell their sex or colour. It was dark and we were covered against the cold air."

"Good. Maybe we can plant the belief that you are staying on with us until the end of our stay. I'll speak to Herold when he gets back. When you get to London Adair Pedersen is planning to take Nancy into her flat in Beckenham, which is near where you have a flat. You and Arthur will stay together for the meantime.

"Adair should be back at the weekend. This is the last week of their three-week holiday. So, until then, I guess Nancy stays with you guys. I've arranged for Arthur to work at the bureau - a menial job doing filing. But he's bright and it's up to you to deploy him as you see fit. Nancy will do similar work at Adair's agency.

"Obviously I want you to write their story. And once that is written and published we'll have to arrange a press conference in London for the world's press to ask their questions. To this end, Adair will groom Nancy to cope with such interviews. I know this sounds patronising but she is naive and will need every bit of coaching she can get.

"I believe Jake Swarts has told you about the possible book deal. Well, Erik is dead keen and wants you to ghost write it. This will mean extra money for you but we will make a plan to lighten your load at the bureau when this comes around. This is a golden opportunity for you."

Daniel knew Steve was right.

"Yes, thank you for that, I am grateful. But we have to get our stuff packed and leave for Jo'burg. What's the plan there?"

"You'll be met by my PA at the airport. She has the tickets and you'll be taken through the VIP section to get aboard - less fuss and less chance of being noticed. You won't even enter the public concourse. Sounds a bit melodramatic perhaps, but better safe than sorry, I reckon," Steve responded.

***

Within the hour everyone was packed, which was easy given that most of the luggage was already in London.

After brief farewells, Herold took the three to the landing strip where the plane was standing. As they taxied down the bumpy runway, Daniel saw a Landrover with passengers passing by - presumably the group from Shabana Lodge on their evening game drive.

"Well," he thought, "London, hopefully, is out of the reach of Jonker and his type. I wonder if Spies being here was coincidence."

By 9pm that night the three were aboard BA056 and heading for London and a new life.

On arrival at Johannesburg airport, their plane was met by a car and they were taken to international departures, given boarding passes and their tickets by Steve's PA - as well as some currency in sterling - and ushered on to the plane after using the border control official who usually dealt with air crew, not passengers. Daniel was impressed at Steve's connections.

On the Boeing 747, Nancy seemed nervous. She was at the window seat with Arthur, in the centre, holding her hand while he chatted to Daniel.

"So, Dan, what are we actually going to do in London? I mean, we'll need money and work, I guess. "I see my passport and Nancy's have two-year work permits in them, which will help."

"Yes," replied Daniel, "I haven't really had time to tell you. Steve and Erik have arranged jobs for both of you. You'll work with me and Nancy will be at Adair's office which, I understand, is quite close to ours in central London. And in the meantime, Nancy will be staying at Adair's flat near ours. That is when Adair gets back. She needs to spend some time with a woman and get to know her way around, I reckon."

"That's a good idea, I agree. But me in a newsroom? That'll be interesting." Arthur chuckled and then settled back to doze.

Daniel sipped his wine and wondered how things would be when he met up with Adair Pedersen again.

***

It was chilly when they landed at Heathrow the next morning. Once through border control and having collected their luggage they entered the arrivals concourse which was teeming with people. Looking around, Daniel saw an elderly man with an A4 sign with *Jacobs party* written on it. He introduced himself and the man, George, whose business was called *Your man in London*, helped them get the luggage to the car. Then they set off for south-east London on the M25, that major road system surrounding greater London. Nancy and Arthur marvelled at the sheer volume of traffic on the motorway as well as the many shades of green - so unlike the African countryside.

"Wait until we get to Bromley," Daniel said. "It's quite a leafy area but the houses and flat blocks are all quite close together. There's not as much space here as in South Africa."

"Oh," said Nancy, "Is that why so many are double-storey?"

"Yes, for that reason and for keeping the heat in," Daniel answered.

After about an hour's travelling George got his party to Shortlands, a suburban area between Bromley town centre and Beckenham. The flat Daniel had rented was in a Victorian conversion about 500 metres from the Shortlands station. After getting the keys from the landlord on the ground floor, they climbed the two flights to a top floor apartment which had a large living area, small kitchen, a bathroom and two bedrooms.

The fridge and kitchen cupboards had been stocked with basics, presumably by Steve's efficient staff.

After unpacking the three went for a walk to check out the area. Heading towards Bromley from The Glen, where the flat was, they stopped off at the Shortlands Tavern, hoping for a light lunch. The pub, in a street adjacent to the station, was dark inside but welcoming with soft lighting. A few older people were sitting at tables while some younger men were at the bar. Some Duran Duran music was playing softly and people at the bar turned and looked at the newcomers.

Daniel found a table near the window and went to order drinks while Arthur and Nancy settled down.

"Two cold beers and a glass of orange juice please," Daniel said to the barlady.

"Hiya, what beer?" she asked indicating the taps.

"Oh, Carlsberg is fine."

A man in his late 30s turned to Daniel. "So, you're from South Africa. What part?"

Taken aback, Daniel said: "The Eastern Cape. Why? How do you know?"

The man smiled and held out his hand. "James Ekron," he said, "Rhodes journ graduate, born in PE. Two things - I recognised the accent and you and your mates looked kind of spare when you walked in. Like you're new in the area."

Daniel shook his hand then paid for the drinks. "Yes," he said, "I'm Daniel Jacobs, arrived this morning form Jo'burg, with my friends. It's their first visit."

"Daniel Jacobs? You work for the Herald. I've tried to get a job there but no joy. So, I'm working for a freesheet here."

Daniel hesitated, drinks in hand.

"Hey, go chat to your friends. I'm here most afternoons if you want a drink and a chat," said James, smiling.

Back at the table, Daniel said: "Small world hey? That guy I was talking to is from PE."

Arthur looked and replied: "Yes, I recognise him, he did some part time work at VW, you know, as students do. Not on the same line as me though."

A hand on Daniel's shoulder made him look around. It was James. "I've got to run. Here's a menu, the fish and chips is great. Suzie at the bar will look after you. And here's my number," he slipped Daniel a card and then, waving farewell, left the pub.

35

MAY 29 - A NEW ROAD TO WALK

It was quite different, going to work in London as opposed to Port Elizabeth. For starters, it was public transport - a train from Shortlands to Blackfriars - not a car. And for Daniel this meant sharing his space with a carriage full of commuters, ranging from bankers and financiers to labourers and office girls.

Arthur found it less different. He was used to crowded minibus taxis and being shoulder to shoulder with strangers on the same commute.

Then there was the short walk to the offices on a pavement that had more people within 10 metres than most of Port Elizabeth's busy streets.

After a few days, however, it was a routine they all quickly settled into - even Nancy. And, after work, Daniel and Arthur would meet Nancy and Adair in the Shortlands Tavern for a few drinks, mingling and making friends with other regulars, including James.

These laid-back, chatty evenings brought the four closer together, with a deeper attraction growing between Daniel and Adair. It was a welcome reward after a hard day of writing the Langa story with Arthur's help and managing the bureau staff. Most of the book was done in draught form and the pair worked long and hard at it.

Then came news about Nelson Mandela.

Sentenced to life imprisonment in June 1964, Mandela and his fellow Rivonia trialists were, effectively, non people in South Africa due to their banning. This meant that most people, mainly whites, in South Africa had no idea about Mandela and they were not allowed to read any of his writings. He was a high-ranking ANC member and was regarded as a terrorist by whites and a future liberator by South African blacks. But by 1985 he had been transferred from Robben Island to Pollsmoor Prison in Cape Town. This was not known to the South African public and it was a surprise for Daniel to be able to read news about the man.

"I can't believe what I've read," he said to Adair, Nancy and Arthur in the pub one evening. "Apparently Mandela has had approaches from the SA justice minister, Kobie Coetsee, about a possible meeting between the government and the ANC. And what's more, FW de Klerk is apparently the man behind this, a move not much liked by PW Botha."

Adair sipped her wine and then responded: "Ah, Dan, you guys have been so isolated in South Africa. News about Mandela's growing influence in the ANC is widespread out here in the real world. ANC leader Oliver Tambo is not in the best health and, even though he is in prison, Mandela, who was a supporter of the armed struggle, seems to have realised that the minority government is too strong to be beaten this way and he has been advocating sanctions and a more passive type of resistance.

"Anti-apartheid support is growing and Peter Hain, a Liberal and fast-rising politician in this country, is one of many who support Mandela and his cause. And others like former bishop Trevor Huddlestone and Canadian Prime Minister Brian Mulroney are also fervent supporters inspired, no doubt, by Mandela's call for reconciliation and not bloodshed."

Daniel was surprised. From 1964 there had hardly been an official word about Mandela and now, 21 years later, the man was a world figure.

"But we all know that South Africa is burning as the black youth and bodies like the ANC, the Black Consciousness Movement and others are leading the violence. And Mandela himself was a co-founder of Umkhonto we Sizwe, the armed wing of the ANC."

"Yes," responded Adair while Arthur and Nancy watched the exchange with interest, "that was after the infamous Sharpeville Massacre and Mandela said, in his famous speech from the dock in 1964, that he had come to the conclusion that as violence in South Africa was inevitable, it would be unrealistic and wrong for African leaders to continue preaching peace and non-violence at a time when the government met peaceful demands with force."

"Well, they did just that," said Daniel. "In 1983, the Church Street bomb was detonated in Pretoria near the Air Force Headquarters, resulting in 19 deaths and 217 injuries. And that was done by MK."

The group sat in silence, digesting what Daniel had said.

"Well," said Adair, "the world sees Nelson Mandela as the true leader of South Africa and pressure is growing for the ruling government to allow the blacks to vote."

Daniel responded, somewhat sadly: "That, we all know, has to come but it will not be without bloodshed. There are many Afrikaners like our friend Jonker."

He was busy telling Adair about the power of Jonker and the Security Police when James walked in. "Hello everyone," he said cheerily as he ordered a round of drinks.

Settling down in a seat he turned to Daniel after a few pleasantries and said, "Funny thing today, I met a guy from Port Elizabeth who said he knew of you."

"Really," responded Daniel, "who is that? Another journo?"

"No, a former policeman, a guy named Jonker. He said you were a respected newspaper man in the region but then you'd just disappeared. I told him I'd met you here in Bromley."

Nancy gasped and both Daniel and Arthur sat upright.

"Did I do something wrong?" asked a worried looking James.

"Depends," said Daniel. "Did he say he knew me, like he'd met me, or knew of me?" He stared intently at James.

"He said he knew of you, did not say he'd met you. Why? What's the panic?"

Daniel did not relent. "And, did you tell him I was here with Arthur and Nancy?"

James smiled and said: "Nope. Hell no. These guys are often racist and he might have taken offence, I guess."

Daniel, Arthur and Nancy breathed a collective sigh of relief and sat back in their seats.

"So, is this the guy you were telling me about?" Adair asked. "The mean cop with more power than he should have?"

"Doesn't seem like it," said Daniel, sipping his wine.

"Hold on," said Nancy thoughtfully after a few moments and she turned to Arthur. "Remember that soldier who came up to us in Langa, before the shooting and told us to go away? He looked like the man who raped me. Maybe he is Jonker's brother."

Nancy's comment brought another silence to the group. Adair and James were not aware of her past.

"Well, I'm afraid I have some bad news then," said James quietly.

"This Jonker guy told me his brother, also a former policeman, is coming over to London in a few days. Apparently he has some people here he needs to look up. And that's not all. The Jonker I met stays in Beckenham near the station and he said his brother was going to stay with him for a few days."

Daniel spoke before anyone else. "Tell me James, are you going to see this Jonker guy again?"

"Yes, we had arranged to get together tomorrow night at 7 for a meal at that Italian restaurant, Luigi's, in Beckenham's High Street. It was his suggestion and I said yes as he seemed lonely and quite keen to get to know me. I can cancel if you want?"

"No, don't do that," said Daniel firmly. "I'd like to come along, if I may. I can just stroll in and look surprised to see you and you can then introduce me to Jonker. I'll take it from there."

36

MAY 30 - PERCEIVED DANGER

The next day was a busy one for Daniel. The first call of the day was to South Africa, a conference call to Jake and Steve to discuss a plan of action following the news that Jonker was en route to London.

"I'm meeting his brother today for two reasons," Daniel told the two. "Firstly, it appears from Nancy that he was in the squad that took part in the Langa shooting. So, depending on how he is politically, I could get some quotes to add to the story, which would be crucial in getting the truth.

"Secondly, it could just be coincidence that the other Jonker is heading this way. But, as you know, I don't believe in coincidence. So it would be worth finding out, if I can, why he is coming to London. If I am the reason he's coming over, maybe I should just meet him, face to face."

"I'll find out from Carl if he can tell us anything and get back to you soonest," said Jake.

Steve interjected: "I can do the same with the top brass up here but perhaps we should unveil our two kingpins sooner rather than later and break the story. What do you think?"

Daniel answered first. "I am ready with the story but it would be great to add anything Jonker might tell me tonight. South Africa is quite topical right now with news of Mandela having meetings on the quiet with the Nat government."

"I agree," said Jake. "Let's see if we can set up a news conference, say, on Monday, June the third. That gives you Dan, and us, a few days and the weekend to get our acts together."

Steve added: "Let's make it impartial and get the Pedersens involved too. Erik was on the phone only yesterday asking about the book and we can get Adair to arrange the conference and use it to announce the book. I presume, Dan, that you, Arthur and Nancy are happy about the book deal? It will mean money for you all. Pedersen has been sounding people out and he reckons interest is high enough for a sizeable advance."

"I agree, and it would be good to move the book deal forward," said Jake.

The call ended with everyone agreeing to an early morning update the next day, including a report on Daniel's meeting with Jonker. Three hours later he received a call from Jake to confirm two important things.

The first was that Frans Jonker had been discharged from the police on grounds of mental instability. Secondly Jake said that he was, according to Carl, due to fly out on the Sunday evening, meaning he'd arrive in London on June the third.

About an hour later, Steve called too. His news was a bit more disturbing.

"Dan, I can confirm that your Jonker friend has left the police force, medically boarded. But, I have also heard from some real deep sources that the Security Branch has set up a covert assassin squad, acting internationally to eliminate ANC leaders in exile whom the government believe are aiding the struggle and pleading for international sanctions. Now, I can't be sure but, given Jonker's contacts, he could be on his way to be part of this clandestine force. On those grounds, I'd seriously advise against meeting the other Jonker. He could be clean but he could be part of this too, we have no way of knowing."

"Yes we do," replied Daniel, "I'll just ask him, his reaction will be enough for me to gauge if he's aware of this. It's the only way we will find out, before it is too late."

That afternoon, with the help of Arthur and a senior journalist on the bureau's staff as proof reader, Daniel finished his feature piece which would be published in South Africa by the group's newspapers on Monday.

"Bloody hell Dan, I didn't know you and Arthur here were onto this, it's dynamite," said Alan Jeffries, the seasoned journalist.

"Yes, it's good stuff," agreed Daniel, "and I could get

some more input tonight. I'm hoping to get quotes from a policeman who was involved in the shooting.

"Geez, this will blow the lid right off," said Jeffries.

"Yes, we hope so," said Arthur, "but please don't tell anyone yet."

"No worries, Arthur, I respect embargoes and a scoop for our group."

***

That afternoon, Adair called Daniel to say the press conference had been set up for Monday at noon. "We have permission to be at St Martins-in-the-Fields on Trafalgar Square. It's next to South Africa House and is a suitably neutral venue. I told the vicar, Geoffrey Brown, what the conference was about and, as a friend of Desmond Tutu, he is quite happy to chair the event."

Daniel updated her with the information he'd received from Steve and Jake and she, too, urged him not to go to see Jonker that evening. When he refused, she said she intended to be there too, going as his date, which pleased Daniel no end. They agreed to meet at a pub near Beckenham Junction after work, just a short distance from Luigi's.

Arthur and Nancy were headed home for a quiet dinner in the flat Arthur shared with Daniel so Arthur wished him well as they parted at Beckenham Junction, a stop before Arthur got off.

"Don't let that whitey scare you off," said Arthur with a grin. "Remember you have right on your side and Adair will be there too, you lucky man!"

For the next 30 minutes or so, Daniel and Adair enjoyed a glass of wine at the pub and chatted about the conference planned for Monday amongst other things. They had grown closer in the short time they'd been in London and so had Arthur and Nancy.

"They're a great couple and well suited to each other," said Adair as she sipped her wine. "I hope the book advance which dad told me about today will give them a good start in life. Dad said he'd try and sort something out for them in Copenhagen. And Nancy has told me how much she cares for Arthur. She also told me you are her hero as you saved her life way back in 1977 when you were in the army and she was attacked."

Daniel smiled in a self-effacing way and tried to brush it off but she went on. "And for that, and what you have done for them since then, you are my hero too." She leant forward over the table and kissed him. Daniel felt like a love-struck teenager. He was looking forward to their time together that evening. And he was even more surprised and pleased when she held his hand as they walked down the road to Luigi's.

As they entered Luigi's, Daniel was struck by how Jonker's ginger hair shone in the restaurant's lights. He was sitting with his back to them, but he did look a lot like Frans Jonker, Daniel thought as they walked towards them. James looked up, saw Daniel and Adair and appeared suitably surprised. Jimmy Jonker noticed and turned to see who James was looking at.

"Ah, what a surprise! Jimmy, this is Dan Jacobs and his friend Adair Pedersen. Would you like to join us?" He stopped and looked at Jonker, hoping he wouldn't mind.

But before he could say anything, Daniel said: "Thanks, let us buy you a bottle of wine we can share. But we have our own table booked, so we'll eat on our own, if that's OK?"

And he moved over to the table, shook Jimmy by the hand and then pulled out a chair for Adair while trying to attract the waiter's attention. After introductions and ordering a bottle of Italian red, Daniel turned to Jimmy. "Well, welcome to the UK. James tells me you're a former policeman from PE. Well, I can tell you, you are the spitting image of a security cop I know, Frans Jonker. I take it you're related?"

Jimmy smiled as he sipped his wine. "Yes, he's my twin. The black sheep in my opinion."

"Good to hear. He's not my favourite person, I'm afraid to say. But if you were a policeman too, how'd you manage to work together if your views are so different? And why'd you leave the police?"

"Wow, you are a journalist, hey. All these questions. It's true, I don't see eye to eye with my brother or my father. Both are staunch Nationalists and believe the country will collapse if the blacks ever take over. I thought being a cop would be better than the army and I could study at the same time. And that time served was enough for me to get a degree and then enrol at university here to do post grad studies in criminal behaviour and forensic psychology.

"As for my brother, I know he had some stressful times. First in the army and then the police. Then drink got the better of him and he was medically boarded. So he's using his pension, he tells me, to travel the world. He will, in fact, be here next week."

Daniel paused, then asked: "So he's nothing to do with the police anymore? I'd heard there was this clandestine squad which the government had set up outside of SA. Given his credentials, your brother would be an ideal recruit."

Jimmy laughed while James looked amazed at the boldness of the questioning. "Hey man, I would be the last to know about that. He doesn't tell me much about his life but I do know he has contacts in high places and did do lots of strange stuff. I only know he's coming here because he needs a place to kip and he's looking for some people here. Whether those people are ex police mates or someone else, I do not know."

"OK," said Daniel, "I understand that. One more question, if I may? Were you part of the platoon involved in the Langa shooting in March?"

"How the hell did you know that?" asked Jimmy, looking surprised. "Yes, I was. I think I fired the first shot. And, if this is for the record, I'd like to tell you my story. Let's meet for a drink after dinner. Just you and me."

187

37

THE PLAN COMES TOGETHER

It was close to midnight when Daniel eventually left the pub with Jimmy. Dinner had finished at about 9 and Adair had gone home, saying she had a busy day to face. James walked her home, leaving Jimmy and Daniel to walk back up the road to the pub near the rail station.

The story Jimmy told was harrowing yet fascinating.

From a bungled order by an inexperienced officer to open fire which led to the vehicle jolting and Jimmy pulling the trigger - a moment he claimed he still had nightmares about.

"Man, I wake up sweating sometimes. We fired on people who were unarmed and did not seem to pose any real threat. The placing of the stones in the hands of the dead was a stupid thing but the brass wanted it to look like we had been attacked. I still see the faces, especially the one of the Rasta guy I think I shot and a young boy. It's not pleasant and I so wish I could undo it all.

"But to a certain extent, you have to see it from our point of view," Jimmy taking a sip of his beer. "We had done patrol after patrol, had stones and even petrol bombs thrown at us. Some of my colleagues and been killed, admittedly when on foot, and many injured. We were always fed information that the people in the township posed a real threat, that they were being helped and trained in guerrilla warfare by the ANC and the Russians. Not that we ever saw any proof of that. But the stress was unreal, never knowing if you'd be injured or worse. Many turned to drink and even drugs, so there was lots of instability and even a few suicides."

"I can understand that. But there would have been, and still are I guess, feelings of stress and anger from the township folk too," said Daniel.

"Yes, I agree with you and I actually feel sorry for them. But I'd had enough. I did not join the army because I did not want to do border duty. I thought I'd be a desk jockey in some remote police station and I knew they'd pay for me to study. But when this nonsense started I waited until I could buy my way out and enrolled to study here," said Jimmy.

"Then, that day in March in Langa was the last straw for me. I was biding my time to get out. I also had to deal with my brother who seemed to have gone off the rails. You know, he mentioned you once or twice. Really seemed to have a grudge against you. But I thought your paper did a great job and when I met James, a journalist who said he knew you and had met you here, I thought it would be great to meet you too. I miss South Africans even though I've only been here a short while."

"So, what are you going to tell your brother, if anything, about me?"

"That's pretty much up to you. Maybe you two should meet and sort out this problem he seems to have with you. Did you perhaps know him in his army days? He seems very pissed off with that time and some people there."

Daniel avoided answering that question and told Jimmy he'd think about meeting up with his brother and let him know next week.

"OK," Jimmy responded, "I'll keep mum about having met you then."

***

The next day at work was another busy one. Daniel told Jake and Steve about the interview with Jimmy Jonker in a conference call. Daniel had added the interview with Jimmy to the feature and it was ready to be faxed to Johannesburg.

"I'm worried about his brother though," added Jake. "Sounds like he's there looking for you. Maybe he's got wind of the fact that you're there with Arthur and Nancy and his twisted little mind wants revenge. Be careful Dan. I strongly suggest you do not arrange to meet him."

"Too right Jake," said Steve. "Dan, be careful. Even at the press conference, don't play up the Jonker angle too much, even though the Jimmy side is a strong anchor for the eyewitness account. Also, I'd keep Nancy out of it at this stage. Just have Arthur there. That would be my suggestion."

"Yes, agreed," Jake intervened. "And to make the Jonker side look stronger, maybe we can get some stats on the injuries for the police, including suicides and so on. Hopefully, if Carl can't get it for us down here, we can get details from headquarters. I'll try to get them to you at the latest by Monday morning. Does Jimmy Jonker know about the press conference?"

"No," Daniel responded, "I didn't tell him. But he knows the story is going out next week and he did say he might consider some interviews, if needed. But only working through me."

"That's great," said Steve. "Maybe we can get Jeffries to do another interview with him."

"I'm not sure about that," answered Daniel. "Let me sound him out next week after the story has broken. He might change his mind. Let me handle this from this side and I'll let you know."

"One more thing," said Jake, "Molly Blackburn has been in the news here as she's investigating police shootings and the disappearance of the PEBCO three. She's really making waves and I found out only yesterday that she's in the UK with family there. I know she'd love to attend the conference so I'll track her down and get her to contact you. Dan, are you happy with that?"

"Of course, that'd be super. She can have a slot to speak about her inquiries and efforts to get the government to investigate the Langa shootings."

"One last thing," said Steve, "Erik Pedersen will be there, as you know, and he is wealthy beyond belief. As part of his announcement of the book, I'll get him to make a cash donation to Molly for her investigations. Oh, and he said he can give Arthur and Nancy about £10,000 as an advance on the advance. But he won't do that publicly, obviously."

Daniel was impressed.

About two hours later the phone rang and it was Molly Blackburn. She was in Cambridge with an old university friend of the family and keen to be part of the conference on Monday.

"As you know, Daniel, Di Bishop and I have been working with Matthew Goniwe and the guys in Cradock to establish their Cradock Ratepayers Association and also as advisors for the consumer boycott. Neither of these has made us popular with the authorities and when I started agitating for an investigation into the Langa Shootings, I started getting death threats so I've decided to take a week or two off and have been in England since the middle of May. I'm going home next week so this will fit in perfectly and allow me to reach an international audience.

"The bad news is that I found out yesterday that a move to have Mathew re-instated as headmaster of his school was thwarted by the local military commander and regional Security Police chief. Apparently they used the words *never ever* when discussing his re-instatement. I worry for his life."

"Well," said Daniel, "perhaps you can mention that on Monday - the clamping down on civic leaders and political activists. Look at the PEBCO three's taking out by the security police."

They arranged for Molly to be at St Martins-in-the-Field at 11am on Monday.

The next phone call was Adair. "So, how did it go last night?" she queried as soon as Daniel answered.

"And hello to you too," he responded.

"I'm sorry he interfered with our date," said Adair. "But before you tell me about the Jonker stuff. I have two things to say. Firstly, the press conference is all set up. We have 25 press, radio and TV journalists attending. Revd Browne will chair. And, secondly, I miss you."

Daniel was pleased.

"OK, I have two things to say, too, before we talk about Jonker. Firstly, Molly Blackburn, the activist, will be there and she needs a slot to speak as she has been asking the SA government to investigate the shootings as a matter of urgency.

"Secondly, I miss you too, and you are now officially booked for dinner and drinks on the South Bank tonight. Meeting at the Founder's Arms at 6."

Then they spoke about the meeting with Jimmy and re-arranged the schedule for Monday's press conference.

Last business of the day was for Daniel to tell Arthur he would not be taking the train home with him.

"Oh, no worries Dan. I'm going to be eating in with Nancy again."

"That reminds me," said Daniel, "I spoke to Steve and Jake today and they are worried about the fact that the other Jonker will be here soon. They suggest that Nancy not attend the press conference on Monday. Are you happy with that? Do you still want to attend?"

Arthur hesitated, only for a short while before responding: "Well, you need at least one of us there for credibility, don't you? So I will be there but I'll only answer limited questions, through you."

"That's fine, thanks very much. And then perhaps we can get together with the Pedersens afterwards to discuss the book. Nancy can be there for that. We'll go to Adair's office."

38

JUNE 3 - BREAKING NEWS

After a relaxing and romantic weekend for Daniel and Adair, in which they hardly left her flat, it was back to work on Monday and preparing for the press conference at noon. Nancy had spent the weekend with Arthur. The train seemed busier than usual on the way in to London, Daniel noted. Probably because school half-term had ended and he had to stand all the way to Blackfriars, jostling with suited office workers, labourers and school children in the narrow aisle of the coach he had chosen on the 8.30 train.

At Blackfriars where the train terminated, departing passengers had to fight their way past others waiting to get on the train for the trip south of the river. In his determination to get to the turnstiles, Daniel kept his head down and forged ahead, not noticing the ginger-haired man with the backpack waiting to pass through the barrier and board the train.

But the man, Frans Jonker, who was on his way to his brother's flat in Bromley to drop his bag, shower and then head back to London to meet his brother in Trafalgar Square for lunch, was quick to spot and recognise Daniel.

He promptly did a U-turn and tailed Daniel out of the station, struggling to keep sight of his target as they emerged into the weak sunlight and headed towards Fleet Street. When Daniel reached and entered the building where the bureau was situated, Frans looked around and noticed a coffee shop nearby where he took a table at the window, ordered coffee and the Daily Mail and prepared for a long morning.

The headlines were full of the Heysel European Cup final football disaster in Belgium where 39 fans died before the game between Liverpool and Juventus. It appeared Liverpool fans had started the whole thing, Frans read, baffled by the European fascination and fervent passion for football, or soccer as he knew it. Rugby was a man's game, he thought, not this sissy sport.

Glancing up, he was just in time to see a smartly attired black man enter the same building Daniel had gone into. Frans wasn't sure, but he did resemble that black man from Uitenhage who had become one of his personal most wanted people.

"No," he muttered to himself, "too much of a coincidence."

Frans knew Daniel had been seconded to the UK office for the newspaper and that the two witnesses had not been seen for sometime.

"Hell, how could two blacks, one from South West Africa, sneak out of the Republic? That's just not possible, the papers don't have that much power," Frans muttered softy, suddenly noticing that the well-dressed man sitting close to him seemed to be listening to his muttering. Frans went back to his paper, casting occasional looks at the building across the road. He ordered a coffee refill. The waitress did not quite grasp his accent and he had to repeat himself. He settled down for a long wait. Even if it meant missing his brother for lunch, this was more important.

***

Across the road Daniel was busy on the phone for most of the morning. Molly Blackburn called to confirm she'd meet Daniel at 11.30 outside the church, and that she was bringing Peter Hain with her. Adair called to say the number of attendees from the media had grown to 30-plus with a Canadian TV crew attending. Arthur then walked into Daniel's cubicle, doing a turn to show off his sports coat and floral tie. "Cool, huh? Got them from a charity shop in Beckenham at the weekend."

Daniel smiled and nodded his approval. "All set then? It's almost 11 and time to go face the media."

The two walked out and headed down Fleet Street towards Trafalgar Square, about a kilometre away.

"I'm actually looking forward to this," Arthur said. "It will be good for this to go public. Nancy and I were talking about it at the weekend. She'll come in later and meet us at St Martin's. She's also quite keen on the book angle too."

"Well", said Daniel, "I have news on that front. Erik will probably tell you and Nancy later but he has arranged a large advance for you and Nancy from the book deal which will set you both up rather nicely."

Arthur was so surprised and shocked that he stopped dead in his tracks, turned and hugged a surprised Daniel. "Man, that's great! Nancy had been talking to Adair and we quite fancy the idea of moving from England. Adair said she and her dad could help us get settled in Denmark or somewhere in Europe where they have offices. A warmer place near the Mediterranean could be good."

About 30 metres behind them, Frans Jonker was surprised and shocked to see the black man and white man hug. Such things did not happen in South Africa. He had followed them from the coffee shop, confirming after a second look that the black man was the guy he was looking for.

"Hopefully," he thought, "they will lead me to the woman from Ovamboland - if she's come to the UK with them."

He noticed they were approaching Trafalgar square, the imposing National Gallery looming to their right and Nelson's column straight ahead. Frans stepped up his pace, getting slightly closer to his quarry as the crowds grew.

"The guide books are right," he thought. "There are a lot of people on Trafalgar Square feeding pigeons, gawking at the monuments and climbing onto those massive lions."

He saw Daniel and his friend head towards the South Africa High Commission, keeping to the left side of the road and not heading for the square itself. They then climbed the steps of the big church there, St Martins-in-the-Field. Halfway up the marble steps stood a group of people. One of them was a young woman with shiny auburn hair who smiled and waved at Daniel. Next to her, Frans noticed to his surprise, was Molly Blackburn. He decided to keep on walking to the corner of Duncannon Street. As he did so, he did not notice the young woman stare at him and then lean towards Daniel.

"Dan," Adair said as she kissed him on the cheek, "I just saw a guy who looks like Jimmy Jonker walk past. Could that be his brother?"

Daniel turned and looked but saw no-one. "Where?"

"He went left at the corner," she said. "Doesn't matter, I could be mistaken."

Speaking louder and turning to the others, she said, "Daniel Jacobs, Arthur Shipalana, this is Peter Hain, Revd Browne and Molly Blackburn."

"I know Daniel," replied Molly. "Good to see you again. And Arthur, it is a pleasure and an honour to meet you. You are a brave man to make your story known."

After handshakes and greetings Revd Browne, looking at his watch, said: "Let's go into the church and to my office. We can have a brief chat there before going down to the crypt where the Press will be waiting."

He smiled at Arthur's nervousness and took him by the arm. "Don't worry, my son, it will be fine. You're in good hands here."

At the corner Frans, who had turned around and retraced his steps, saw them enter the church. "Now what?" he mused. He knew he could not go in. He'd be noticed. Turning around, he saw a red telephone booth on the opposite corner of Duncannon Street. He decided he'd wait there for a while and see what happened. It was still an hour before he was to meet Jimmy at Nelson's Column and, if Daniel and company had not emerged, Jimmy could help him.

39

THE WORLD LISTENS

Downstairs in the crypt, it was packed. Television lights glared towards the empty top table where five chairs were placed. In front of it, photographers crouched on the floor ahead of the front row of seats, ready to take pictures of the main players. Every seat was filled with journalists of different nationalities. Others stood at the back jostling for space between the TV camera crews.

The chatter died as Revd Browne led Daniel, Arthur, Molly and Erik into the room and they took their places at the main table. Adair and Peter Hain stood to one side.

"Ladies and gentlemen of the media," started Revd Browne, standing at the podium near the table. We are gathered here today to hear an amazing story. An eyewitness account of a horrific killing, massacre if you will, of unarmed people by the South African armed forces earlier this year at Langa near Port Elizabeth. Most of you have heard of the shooting itself but Arthur Shipalana here," he indicated Arthur seated closest to him, "and his companion saw it unfold.

"Beyond that, you will hear a story of a manhunt and intimidation as a South African newspaper group, represented here by Daniel Jacobs," again Revd Browne indicated to whom he was referring and Daniel lifted his hand in acknowledgment, "planned to move Arthur and his companion to safety, facing harassment from the Security Police."

A rumbling murmur grew in volume from the gathered journalists and cameras flashed as photographers took shots of Arthur and Daniel. Revd Browne held up his hands and silence descended.

"Then we have Molly Blackburn, a respected human rights campaigner in South Africa, who has been fighting to have this shooting properly investigated. The other gentleman is Erik Pedersen, a Danish publisher and owner of an international news agency who many of you might know. He is also a firm believer in civil rights and justice. Today he will make two important announcements. But first, I hand you over to Daniel Jacobs, bureau chief for SA Associated Newspapers here in London and his story."

More cameras flashed as Daniel stood and moved to the podium, a few notes in his hand.

"Good afternoon. A few months ago, I did not expect to be here. In March I was news editor of the Herald in Port Elizabeth and my friend Arthur was a car factory worker in Uitenhage, a small town nearby. We did not know each other then. But the events of March 21 have linked our lives in a way we never expected.

"I was tasked with getting the news of the day, something you all know about," he said with a smile. Arthur here was just going about his daily life in the township and about to go to a nearby shop with his friend, Nancy Nujomba from Ovamboland, South West Africa.

"It was a warm morning and, again as many of you know, the SA police and army were often patrolling the townships to keep the peace. Arthur and Nancy came upon a police motorised patrol and one policeman told them to move away as a funeral in the area had been banned and there could be some trouble. They then moved off. But within minutes a large crowd of people wishing to attend the funeral arrived on the road. Again only a short while later, when Arthur and Nancy were about 200 metres away, shots rang out and several people were killed.

"Arthur and Nancy witnessed this. They saw that the police were armed, that the crowd was peaceful and unarmed. They saw many in the crowd turn and run after the first few shots. Many were shot in the back, even innocent young children who were part of the crowd."

He paused as the murmur grew once more and more pictures were taken of him and Arthur. Looking around, Daniel saw tears in Molly Blackburn's eyes. Arthur had his head down.

"Then to his horror Arthur saw, after the shooting had

stopped, that policemen had disembarked from their vehicles and walked around putting stones in the hands of dead people."

Again he paused. This time the room was silent. Faces stared at him.

"That was March 21, ironically the anniversary of another shooting by the SA police of unarmed people at Sharpeville in 1960."

Daniel spoke on for about another 10 minutes outlining events from then to eventually leaving South Africa.

"And now, more than two months later, Arthur can really tell his story to the world. We, our newspaper that is, had to sneak him and Nancy out of the country. In the interim, there was intimidation and harassment by the security police. We had used some of what they saw in the initial newspaper coverage.

"It is my belief that the security police wanted Arthur and Nancy permanently removed from society to prevent the whole story coming out. That is why they are now here. Yes, Nancy is here too but not attending today. I have also, in recent days, spoken to a policeman who was part of that fated patrol and his comments, along with quotes from Arthur, Nancy and others, are in a press release we will hand out at the end of this conference.

"Molly Blackburn will now speak about her goals in trying to get the authorities to officially investigate the shooting."

The elegant grey-haired woman stood, moved gracefully to the podium and said: "Arthur Shipalana, I salute your bravery, your conviction and your willingness to let the truth be known. While people like Steve Biko will be remembered as martyrs and heroes. History might never know that it is the unsung few like you who will be the ones who helped bring about real and significant changes in South Africa.

"Events like the Langa Massacre - and that's what is was, a cold-blooded massacre - need to be investigated. The security forces in South Africa are becoming a law unto themselves and this cannot be allowed to continue.

"Evidence gathered by Daniel and his team on the Herald would, in normal times, be enough to warrant a full-blown and official commission of inquiry. But no. The authorities think they can sweep it under the carpet, like Biko's death and so many other mysterious disappearances, assassinations and use of excessive force.

"Through the recently imposed state of emergency the government has imposed curfews, made thousands of arrests, restricted the movement of individuals, and ordered the South African army to occupy townships in support of the police. In Port Elizabeth blacks have instituted a consumer boycott of white businesses. This is in response to the state of emergency with demands like ending the state of emergency and the release of long-term political prisoners, such as Nelson Mandela.

"The hope is that white business owners will become desperate and call upon the government to meet the demands of the black South Africans. Already the boycott is hurting the white businesses in Port Elizabeth greatly. The boycott committee has told the chamber of commerce that the boycott will last until March next year unless the business owners arrange for black leaders to be released. And, as a show of faith, they have agreed to suspend the boycott over the Christmas shopping period."

Molly Blackburn then spoke about the efforts to have the government convene a commission of inquiry into the shooting and her worries that, if not investigated, the police would step up its already extensive reliance upon covert operations.

"Yes, there is a little-known side to the police called the *Third Force* and another one known as *Koevoet*, or the *Hammer Unit* and perhaps even other official and quasi-official arms of the security forces which specialise in causing trouble in the townships and eliminating potential problem people like Steve Biko. My worry is that the State could start its own reign of terror through these covert operations which would help justify their covert actions.

"An example of that came earlier this month when three

black civic leaders in Port Elizabeth were lured to the local airport and then disappeared, kidnapped by the security police. Human remains were found at a remote police retreat near Port Elizabeth and we believe these three were murdered and set alight by the security police.

"As you can see, the situation is getting out of hand."

Erik Pedersen's talk was short and sweet.

He announced that the Pedersen Foundation would assist in funding Blackburn's efforts for justice and that he would also help fund a book, to be written by Daniel.

"This way, if nothing else, there will be a record of what happened on that fateful day, March 21, 1985. But my hope, and that of many right-thinking people, is that South Africa will be a true democratic country in the not-too distant future."

The next 40 minutes saw Daniel answering questions while Molly and Erik were interviewed by TV crews. Daniel refused to do any TV interviews featuring himself or Arthur. By 1pm it was all over.

Molly Blackburn and Peter Hain had left, Nancy had arrived and Revd Browne had other commitments and took his leave too. Erik offered to take Daniel, Adair, Arthur and Nancy to lunch.

As they left the church and turned towards Trafalgar Square, Daniel automatically looked towards the towering Nelson's Column and the huge lions at its base on the far side of the busy road. They turned left and headed towards a restaurant in Pall Mall. Near one of the lions he saw a flash of ginger hair highlighted in a beam of bright sunlight and spotted the two Jonker brothers engaged in what looked like a heated argument.

201

40

NEW BEGINNINGS

A red mist descended over Frans Jonker's eyes shortly after meeting up with his brother. Jimmy had refused to help him contain the threat that he perceived Daniel and the two Langa witnesses to be to the further security of South Africa. Speaking Afrikaans after spotting Jimmy in the square, Frans had urged him to help, telling him how he'd followed Daniel to his office, kept watch and then followed him to the church.

Responding in the same language, Jimmy had said: "But Frans, you are being silly and stupid. How can these three be a problem? Daniel Jacobs is a respected newspaper man and the other two, even though they might have seen the Langa shooting, what can they do now? They have no real influence. And anyway, I spoke to Jacobs last week. He's a really nice guy. So I told him my side of the story about Langa. How I think I fired the first shot and how bad I feel about it. It will be used in a further news story."

This was when the red mist arrived and Frans really lost it. Swearing, he grabbed his brother as if trying to shake some sense into him. "You bastard! You've become a sell out. It is important we keep such people under control. They must not live! And why did you not tell me this morning you'd met that shit, Jacobs. He's the real cause of all this trouble. It's because of him that I left the army."

Jimmy grappled with his brother and struggled to loosen his grip on his jacket. Then it sunk in.

"Because of him? What do you mean?"

As Frans relaxed his grip, Jimmy managed to break free.

"Let's go have a drink and talk about this. Hell, it's your first day here and we're fighting already," he said trying to remain calm.

The wind seemed to go out of Frans's sails and his

anger dissipated.

In the pub at Charing Cross, Jimmy bought Frans a beer and they moved to a quiet corner away from the door.

Frans referred to an incident in the army in 1977 and how a confrontation with Daniel, then an officer, had let to his court martial.

"So, what really happened? What was this incident? It must have been serious for you to be court-martialled."

"Well, that bastard walked into a hut during a raid where I had found this half-naked woman. I was trying to help her when Jacobs walked in. She had grabbed me and ripped my trouser flies open. I was trying to repair that when he saw me and jumped to the wrong conclusion. He said I'd raped this woman, this black bitch."

He stopped talking and took a deep swig of his beer. "Hell, this Pommie beer is crap. No bite and not even properly chilled."

While Frans ranted about the beer, Jimmy thought of his story. Hardly a plausible reason for a court martial. Maybe Frans was hiding something? He'd have to speak to Daniel about this but, until then, he needed to keep Frans under control and try and dissuade him from taking vengeance.

"Let's have another drink, then I'll take you to a great pub on the South Bank, the Founder's Arms, for some wine and traditional British battered fish and chips. You'll like that."

Frans readily agreed and changed from beer to brandy for his next drink.

***

Erik Pedersen had booked a table at the restaurant at 116 Pall Mall, that imposing Georgian building, home to the Institute of Directors, designed by architect John Nash in the early 1820s. First stop was the elegant cocktail bar with its sumptuous leather sofas where a bottle of chilled Moët and Chandon champagne awaited them.

"Cheers to a successful day, a great event and the launch of what will be a great book," said Erik, raising his glass to Daniel, Arthur, Nancy and Adair.

"Book?" asked Nancy, "How is that progressing? I know Arthur and Daniel have been busy with it but Arthur hasn't kept me up to date."

"Yes, I've finished the writing," said Daniel, "and we should get a proof copy in a few weeks, Adair tells me. Arthur and I did put in long and hard hours and I'm happy with the result."

Adair turned and smiled at Nancy. "It was to be a surprise, I was going to give you a copy."

"Never mind surprises," said Erik brusquely. "More important is the fact that early interest is already high with pre-orders from bookshops around the world bringing in a substantial amount. So much so that I already have taken an advance on that and I would like to present Nancy and Arthur with £10,000 to help set them up in a new life together.

"Adair also tells me you would like to move to Europe. Well, I can pull a few strings and get you into my office in either Copenhagen or Italy. I have a new bureau which has just opened in Rome. We have a company flat there and that would probably be the best. She also tells me Nancy has a flair for office admin and Arthur could develop into a fine feature writer, I hear from Daniel. So, that's my offer. It's the least I can do for two people who have risked their lives and given Pedersen Publishing a book that will do extremely well. Ideally, I'd like you to come to Copenhagen next week, learn the ropes there and then by the end of July you could be in Rome."

Arthur beamed and held Nancy's hand. He could hardly believe how much their lives had changed in such a short time.

Lunch was a grand affair. More wine and a tasty and well-presented three-course meal in a restaurant where massive paintings belonging to Queen Elizabeth looked down on the diners. Daniel was impressed by how many people Erik knew, top businessmen who came over and said hello. It made him realise just how influential he was and that offers of jobs and books were easily within his power. It was a pleasant meal, but by 2.30 Erik was glancing at his watch and saying he had to go.

"Daniel," he said as he took his leave after signing for the meal, "why don't you come over to Copenhagen with Arthur and Nancy? I'm sure you can take a day or two off and I have an opportunity I'd like to discuss with you."

"I'd love to come over," said Daniel, "let me check with the office and I'll confirm by tomorrow."

The group then split up, Arthur and Nancy heading back to Shortlands, Erik to his meeting and Daniel and Adair to their respective offices after agreeing to meet after work at the Founder's Arms.

As he walked back to Fleet Street, Daniel had a lot on his mind. "What could Pedersen's opportunity be? What was going to happen next with Arthur and Nancy? Will they be safe in Rome? Will the security police leave them alone now that the news would be international by the evening? And, what will my future be? Would we all be safe?" He knew he would have to seriously look at Pedersen's offer and possibly relinquish thoughts of going back to South Africa and becoming an editor.

41

SOUTH BANK SHOWDOWN

Frans was not too sober - but he carried it well - by the time Jimmy got him to the Founder's Arms. From the pub at Charing Cross train station, they had taken the Tube to Blackfriars and crossed the river to the Founder's Arms near the disused Bankside Power Station with a view across the river of St Paul's. Here they settled down in the balmy evening sunshine on the deck overlooking the Thames.

"Do you realise you're sitting where history unfolded," Jimmy said as they sipped their drinks.

"Serious? Why?" asked Frans, not really interested and inwardly still wondering about Daniel and company.

"Well, Shakespeare's Globe Theatre is just down the road a bit and that church across the river is the famous St Paul's, designed by Christopher Wren."

"Interesting," said Frans. "So, tell me, what are we going to do about Jacobs and these people he brought to London?"

Jimmy was taken aback. "Why are you fixated on them and so hell-bent on revenge?

"Can't you just forgive, forget and move on? After all, you're out of the police now and being boarded has given you some money. So relax, travel the world as you planned and enjoy life. You've probably earned it."

Frans knocked back the rest of his brandy and coke and then said: "OK, get us another round and I'll tell you why. I mean really tell you why I hate that guy so much."

He stopped and looked out over the river. It was just before 5.30 and the river was flowing quietly out to sea. The weather was surprisingly pleasant. The temperature had reached 25C, Britain seemed set for a hot summer and there was rising speculation about Bob Geldoff's planned Live Aid concert. Frans liked modern music and he thought he might try and see the concert.

Jimmy returned with the drinks and Frans, accepting his said: "Why don't we go to this Geldoff concert at Wembley next month? I'll pay and then head off later for Thailand, I hear it's good out there. Hell man, we can see Status Quo, Queen, U2, The Who and Paul McCartney."

Jimmy was surprised by this change in tack. "Yes, great, I'd like that. But now, what were you going to tell me about Daniel Jacobs?"

Sipping his brandy, Frans said with a smile, "I'm prepared to pay good money to see those artists, even though they're raising money for some black kids in Ethiopia.

"Jacobs? He's the shit in the army who caught me with that woman."

"Yes, I remember, you told me earlier this afternoon."

"Did I?" Frans paused and looked confused. "Anyway, He was a Lieutenant in the same unit as me on the border, way back in 1977. We'd been there almost three months and I was sick and tired of the whole thing. It was a lot sitting around doing nothing or otherwise long, meaningless patrols to show the locals that we were there to keep them safe from SWAPO. What rubbish! They didn't care and some were quite arrogant. They did not know their place.

"Anyway, one day we did this raid on a village where, we'd been told, some SWAPO insurgents had taken refuge. The night before me and some of my mates had been talking about life back home and, man, we were missing our girlfriends. So, on this raid, my platoon had gone ahead with Captain du Toit and I was bringing up the rear. The platoon had gone past some of the huts and was inside the village, shots were being fired so I knew there were terrorists there.

"Then I saw a movement in one of the huts and with my rifle ready, went slowly towards it. A man came out, saw me and turned as if reaching for something. It could have been a weapon, so I fired. He fell back into the hut and as I advanced, I heard a woman whimper and, on entering, I saw this black woman, half-dressed with her boobs

207

hanging out.

"She said something to me in her language which sounded insulting and rude so I grabbed her. I was going to teach her a lesson and how to treat white people. Next thing I knew, I had my hand over her mouth and I was ripping her dress away, feeling her all over. She struggled but she felt so soft and feminine."

As he paused, Jimmy sat shocked, unable to speak. He was glad there were no people sitting near them to hear his brother's tale.

"So, I think I must have had sex with her. Everything just went red and I suddenly was aware of standing over her. I had come and she was crouching there staring at me. Man, she was going to be big trouble, I could tell. I was thinking maybe I should just shoot her, then no-one would know what happened.

"Next thing, I was struck from behind. This Jacobs guy had come in and seen me. He hit me with his rifle, that's how my nose was broken. So, before I knew it I was under guard, then court-martialled, put in detention barracks and kicked out of the army - and it's all because of that bloody Jacobs. He could have just let it go, after all, it was only a black woman. But no, he had to prove a point."

He stopped and finished his drink in one swallow.

Jimmy said, softly, "Frans, I cannot condone what you did, I'm sorry. But if I'd been Jacobs I would have done the same thing, believe me."

Frans stared at his brother, his mouth hanging open. "Well, screw you then," he said softly but forcefully.

Frans pushed back his chair to stand, stumbled and then walked off, swaying slightly, swearing softly. Jimmy sat, stunned.

After a few seconds he'd thought he better follow his brother and get him home.

***

Daniel and Adair walked hand in hand along the South Bank towards the Founder's Arms. It was just past 5.30.

"Isn't this weather great?" said Daniel, feeling very happy with life. Just upriver of Blackfriars Bridge, they stopped and looked out over the Thames.

"Dan, I think you should seriously consider my father's offer when you go to Copenhagen. I think he is looking for an editor-in-chief for his news operations and you'd be great at that. Means you'd be my boss!" Adair nudged Daniel playfully in the ribs.

"Seriously? That's quite a big task. I see he has three bureaux in Europe, Copenhagen, Paris and Rome as well your one here in London. Then there's New York, Toronto and a small one in Johannesburg in South Africa,"

"Yes, and I know he's looking to set up in the Asia Pacific area too, probably Melbourne in Australia, Singapore and Tokyo. So that's 10 offices you'll be looking after. He currently does that himself but it's a lot of work along with his other management tasks. I think he's tired now and wants to pull back a bit from the day-to-day stuff and concentrate on his philanthropic campaigns and the publishing house.

"After he met you on safari, he told me he liked you and he's since had glowing reports from Steve Russell about you. He's also really impressed with the book and I think it was that which made his mind up to make an approach, which he'll do next week."

Daniel looked up at the trains going over the bridge into Blackfriars station.

"Well, I do love the world of journalism, as you know, so I'll seriously consider what he has to say. I told him this afternoon I'd be able to make the trip with Arthur and Nancy. But now, it's been a long and fulfilling day, let's go share a bottle of wine and then head home."

Daniel took Adair's hand again and they turned to walk down to the Founder's Arms, heading into the covered walkway under Blackfriars Bridge where a busker was strumming his guitar and singing his version of the Foreigner hit *I want to know what love is*. As they did so they both noticed a man stumbling towards them, seemingly slightly the worse for wear. He was just a silhouette in the darkness with the sunlight behind him but just entering the walkway behind him was another man. The first man got closer and stopped.

"You bastard!" he screamed and lunged towards Daniel.

It was Frans Jonker. He took a swing at Daniel's face, a wild haymaker of a blow. But as he did so, his foot slipped in the cobbled paving and he was off balance enough for the blow to hit Daniel's shoulder.

Adair screamed, the busker stopped in mid song and Jimmy started running towards the scuffle. Daniel managed to let go of Adair's hand and push her to one side as he fell against the side of the walkway as the force of the blow pushed him off balance too.

Still stumbling, Frans grabbed at Daniel's legs in a loose rugby tackle and Daniel lost his balance fully, falling forward onto Frans. Despite being drunk, Frans's strength was fuelled by his anger and he rolled over getting on top of Daniel and managed to claw at Daniel's face, raking his nails down his left cheek. Daniel felt the sting and then blood starting to flow.

He managed to lift his right leg and his knee hit Frans in the testicles with enough force to make him scream and fall sideways. As he fell, Jimmy who had dived forward in an effort to knock Frans off Daniel, landed fully on Daniel, winding both of them.

Next thing Daniel knew he was being kicked in the ribs as Frans had managed to get up and was taking wild kicks, hitting both Daniel and Jimmy. Adair then entered the fray, swinging wildly with her handbag, striking Frans about the head with several hefty blows, forcing him to shift his attention to her.

By this time, other people had entered the walkway and two young men intervened trying to stop the fighting. As one helped Daniel and Jimmy to their feet, Frans managed to break free from the man who was holding him by the arms and ran off towards Waterloo station.

Sobbing, Adair turned to Daniel and was shocked to see the blood running down his cheek. Frans had just missed Daniel's eye but there were two long cuts which were bleeding freely. Jimmy stumbled over, obviously in pain from the blows to his side.

"Hey man, I'm so sorry. He's not all there. Frans is mentally unstable, I'm sure of it. Are you both OK?"

Adair was hugging Daniel. She nodded.

"I think I'm fine, besides these cuts to my face and some bruising on my ribs it feels like. Guess my new suit is ruined," Daniel said he looked down and saw the left trouser leg was torn.

"Should we contact the police?" asked one of the two who had intervened.

Daniel looked swiftly at Jimmy and then said: "No, thanks anyway, just an argument that got out of hand after he'd had one drink too many. Thanks for your help."

As the pair walked off, Daniel, Adair and Jimmy moved to a nearby bench outside the walkway and sat down.

"Now what?" asked Adair, still looking shocked by the sudden attack.

"Well, I guess I'll find Frans at my flat when I get home. What would you like me to do?" Jimmy looked at Daniel for help.

"Nothing for now, I guess. Ideally we should sit down and sort this out once and for all, but I don't think that's likely to happen."

42

JUNE 5 - A CHANGE OF SCENERY

It had been a busy Tuesday dealing with follow-ups to the Langa shooting story from newspapers and TV networks around the world, during which time Daniel had little time to think about Frans Jonker.

Wednesday, June 5, was an easier day. The mid-morning conference call with Steve and Jake started well but ended with an ominous warning.

"Dan," said Steve, starting the meeting, "the repercussions of our story have been amazing. In most papers it took up the front page with inside spreads too. Even the Afrikaans papers have given it unusual prominence."

Jake chipped in: "Yes, way more than we all anticipated. Sidebars included Molly's campaign, with comments from Van Zyl Slabbert and church leaders like Tutu backing her call. Even some senior judges have added their weight to the call for a Commission of Inquiry. And we were told today that the Government is seriously considering this, which is a feather in her cap - and ours!

"On the negative side, we've had what we expected with the police saying our story is biased and exaggerates the planting of stones and pangas among the dead to make it look worse for them. But the comments from Jimmy Jonker have kind of taken the wind out of their sails quite considerably, even though the police have added that he suffered from stress and that his comments could not be taken as the truth and were exaggerated too, which is laughable. We're waiting for official comment from the Ministry of Law and Order and PW Botha's office."

"Yes, given that Botha made a policy address earlier this year in which he had refused to give in to demands, including the release of Mandela, and his defiance of international opinion which has further isolated South Africa and led to economic sanctions, it will be interesting to see how he reacts to this. Silence so far," said Steve.

"Well, we hear from here that Ronald Reagan is to issue comment later today as is Margaret Thatcher. Both, we understand, will be hard-hitting and call for an inquiry and further sanctions," added Daniel. "Most nations want an answer or some form of response from the SA Government."

"Well, it's all good and we're riding the crest of the wave right now," said Steve. "Well done Daniel."

"Yes, good stuff but, a word of warning, and this comes from your friend Carl Strydom," said Jake. "He says he believes Frans Jonker is working undercover for the security police and needs to be treated with extreme caution.

"He had to say he believes because no-one would tell him officially, for obvious reasons. But he said a friend of his in the force told him that Jonker is still on the books and has made contact, as recently as yesterday, with people in the IRA who are helping the security police in their covert work outside of South Africa.

"Daniel, this is serious. If Jonker is unstable but still in their employ, he could get access to weapons from the IRA and this spells danger for you, Arthur and Nancy. Now I know you are all going to Copenhagen next week, and I've spoken to Erik Pedersen about it. He has contacts in the Rigspolitiet, the national police force, and he insists you will be safe over there.

"So, we seriously advise that you lay low, do not try to confront him or even make contact with his brother for a while," urged Jake. "It's only for six days as you fly out on Monday, I believe."

Steve intervened: "Daniel, Jake is right. Why don't you all leave London for a while? I mean go today and return on Sunday, take a drive down to the coast, head for the New Forest, Wales or Cornwall or somewhere like that but don't tell anyone where you are going."

This agreed, the call ended and Daniel set about handing over his administrative duties to Alan Jeffries. He realised that he had not even told Jake and Steve about the confrontation with Frans. Probably just as well, he thought.

His next phone call, while he was briefing Jeffries, was from Jimmy Jonker.

"Hello Daniel, I'm calling from University and I have some bad news regarding Frans. I think he's still working for the police. He was out most of yesterday and I answered two phone calls for him. One was from Arrie du Preez, his captain in the security police, who said he had some contact information for Frans. I offered to take a message but he refused. The other was from an Irish sounding guy and also no message.

"Anyway, I know Frans is still pissed with you and I really cannot say he won't do something silly. He knows where your office is, so all I am saying is watch your back and be careful."

Daniel thought for a moment before answering: "Well, thanks but we're all going to France tonight - Adair, Arthur, Nancy and myself. We're taking the ferry from Dover, so he won't be a bother for a few days at least."

"France? OK, I don't think Frans would follow you. He doesn't even know the ferries go from Dover."

After the call ended, Jeffries said: "France? I didn't know that."

"Not necessarily true," said Daniel, "but I don't know how close the two of them really are. So if Frans finds out, then he's off on a wild goose chase isn't he?"

But, in Beckenham, as Jimmy put the phone down, he saw that Frans had silently slipped into the kitchen behind him. "He might have heard what I said," he thought.

"Hey, how are you doing? You slept late," said Jimmy.

"Yes, I had a tough night. Who was on the phone? Another call for me?"

"No, some wrong number."

***

At lunchtime, Daniel told Arthur about the plans to go away and suggested Arthur visit Nancy at Adair's office and then head home to pack. Daniel then phoned Adair and asked if she could take a few days off.

"Well, sounds tempting Daniel, but I'm not sure. Why? I have quite a few things to organise here."

"Trust me, Adair, it is important, that's all I can say. I'll call your dad if you want, and tell him too."

"No don't worry, I have to call him anyway so I'll tell him then. If you say we need to get away then he'll believe it. Is this about that Jonker man again?"

"Yes," said Daniel, refusing to say anything more on the phone.

Daniel then realised he'd not thanked Revd Browne for the use of the church facilities and, feeling the need to stretch his legs, decided to walk to St Martins-in-the-Fields. Remembering Jimmy's words, he left the building through the fire escape at the rear and walked down to Embankment and then up Villiers Street and to the church. He found Revd Browne in the crypt where a choral performance had just ended. The two sat and had some coffee in the cosy café area.

"What happened to your face?" Revd Browne asked.

Daniel told him about the attack by Frans Jonker and then told the vicar about the warning he'd received from his office in South Africa.

"Oh, I firmly agree. You should get away, all of you. I have a cottage in the New Forest, near the village of Bransgore, which has been in our family for years. It has two bedrooms and is quite remote, without being too far from the amenities like the village shops and pubs. Why don't you go there? I have a set of keys upstairs in my office. It's yours for a while, quite a few weeks, if you want. I know when the summer holidays start early in July my sister and her family are going down."

Daniel readily accepted and told Revd Browne he'd have his keys back on Monday morning.

"It's just a few days until this blows over. Then we're off to Denmark."

In the afternoon, Adair called and told Daniel her father had agreed to the days off for her.

"He even wants me to fly to Copenhagen with you all next week, which I'll do because he wants to have a staff meeting and it's my mother's birthday on the Wednesday. He's arranged that we're on the same SAS flight."

Daniel then told her about the trip to the New Forest and Revd Browne's generous offer of accommodation.

"Wow, that's great and we've just taken delivery of a new company car so we can use that for the trip. At least Jonker won't know the car. In fact, why don't we leave this evening? It's less than three hours to the New Forest and we can be there before 9. Arthur and Nancy are already heading home and I can be there by 5 and can pack in a few minutes."

Daniel agreed, realising that speed was of the essence if Jonker was armed and still looking for them.

43

TREES AND TREASON

By 6pm they were driving south past Gatwick Airport using the M23 and A23 roads before heading south west to Petersfield and across to Southampton and then on the M27 towards Ringwood. They reached Bransgore by 8.30pm, unpacked into the two upstairs bedrooms and by 9 they were in the Three Tuns pub nearby, having a meal and sharing some wine. On the trip down Daniel had filled them in about the possible threat posed by Frans Jonker and the advice he'd received from Steve and Jake.

"Wow, this is getting like a spy novel," Arthur said as they relaxed in the 16th century pub.

"Yes, it is, but I don't like being the hunted," commented Nancy with a laugh.

"I know, I know, but this is serious. There's no telling what Frans will do or is capable of doing in his state," warned Daniel.

"Well, I say let's leave him be for a while and enjoy our long weekend here in the New Forest," said Adair. "Let's have a quiet night and then head off for a long walk tomorrow, maybe stopping at a pub for lunch?"

"Is there a lot to see here?" asked Nancy.

"Well, there are several kinds of deer here and have been since the 11th century when it was a royal hunting ground. With the exception of the inevitable road and rail networks, the forest has remained largely unchanged, which is quite impressive," answered Adair. It's also known for its many walks so if we head from our cottage towards Burley, we'd get a good walk in, see some ponies and hopefully some deer."

As their cottage was just outside Bransgore, on the road to Thorney Hill and Burley, her choice of walk seemed good to everyone. The decision made, they finished up and headed back to the cottage, their troubles seemingly forgotten.

***

But, earlier that afternoon Frans Jonker, having found out that they were planning to leave London, made his way to Daniel's office and called upstairs from the concierge desk to speak to Daniel.

"Hello, Jeffries," came the response.

"Hello, this is Jimmy Jonker," said Frans, "may I speak to Daniel Jacobs please?"

"Aah, Jimmy, yes I've heard about you from Daniel and Arthur but I'm afraid Daniel's not in. Can I take a message?"

"Well, I'm downstairs in the lobby, I'm here to give Daniel some information about my brother. It is rather important."

"Downstairs?" asked Jeffries. "That's good. I'm on my way out now, I'll come down and speak to you."

A few minutes later, Jeffries and Frans were face to face.

"I must say, it's a pleasure to meet you. I've heard so much about you and your harrowing story from Daniel," said Jeffries, shaking hands.

Frans said nothing, just smiled and shook hands.

"Now, I know you need to make contact with Daniel but he's out of town. I think they are actually leaving this evening, if not already on their way. And, because they're worried about your brother, they're going to be away until Monday."

Frans put a worried look on his face and then said: "So there's no way to make contact? If they've gone to France, I guess not."

He paused and then added: "But my brother seems to have got wind of the fact that they are going away for about five days. I would like to be able to contact them and let them know they are in danger. But if I can't, well let's just hope he doesn't track them down. I have good reason to believe he's on his way to Dover."

He then stopped, put the worried look back on his face

and turned as if to leave.

Jeffries put his hand on Frans's shoulder.

"He's gone to Dover? Well, that's great, he won't find them there,"

Frans turned back.

"Yes," Jeffries added, "it seems he fell for the bait, or Daniel changed his mind. "Would your brother go to France to find them? Is he that desperate?"

"Oh yes, he seems really fixated on tracking them down," responded Frans.

"Good. Because if he does, then they'll be OK," Jeffries paused, a smile on his bearded face.

"And why is that?" asked Frans.

"Easy, They're miles from there. I overheard him on the phone to Adair, his girlfriend and it appears the vicar at St Martin's, Revd Browne I believe, has given them the use of his family's cottage in the New Forest."

Frans just managed to stop himself from smiling, happy that his plan had worked.

"Oh well, that's good to know. I'm sure they'll have a great time relaxing while my brother goes silly trying to track them down. Thanks then for your help, but I have to go."

Frans shook hands again and hurriedly left the building. He started retracing his route from Monday, along Fleet Street and back to Trafalgar Square. It was just gone 5pm when he got to St Martin's, only to be informed that Revd Browne had already left for the day. The curate asked if he could be of assistance.

"Well, yes, I hope you can," said Frans. "My friends are using Revd Browne's New Forest cottage and they asked me to meet them there at the weekend. But I seem to have lost the piece of paper on which I wrote the directions." He tried his best to look forlorn.

"Oh well, I guess I won't be seeing them. A pity because I have to go home to South Africa early next week and it would have been nice to spend some time with them."

"That's the newspaper man who held the press conference here on Monday?" asked the curate.

"Yes, Daniel Jacobs, my friend from Port Elizabeth in South Africa."

"Fortunately, I have been to the cottage. We went here about a year ago for a weekend retreat. I can tell you just how to get there. Hold on! Come to my office and I'll write out directions. You are going by car are you?"

Two hours later, Frans Jonker was driving to Jimmy's flat, having taken a train to Elmer's End nearby where he paid cash for a hire car, an old black Toyota Corolla. He spent the early part of the evening making calls. Jimmy was at a tutorial and would only be back after 10pm.

By 9.30, he'd made contact with his IRA connection, arranged to pick up a 9mm pistol with a full nine-shot magazine from a contact in South Croydon, packed some clothes and left a note for Jimmy saying he was heading for Dover and possibly France and that he hoped to be back by Sunday.

"Let him worry about that," he thought to himself as he drove towards Croydon to pick up the gun and spend the night drinking with his contact.

***

At 10.30pm Jimmy Jonker walked into his flat and found the note from Frans. He knew then that Frans must have overheard the call to Daniel the previous morning. Jimmy had a restless night, wondering how to find Frans and warn Daniel. Or if he had the time.

"On the other hand," he thought, "by the time Frans gets to Dover the ferry could have gone, if they left today. If not, how's he going to check every car?"

He decided that, first thing in the morning he'd call Daniel's office to see if there was any news. Awake early, he waited anxiously until 9.30am when he could call the newspaper bureau office. He was put through to Alan Jeffries.

"Jeffries here," said the journalist.

"Good morning, I'm Jimmy Jonker. We haven't met but I'm looking for Daniel Jacobs. It is urgent."

"Haven't met? Yes we have. I'm the guy who met you downstairs yesterday evening and told you they were going to the New Forest. I remember you, ginger hair, well built."

"That was not me. It must have been my brother and now he knows where they are. Is there any way we can get hold of Daniel? We need to warn him."

"Your brother? The one who's after Daniel and Arthur? He said he was Jimmy Jonker. Oh, shit, what have I done? Give me your number and I'll call you back. I need to check if there is a phone where they've gone."

Within 30 minutes Jeffries called Jimmy.

"Good news and bad, I'm afraid," said Jeffries. "The good news is that there is a phone there. I rang but there's no reply. The bad news is your brother knows where they are. He went to the church yesterday and got the details, again pretending to be you. Here's the number and I'll try again. I suggest you do too. I can't go down there because I'm tied up here. Any chance you can, if you don't get hold of them?"

Jimmy paused, remembered James Ekron had a car, and said: "If I have to I can, I'll let you know either way. But I think I can get there."

***

The morning was clear and sunny in Bransgore and, after a leisurely and light breakfast, the four drove to the Thorney Hill intersection, parked the car and set off on their walk towards Burley. The first leg, along the east side of Burley Road towards Whitten Pond, was in open moorland with gently undulating hills. By 10.15am they'd reached the ponds where some New Forest ponies were drinking and standing in the shade. After some time there, just relaxing and soaking up the scenery and tranquillity of the area, they walked back to the roadside and continued on towards Burley and the Burley Inn at the heart of the village. It was about a 45 minute walk.

At the same time, just after 11.30, Frans Jonker was

driving down the A31 towards Ringwood and took the turn off to Burley. He reckoned from Burley to the Browne cottage was about another 5 miles and he'd be able to find a place to park and keep watch on the cottage.

As he drove into Burley and then turned right into Pound Lane towards Bransgore, he caught a glimpse of four people, two of them black, walking up the steps to the inn. He only saw them from the back but, he reckoned, chances were it was Daniel Jacobs and company. The road he was on was busy and he had to drive about 200 yards before he could pull off and park the Toyota. Tucking his pistol into his waist band and pulling his jacket down to cover it, he walked briskly back to Burley. But then he saw a tourist coach pull up and about 40 people disembark and enter the Inn.

"Shit! Now what?" he muttered to himself and then realised he was being irrational in trying to confront them in a public restaurant. "Better to wait until they finish lunch."

His mind made up he went to the coffee shop over the road and ordered a light lunch and then decided to drive on to the cottage where he would wait. He knew an ambush would give him the advantage. As would his weapon as he assumed they were not armed.

It was 12.45pm. He reckoned they'd be done by 1.30 at the latest, giving him plenty of time to set up, maybe even get into the cottage and take a look around.

44

THE CHASE IS ON

By 10am Jimmy had tracked down James in Petts Wood, told him what was happening and was soon on a train from Beckenham Junction via Bromley South to Petts Wood station where James met him.

"Man, we're on deadline here and I can't go with you. But, please, take my car. It's an old VW Golf but it's a GTi so it does go rather fast. There's a road map under the front passenger seat. You'll need to fill up and I'd like it back tomorrow if you can, I have a hot date."

James handed over the keys after telling Jimmy the quickest way out of Petts Wood and south of the greater London area. Within an hour, Jimmy was headed down the A23, having studied the map and made sure he had the route firmly lodged in his head. He'd taken time to fill the tank and he was travelling at quite a speed, traffic being light. With the weather being clear too, Jimmy made good time and by noon he was passing Portsmouth and reckoned he was about an hour from the cottage.

"I hope I'm not too late," he thought to himself as he drove on.

Jimmy realised that Frans might be armed but his theory was, if he got there in time, that he, Daniel and Arthur would be able to deal with him. At 12.45 he turned on to the Ringwood road and headed towards Bransgore, recalling that he should turn off towards Burley and then head south-east towards Bransgore and the cottage. As he approached the forested areas, Jimmy marvelled at the amount of uninhabited land there seemed to be in England.

"Strange," he pondered, "some 56 million people, wide open spaces like this and Dartmoor, yet it was easy to bump into people - like meeting up with Daniel and company."

Having told his side of the story regarding the shooting

had been cathartic. He felt better as a result and was thankful to Daniel as well as in awe of the bravery shown by Arthur and Nancy. But he was worried about his brother.

Frans, he realised, was slightly unstable and prone to go off pop without any apparent reason.

His red mist episodes, Jimmy recalled, had become more frequent in the last few months in Port Elizabeth and this, with his drinking, was worrying.

He suddenly braked hard, realising he'd almost missed the turn to Burley.

It was just gone 1pm.

Jimmy was tired and hungry but he knew time was of the essence and he could not afford to stop.

***

Daniel finished his Ringwood Fortyniner, a lovely golden brown, full-bodied and bittersweet ale. Smacking his lips, he turned to Adair.

"You should have tried that, way better than the cider you're drinking, I'm sure. So sure in fact that I might have another."

Arthur, who'd opted for a lager, agreed to another drink, saying he'd try the darker Ringwood Old Thumper. But just a half pint. The meals had been wholesome yet simple, beef and ale pies with chips for the men and two ploughman's platters with local cheeses and ham for Adair and Nancy.

By 1pm they'd finished their drinks, paid up and were walking back towards Bransgore. About half a mile down the road, they were passed by a battered, faded red Golf GTi. The first car they'd seen heading in their direction since leaving the Burley Inn.

"Hey, we should have thumbed a ride," joked Arthur. "Then we'd be back in time for a nap before dinner."

Everyone laughed but all stopped when the car pulled up a short distance ahead of them and they saw its reverse lights come on.

"Maybe he heard you," said Daniel as they stopped

walking and waited.

"Or maybe he's lost," offered Adair.

"Or maybe it's someone we know," added Daniel, catching sight of the red hair above the driver's head rest.

He stared hard into the car and recognised Jimmy just as he feared it might be Frans Jonker. The car reversed towards them and Jimmy jumped out.

"Hey, what a fluke! But am I glad to have found you. My brother knows you are down here and I think he's either on his way or already here."

Adair clutched at Daniel's arm and Nancy gasped.

"I thought we were finally finished with him," she cried.

"Not yet," said Arthur as he put a comforting arm around her, "but don't worry, we'll be OK." He sounded more certain than he felt but he knew Nancy needed some bravado.

"Yes," said Daniel, "let's try and finalise this now. I suggest we go to the cottage but, just in case he's there, I'll go with Jimmy and the rest of you walk. If he's not there I'll send Jimmy back to fetch you." With that he got into the car and they drove off.

"Hell, I am so sorry about this," said Jimmy. "He's more dangerous than we think. I think he might even have a gun or two."

"Well, we will just have to deal with it. I'm tired of looking over my shoulder and I'm sure Arthur and Nancy are too. Fortunately our cottage is quite isolated, so we should be able to see if he's about. Presumably he has a car if he's here or on his way."

***

Frans parked his hire car on the side of the road just past the cottage and walked back towards it. The cottage was set just off the road, the front door about three yards from the road itself. Even though he knew they were not there, he was cautious and scouted around carefully.

The cottage seemed quiet enough and appeared deserted. He walked round to the back and found a window near the kitchen door that was open enough for him to get his hand in and reach the key to unlock the door and gain access. A quick look around showed he was protected from view by a tall hedge badly in need of cutting. No one would see him unless they were in the garden too.

The door squeaked slightly but was not too loud and, within seconds, Frans was inside, and he locked the door again. He moved silently through the ground floor, noting the sitting room facing on to the road and a small bathroom between that and the kitchen and dining area.

Upstairs, despite some creaky stairs which he locked into his memory - miss the third and the seventh to avoid any noise - Frans found two bedrooms facing the road, a bigger bathroom and a study overlooking the back garden.

In the first bedroom was a rocking chair near the window. Frans estimated the window would be in shadow in about five minutes. An ideal place to sit and watch for return of the four.

In the next room, Frans found a travel bag with Arthur's name on it and another bag which obviously belonged to a woman.

Back downstairs for another look around, skipping the creaky steps, Frans went into the dining area and saw a Welsh dresser with an almost full bottle of Famous Grouse whisky and a crystal decanter which he discovered, after sniffing and taking a sip, contained port. Frans grabbed the Famous Grouse and headed back upstairs. Halfway up, he stopped, went back down and unlocked the back door.

"Might need that as a quick escape route," he said to himself as he took a deep swig from the bottle, enjoying the burn of the spirit in his mouth and that pleasuring warmth as it slid smoothly down his throat. Within two minutes he was settled into the rocking chair, his 9mm pistol on his knee and the whisky in his right hand.

His calculation about the sun and shadow was incorrect though and, after another 10 minutes and several sips of whisky, the sun was still warming his face and chest and he nodded off.

Shortly after this, Jimmy and Daniel took the turn towards the cottage with Daniel estimating they'd be there at least 30 minutes ahead of Arthur and the women. Enough time, he hoped, to sort out Frans if he was in the area.

"If he's armed, we could have a problem," said Daniel, only realising he'd spoken aloud when Jimmy replied: "Maybe, but we might have the element of surprise in that he does not know that you know he knows where you are. Also, I'm here too, so there are three males to take him on, armed or not."

"Yes," said Daniel, "but this is not your fight. He's your brother after all is said and done."

"Perhaps, but he's wrong here and I don't think he has any justification in doing what he's doing. So I'm on your side."

As they approached the cottage Daniel said to Jimmy: "Stop here. Let's park short of the cottage, near this nursery entrance. Then, if he is still coming, he won't know this is our car."

After Jimmy parked, the two locked the car and walked on another 100 yards or so to the cottage. It all seemed quiet and normal as they approached. No car parked too close and the cottage looked peaceful.

"So, if he's not here but knows where you are, how are we going to know when he gets here?" asked Jimmy, looking around. "There's no place where we could keep watch, except from inside the cottage itself. What's at the back?"

"I'm not too sure," said Daniel. "I had a look outside this morning and we seem to back onto another property with the house set about 50 yards away. The only way he can get to us is along this road, so we just have to watch the front."

They got to the front door and Daniel opened it with the key he had.

As the door opened quietly, Jimmy looked inside and said: "This looks cosy, just like those cottages you see in English magazines like *Home and Country* or something like that."

Daniel chuckled softly then said: "Well, no car outside, no sign of anyone being here. I suggest you head back and I'll wait for you guys, keeping watch."

Jimmy turned and set off as Daniel closed the door and walked quietly through to the kitchen. A quick glance around and he noticed the bottle of whisky was missing from the dresser. He checked the back door and it squeaked softly as it opened and shut it again. He stopped as he heard a noise, then a thud, from upstairs followed by a curse in Afrikaans.

Daniel said to himself: "He's here! Now what?"

Quickly he moved back to the lounge, stopping to take a fire poker from the large hearthstone. He had to disable Frans somehow and hopefully do that before the others came back.

45

SHOWDOWN

Frans awoke with a start and grunted as the whisky bottle slipped in his hand and he felt the liquid spill into his crotch, wetting his trousers. As he bent forward to grab the bottle, the pistol slipped of his knee and landed on the carpet with a thud. This time he swore and felt his tongue stick to the roof of his mouth. The bottle was almost empty. How much had he drunk? He did not feel too good. His eyes were sore, his mouth was dry and there was a dull ache at the back of his head.

"Man, that bottle was almost full," he said softly as he stopped to pick up the pistol. "No wonder I feel shit."

He glanced at his watch. He'd been in the cottage for just under two hours. "Damn, that was stupid."

Then he realised he'd heard a noise downstairs that had awoken him. Dimly he recalled the squeak of the back door. "That was it! The door had been opened. Someone was inside or had someone left?" With the pistol in his right hand, Frans moved to the top of the stairs and peered down. He saw nothing but he did notice that things seemed a bit blurry. He rubbed his eyes as if to regain focus and then moved as silently as he could downstairs.

He paused after one step. "Shit, which one creaked? Was it seven or eight?" he thought to himself. "Seven and three." He counted up from the bottom and found he was one step away from the first creaky one. So he took a huge stride and skipped step seven. "So far, so good," he thought. Down again. Six. Five. Four. Pause. Preparing for missing step three, Frans focused on the steps in front of him and put his left hand on the banister, the right still holding the pistol which was pointed in front of him.

Suddenly, excruciating pain in his left hand and he looked down to see a black metal rod on his hand. "Shit!" he screamed and as the rod was lifted, he saw two of his fingers were broken, and possibly his knuckles. He fell forward and landed in a heap on the floor, out of breath and in agony.

***

With the poker firmly in his hand, Daniel had moved to the side of the stairs, waiting in the shadows. He could almost sense Frans on the top step and then, straining his ears, heard his feet shuffling down and the policeman's breathing.

Frans's legs came into view as he skipped a step and paused again. Daniel could see he was looking straight ahead and seemed to be concentrating on the steps ahead of him. He watched as Frans took three more steps then paused. Daniel took a step forward but was still behind Frans when he saw the gun in his hand.

Then Frans put his left hand on the banister, just a few feet ahead of Daniel. Instinctively, Daniel lifted the poker and brought it down as hard as he could on the policeman's hand. He felt, and heard, the bones crack and as he lifted the poker, saw Frans tumble, screaming to the floor.

"Now's my chance to disarm him," Daniel thought as he moved quickly forward, the poker raised again, preparing to hit Frans across the back as he lay there in an untidy heap. But as he moved swiftly forward, his feet caught on the rug and he lost his balance, tumbling to the ground and dropping the poker.

As he landed, sprawling forward with the rug between his feet, Daniel's face ended up inches away from Frans's left hand. He could see blood on the knuckles and even some white bone where the poker had shattered the knuckles and broken the skin.

Two fingers, the index and middle fingers, stuck out at an awkward angle.

Unable to get to the poker, Daniel swung with his left hand and punched Frans's injured hand as hard as he could, rolling away straight afterwards. As he rolled, Daniel heard Frans scream again, cursing Daniel, his parents, ancestry and anything else that came to his pain-filled mind.

Daniel's only thought was that Frans had a gun and would not hesitate to use it. He also knew that Adair, Arthur, Nancy and Jimmy would be close to reaching the cottage and he wanted to neutralise the threat Frans represented to all of them. As he rolled, Daniel hit the back of the sofa with his back to Frans. He heard the policeman cursing and shuffling around on the floor. "You bastard, I'll get you first. Then the others," said Frans, his voice hoarse with pain.

He must be about a yard away, thought Daniel, impossible to miss at such close range.

Pushing hard against the sofa's back, Daniel rolled closer to Frans, seeing the flash of the pistol and hearing the shot as he rolled.

His ears ringing from the shot at such close proximity, Daniel heard noises as if cocooned in cotton wool. There were strange noises, bangs and voices it could have been. He was not sure as survival was uppermost in his mind. He knew he had not been hit by the bullet and he had one more chance.

Swinging around on the floor so his legs were closer to Frans, he lashed out with both, aiming for his assailant's chest as he saw Frans aim again. His left foot struck first, hitting Frans's injured hand and pushing it into his chest. Frans screamed and stumbled backwards, firing as he did.

Daniel dimly heard another scream. Or was it his hearing playing up? He saw Frans aim at him once more and he kicked out again, hitting the right hand this time but a little too late. There was another muzzle flash and a bang followed by a sharp, searing pain in his left thigh.

As he lay there, shocked and stung by the pain, he saw Arthur flying through the air above, tackling Frans with outstretched arms and the pair of them falling back against the wall and pistol going off a fourth time. Daniel felt dampness soaking through his jeans but, strangely enough, not as much pain as he expected. He knew he'd been shot and he was bleeding but it didn't seem too bad.

His ears started to clear and he could hear shouts and screams. The screams were coming from Nancy and Adair, somewhere behind him. The shouts came from Arthur and Frans as they fought on the floor a little ahead of him. Daniel struggled to his feet, only to find his left leg crumpled under him and he fell against the sofa.

"My God, you're shot!" cried Adair as she crouched on the floor near the front door.

But it wasn't Daniel she was talking about. She was kneeling over Jimmy Jonker who lay across Nancy.

"Who's been shot?" Daniel asked hoarsely. She did not seem to hear him as she bent forward peering intently at Jimmy. Daniel then saw blood on Jimmy's throat and heard Nancy whimpering, trying to move Jimmy's deadweight from her body.

As he was about to move around the sofa to help them, he heard another shot, a grunt and a thud behind him and he swung around to see Arthur lying on the floor and Frans making a beeline for the kitchen doorway to his left.

"Is Nancy OK?" Daniel screamed at Adair as he bent to pick up the poker.

"I think so," he heard Adair say, "she's covered in blood but I can't tell if it's her blood or Jimmy's. Jimmy's unconscious but breathing."

With the poker in his hand, Daniel hobbled to the kitchen, hopping over Arthur's prone body as he did so. Unable to open the door with his injured left hand, Frans had been delayed in his attempt to get away. He'd put the pistol on the kitchen counter so he could turn the handle with his right hand. He then saw Daniel as he opened the door and grabbed at the pistol.

"Ready for more?" he sneered as he looked at the blood seeping through Daniel's jeans. "I've shot the black bitch and the guy. Now it's your turn." He lifted the pistol and aimed at Daniel's head pulling the trigger too soon and the bullet hit the kitchen wall near Daniel's shoulder. Chips of plaster and brickwork stung Daniel's cheek, drawing blood.

Daniel flung the poker at Frans and watched,

unbelievingly, as the poker seemed to cartwheel in slow motion towards the ginger-haired man at the door. Frans saw it coming and instinctively lifted both his hands like a boxer to protect himself. There was another scream and a shot as the poker hit Frans's injured left hand and the policeman involuntarily pulled the trigger yet again.

The bullet ricocheted off the quarry-tiled kitchen floor as Frans stumbled through the open door way and disappeared from sight. Realising he was in no state to give chase, Daniel turned back into the living room area. He paused to look at Arthur and saw the man stirring slightly with no sign of any bullet wound. Stepping over him, he saw Nancy had managed to extricate herself and was helping Adair try and staunch the flow of blood from Jimmy's throat.

Jimmy was still lying on his back on the floor but was awake and the two women were using a cloth from the coffee table to stem the flow.

Adair looked up at Daniel. "Are you alright?" There was anguish in her eyes and her hands were shaking. "As we got to the door, we heard screams and a shot. Arthur opened the door and we saw Frans pointing his gun, presumably at you on the floor. Then your legs kicked out and hit Frans on the chest and he shot again. Then he looked up and saw us and aimed at us. Suddenly Arthur dived forward, like Superman, flinging himself at Frans and the madman fired another shot. That one hit Jimmy in the throat as he moved in front of Nancy and me, to protect us, I think."

Adair paused and drew a shuddering breath, wiping her face and unaware of the blood streaks her fingers left on her cheeks. "I wasn't sure if Frans had shot Nancy too because she fell back with Jimmy on top of her. There was blood everywhere." She stopped talking, by now almost incoherent and sobbing, looking at Daniel with distraught eyes as he stood there, blood running down his cheek and his leg.

Just then there was the scream of a highly revving car engine and a massive crash as the front of the cottage caved in and a black Toyota appeared where the front door had been. Fortunately, no one was close enough to be hit by the car or the debris. As Adair flung herself to the floor screaming, Daniel saw Frans stumble from the car, the pistol in his hand.

"Here, shoot me!" Daniel shouted, trying to draw Frans's attention from the women and his brother who were less than two yards from him.

"No, shoot me, you child killer," Daniel heard Arthur say from behind him and he looked round to see Arthur at his shoulder.

As Frans lifted the pistol and took wavering aim, Daniel saw one of the dislodged cottage bricks above the door's ancient lintel wobble and then, again almost in slow motion, fall. Frans saw Daniel look up and instinctively did the same, as the brick struck him in the face and he crumpled, unconscious to the ground.

The sound of a police siren got closer and the last Daniel remembered before collapsing was Arthur embracing him as the two of them fell onto the sofa.

46

AFTERMATH - COPENHAGEN, THREE DAYS LATER

It was still light at 10pm when a bruised and tender Daniel got into bed in the guest room of the Pedersen family home overlooking the extensive landscaped gardens of Frederiksberg Park with its follies, waterfalls, lakes and decorative buildings.

It had been three days since the incident in the cottage. He was exhausted, both mentally and physically, and fell asleep within seconds of his head hitting the pillow. So sound asleep was he that he did not hear Adair and her father knock and then enter the room about 15 minutes later.

"This is your hero? Your knight in shining armour?" asked Pedersen as he and his daughter looked at the snoring South African whose face still showed the scars from the brickwork which had hit him three days earlier as well as now diminishing bruising from his showdown with Frans a few days prior to that.

"Yes he his, daddy," said Adair. "You don't know what he, and the rest of us, have been through."

Pedersen smiled wryly. "I have heard and it appears he got off lightly." Daniel had been lucky with only a flesh wound to the thigh, some cuts to his face and bruising. Arthur, on the other hand, had internal bleeding from a shot to his stomach and Jimmy had damage to his vocal chords after he was shot in the throat. Both were in a Bournemouth hospital. Nancy was in a hotel nearby waiting for them to be discharged.

Adair looked at Daniel. "Yes, maybe he did get off lightly but he was the man who decided he'd tackle Frans while we were still walking to the cottage.

"Talking Frans, what is happening there?"

Daniel stirred in his sleep and Pedersen smiled and said to his daughter: "Let's go downstairs and leave Dan.

I'll tell you over a glass of wine, that South African red wine we brought back from the safari trip."

Minutes later, with a glass of a smoky and robust Meerlust Rubicon in hand, Pedersen sat on the sofa near the window overlooking the gardens and his daughter sat opposite, delicately sipping her wine.

"Hmm, no wonder this is one of Dan's favourites," she said, appreciating the taste and mouthfeel of the wine.

"So, he has taste then," said Pedersen, "good wine and you.

"But, back to Jonker. Interestingly enough, after he was arrested by the police for attempted murder, assault, grievous damage to property and carrying an unlicensed firearm, he demanded to make a call to the SA Embassy in London, I was told.

"He claimed he was working on behalf of the South African security police. A silly claim to make as they have no right to operate in the UK, unless with the co-operation and knowledge of Scotland Yard. Perhaps his brain was a bit scrambled after being knocked out by that brick you told me about.

"Anyway, he made his call and about an hour later the police in Christchurch, where he had been taken, received a call from the embassy informing them that Jonker was a renegade and acting on his own, without sanction from the security police who told the embassy he was on sick leave.

"Now, perhaps he was undercover and they don't want an international incident, it does not matter. The point is, he is now in custody in Christchurch after an initial magistrate's hearing and will be held as such until his trial. One of you might have to give evidence and I'd suggest Daniel do it as he'll have to give notice from his job."

"Give notice? Why?" asked Adair. "You still want him to be your editor-in-chief? That's great!"

"Well, remember in London I said I wanted to discuss an 'opportunity' with Daniel?" He made the quote signs with his hands as he spoke.

"So, I have been giving it some thought and I must say I like Daniel's mettle and character. So much so that he could take over my business, not just as editor-in-chief but in my role.

"Having chatted to people like Molly Blackburn and others of similar mind around the world, I want to involve myself more in human rights.

"And, quite frankly, I'm tired of the hustle and bustle of daily newspaper work and the pressure of running the agency.

"Now, I must say I did have you in mind but, honestly Adair, you're still too young. Too young," he added as he saw the fire in her eyes, "to run it alone."

She took a deeper gulp of her wine this time and looked at her father questioningly.

"Yes, you and Daniel make a good team and you should work together, not every day, but at the same task.

"So, I want to ask Daniel if he's happy to be MD of Pedersen's with you as publishing director. That way, you run the books division - which, as you know, makes big money - and he runs the news operations. My offer to Arthur and Nancy remains the same too. I'll stay on as chairman for a while, but in a non-executive role, and see how it pans out. What do you think?"

She paused before answering.

"Well, It's an obviously attractive prospect and you know I want to stay in the family business but I'm not too sure, at this stage, what Daniel will say. His heart is set on returning to SA where he hopes he can make a difference in the struggle for democracy. But maybe I've got a part of his heart too and that could change things."

She smiled and finished her wine before pouring more for the two of them.

"Oh, I'm sure you do have a big part of his heart.

"At the same time, we need to establish a bigger presence in Southern Africa because that will be the hub of news for the next 10 years or so. My first task for Daniel will be to set up two offices there. One in Cape Town and one in Johannesburg, staff them with good people, help get the real news out and make a real change to how the world sees South Africa and its efforts to change."

There was a noise at the doorway and they turned to see Daniel standing there, looking groggy but alert.

"Couldn't sleep," he said, his eyes lighting on the wine, "and I thought I smelled Meerlust, so I needed to investigate."

Clad in a vest and sleep shorts with his thigh bandaged, he moved to join them as Adair poured another glass.

"It's the last one," she said, handing it to Daniel as he sat next to her on the sofa, facing Erik.

"No it isn't," smiled Erik, "I have more and we can open another bottle."

As he moved to get up, Daniel raised his hand in a stop motion.

"What, no wine?" asked Erik.

"Please, more wine would be most welcome but, I have to admit, I heard the last part of your conversation with Adair. She does have a large piece of my heart and I see us spending the rest of our lives together. What you said about the agency makes a lot of sense and I'd say yes, thanks very much. But, only in two months' time, if that's OK?" Daniel paused and sipped the wine, a blissful expression on his face.

Erik nodded his assent but looked querulous and Daniel added, taking Adair's hand in his: "Quite simple, really. I'd need to do a month's notice in my current job and I would like us to spend our honeymoon in Cape Town, at Meerlust and in the Robertson area where there are also great wines and scenery."

Adair looked mildly surprised. "Well, if that's how South Africans propose, I accept." She leant over and kissed Daniel on the cheek.

Erik smiled and raised his glass, "I think another bottle is called for."

EPILOGUE

A 1987 newspaper report in South Africa stated the following:

In what amounts to an admission of liability, the Minister of Law and Order has paid out R2,3-million to 51 people injured or widowed in the 'Uitenhage massacre' of March 21 1985.

The payment is accompanied by a rare concession notice which states the minister 'unconditionally pays the sum of R1,3-million'.

"It means the police have admitted they acted wrongfully and negligently and that this was the cause of the incident " a Johannesburg attorney said. "It means the police are open to charges of culpable homicide."

More than 21 people were shot dead - many in the back - when police opened fire on a crowd of funeral-goers on the anniversary of the Sharpeville shootings in Uitenhage's township of Langa. It was the first mass police killing in a year which was marked by other 'massacres' in Queenstown, Mamelodi, Winterveld and Alexandra as spiralling unrest turned into bloody conflict.

The Uitenhage shootings evoked a national and international outcry, and the South African government appointed a judicial commission of enquiry under Judge Donald Kannemeyer to investigate the circumstances surrounding March 21 1985. Legal papers in the civil application which was due to come before the Port Elizabeth Supreme Court on Monday, recreated the fateful march down Maduna Road, Langa, and the contrasting versions of these events presented to the Kannemeyer Commission.

But while the settlement contradicts the police version presented to the commission, it does not contradict Judge Kannemeyer's findings as such. Kannemeyer absolved the police unit, led by Lieutenant John Fouche, which opened fire on the crowd, from culpability for the deaths. But he found the banning of funerals on doubtful grounds and improper riot control equipment were the main factors which led to the Langa deaths.

Although by opting for an out of court settlement, the Minister of Law and Order has effectively admitted police culpability, it is not clear which group of policemen it admits was to blame. The plaintiffs were represented by Johannesburg advocates WH Trengove - who also represented Langa residents in the Kannemeyer inquiry - and Bob Nugent who were instructed by Johannesburg attorneys Cheadle, Thompson and Haysom.

They claimed Fouche's men were not adequately equipped for riot patrol - instead they were equipped with R1 rifles, shotguns, 9mm sidearms, sharp ammunition and SSG cartridges. The complainants contended the police had failed to disperse the crowd when it gathered at Maduna Square, but had instead provoked Langa residents. In addition, a police major had sown confusion by applying for and obtaining orders prohibiting four funerals planned for March 21.

In replying papers, the minister denied the police acted negligently and claimed they had opened fire - using a degree of force necessary in the circumstances - in 'legitimate self defence as well as in defence of the lives of the public of Uitenhage and in the protection of their property'. The papers also denied the police major, who applied for an order prohibiting funerals, had acted negligently. In a surprise move last week, however, attorneys representing the minister approached the plaintiff's lawyers and made offers of settlement for all the civil cases, which virtually amounted to the full sum claimed.

The largest single amount of R450,000 was paid to Lawrence Gqubule, 25, who has been paralysed from the waist down as a result of a bullet fired by police on March 21, which severed his spinal cord. Gqubule's parents were among those forcibly removed from Langa to a squatter settlement called Tjoksville in Uitenhage's KwaNobuhle township in 1986.

Living in conditions which were unhygienic, deprived of expensive personal and medical care and physiotherapy,

Gqubule was admitted to Uitenhage hospital early this year with septic bedsores, stiffening joints and severe depression.

"His compensation will enable him to buy a house and obtain the necessary facilities and treatment—it could mean the difference between life and death," his attorney commented.

One of the central figures to the Kannemeyer Commission, the boy-on-the-bicycle, Moses Kwanele Bucwa, received a pay-out of R17,000. Affidavits collected by the Progressive Federal Party soon after the shooting contained graphic accounts of the bike-rider's death and his brains spilling over the road. But early in the preparation for the Kannemeyer Commission, 15-year-old Bucwa came forward - with a bullet lodged in his head, but minus his bicycle which had been confiscated by the police.

During the inquiry Bucwa scotched all doubts about his identity by describing the tiny intricacies of his bicycle. Kannemeyer found the police version that the boy on the bicycle had arrived on the scene only once the crowd had dispersed to be 'false'.

ABOUT THE AUTHOR

André Erasmus is an experienced journalist with over 30 years of newspaper and magazine experience. He worked in South Africa and latterly in the UK where he has lived since 2001. Real Change, his first novel, draws on his time as a daily newspaper's news editor in Port Elizabeth and also as a conscripted soldier in the South African Defence Force, doing active border duty in South West Africa (now Namibia).

Besides writing, he's into music and plays bass guitar. He also enjoys the outdoors and camping - despite his time in the army; good food - probably because of his time in the army - and travel. André is married with four adult children and three cherished granddaughters.

Made in the USA
Lexington, KY
29 November 2014